The Party Agent

Nigel Pickford

BLACK SWAN

THE PARTY AGENT

A BLACK SWAN BOOK 0 552 99389 1

First publication in Great Britain

PRINTING HISTORY
Black Swan edition published 1990

Copyright © Nigel Pickford 1990

The right of Nigel Pickford to be identified as author of this work has been asserted in accordance with sections 77 and 78 of the Copyright Designs and Patents Act 1988.

This book is set in 11/12 pt Mallard by Colset Private Limited, Singapore.

Black Swan Books are published by Transworld Publishers Ltd., 61–63 Uxbridge Road, Ealing, London W5 5SA, in Australia by Transworld Publishers (Australia) Pty. Ltd., 15–23 Helles Avenue, Moorebank, NSW 2170, and in New Zealand by Transworld Publishers (N.Z.) Ltd., Cnr. Moselle and Waipareira Avenues, Henderson, Auckland.

Made and printed in Great Britain by The Guernsey Press Co. Ltd., Guernsey, Channel Islands.

For Ros

1

When did things first start to go wrong? My marriage, my birth, the Industrial Revolution, the Garden of Eden, the Big Bang? It wasn't that easy to put your finger on it. But there was this phone call to my ex-wife which, looking back, was something of a turning point.

It was a warmer than average day. I'd been thinking about phoning Andrea all week, but putting it off for one reason or another. All the same I knew eventually there was no way round it. Sooner or later I'd have to tell her. So, lulled into a false sense of optimism by the unseasonable spell of hot weather, I took the bull by the horns, or the phone by its handle, and tapped in those wrenchingly familiar digits.

As it happened the first time I tried she was engaged. What's more she persisted in that exasperating condition for approximately the next hour and a half. I'm at a loss to explain what she can find to talk about at such length. My own calls last on average forty-five seconds. But then again I'm forgetting how Andrea can hardly ring the speaking clock without getting into why it is she needs to be wherever she's going on time. And this inevitably leads into why her whole life she has felt harassed by external pressures. A subject not entirely unrelated to the mainstay of all her conversation, namely, what an oppressive bastard I am.

I crashed the receiver back into its cradle in the manner of a really oppressive bastard. I'm not too fond of phones. I don't find them exactly user-friendly. Being somewhat on the socially insecure side, I need to be sure whoever I'm talking to isn't pulling a face, reading a novel or indulging in some obscure sexual practice at my expense. But Andrea, bless her little designer socks, has none of these inhibitions. She just pours her soul out like British Telecom was the best thing since Roman Catholicism. No wonder her ears fit so snugly against her head. It must be the continual pressure of having a lump of plastic clamped against them.

'6113011.' A faint, rather crackly voice that I didn't immediately recognize took me by surprise. Then it clicked. It was Livingstone, my son. The fleshly witness of our ill-fated union. How oddly grown up he sounded.

'Whatcha Livers. Dad here. How you doing?' I slipped into the jovial paterfamilias act that was the only way I knew how to talk to him.

'Sorry. Could you repeat that please?'

'It's Dad. How are you? How's the football coming on? We must have a kick about again soon.'

'This is 6113011. Mummy is in the bath. Could you please leave your name and telephone number and she will return your call as soon as she can.' He sounded like a rather nervous pre-recorded message.

'Livers. This is Dad. Your father. Remember? Tell mummy I know she's lying and I need to talk to her urgently, OK? There's a good boy. Oh, and see you Saturday. Don't forget. I've got a big surprise planned.'

Silence. Not an ordinary, hopeful sort of silence, the necessary pause that occurs in any conversation, but a yawning great chasm of the stuff. I uttered the odd imprecation, followed by a series of frantic dingings on the dinger. Nothing. I had this upsetting image of my disembodied voice swinging on the end of a cord in the front hall, tweeting like a castrated sparrow.

'Well, what is it?' Andrea came on at last in her strong no-nonsense mode.

'You've been having a busy morning.'

'I think that's my business, don't you?'

'Is Livers OK?'

'Fine.'

'I thought he sounded rather strange. You don't think he's becoming withdrawn do you? I noticed it last time he came over.'

'With you perhaps. With me he's fine. You might find he responded more positively if you didn't insist on referring to him as if he were a bowl of offal.'

'But I've always called him Livers.'

'Just because you've always done it doesn't necessarily make it OK behaviour.'

'I just wish he wasn't so polite the whole time. Doesn't seem natural somehow in a child his age. On the phone just now he sounded like he was someone's secretary more than a little boy.'

'You'd rather he was going around raping old ladies, I suppose.'

'Not exactly, no. But perhaps there is a happy medium.'

'Oh, the famous British compromise. The middle way. Look, is that what you rang me up about? To discuss Livingstone's telephone answering technique? Because I happen to be very busy.'

'Well, there was something else.'

'Yes.'

'I've decided to go to the Ronaynes' potluck supper tonight.'

'So?'

'I thought you might like some prior notice.'

'Decent of you.'

'You don't have any objections then?'

'Why should I have objections?'

'No reason.'

'Joseph, you're an adult white male. You can go where you like. The world is your bloody oyster.'

'I don't like oysters,' I said.

'Tough shit. Is that all you wanted to say to me?'

It was and I don't know what made me utter my next remark. It was quite unnecessary. It just slipped out on a self-destructive impulse.

'You don't have any suggestions as to what dish I

might take along do you? I mean dish as in item of cuisine, of course, not female escort.'

There was a pause.

'Women are not equated in my mind with objects for consumption, Joseph.'

'Sorry. Silly joke.'

'Perhaps you wouldn't find it so funny if you'd been a victim of male appetites for the past several thousand years.'

'Yes, I'm sure you're right.'

'And why the hell do you think I want to start putting your nappies on for you again? I had more than my fill of that when we were married, thanks very much.'

'Er, excuse me, but what exactly do you mean by that last remark?' I asked in tones of great intellectual curiosity. Actually I knew exactly what she meant by it and I really didn't want to listen to Andrea going over the same old ground yet again. Fortunately, she chose that moment to put the receiver down on me.

All in all, apart from my one major lapse in non-sexist protocol, it was a moderately satisfactory outcome. The main burden of my message, namely my forthcoming appearance at the Ronaynes', had been received with the most unexpected equilibrium. The coded significance of such an appearance could hardly have been lost on Andrea, who had always been terribly into coded significances, hidden meanings, symbolic gestures, Freudian motivations, and all the rest of it. Which could only mean that she had made up her mind to take a Realpolitik attitude towards my staying on as the Party Agent. So far so good.

A little background might be helpful here for those less au fait with coded significances than Andrea. I had been the Party Agent for Docklands East for the past fifteen years. For most of that period it had been an averagely corrupt little rotten borough, rock solid Labour, with a sitting MP who might be more aptly termed the lounging MP, or sprawling flat on his back and out for the count MP.

Ronnie Mullins wasn't the sort of man who would walk a hundred yards if the limousine was available, and no-one could ever recall seeing him on a march. Marches were for cranks in Mullin's book. He was one of the old school of Labour politician; a fixer, an operator, a man who prided himself on his ability to deliver the goods and boasted of his ignorance of anything that smacked of the intellectual or artistic. And I have to admit I do tend to look back on those early years of Mullins' reign as a honeymoon era. They were the days when you could stitch up a selection meeting by wheeling in three tame old age pensioners and a trade union lackey, no problem. But then, towards the end of the Seventies, for some mysterious reason that no-one has yet satisfactorily explained, but I rather suspect it will prove to be viral, grass roots activism emerged, or Trotskyist infiltration, depending on your point of view. End of peace and tranquility and cosy deals behind the scenes. Start of democratic accountability and the struggle for socialism.

In my little neck of the concrete jungle this had culminated in Mullins being ditched as candidate for the next election, in favour of Alan Sayeed, a handsome young protagonist of the Post New Left. Now I had nothing against Alan personally. It was just that he also happened to be the latest in my ex-wife's long line of lovers. The relationship between an agent and the candidate, particularly a new and inexperienced candidate, is necessarily a close one. The domestic tangle could prove embarrassing.

Andrea clearly thought so, because she was on the telephone to me within twenty minutes of Alan being selected demanding to know whether I was going to do the decent thing and hand in my notice. It had been Andrea who had originally suggested that I apply for the Party Agent job in the first place, and she'd always rather regarded it as sort of in her gift for the taking back whenever she felt like it, along with the hi-fi system and the Habitat sofa. I told her I'd think about it.

11

Since then, until my return call, I'd done very little else.

OK, being a Labour Party Agent isn't exactly everyone's idea of a big deal. True, it does mainly consist of organizing tombola stalls and writing up the minutes of meetings that are so indescribably tedious the telephone directory makes more interesting reading. And also true, I have done very little else but moan about my conditions of employment ever since I started. But fifteen years is a long time and being an agent was pretty well all I knew how to do. Besides, if my job opportunities were to be circumscribed by an avoidance of all Andrea's lovers, present and past, wasn't I putting myself at a severe disadvantage in comparison with the rest of the labour force?

So, having made my decision to stay on, what better way of signalling it to the outside world than by putting in an appearance at the Ronaynes. The Ronaynes' potluck supper was an annual fund raising event, but this year, coming as it did only a week after Alan's selection, it was also to be an inauguration ceremony and campaign launch, all rolled into one glorious socialist jamboree. Anyone planning to defect would obviously not be going along.

12

2

I had hardly put the phone down when the front door bell rang. It was Charles Ronayne, I discovered him staring shiftily at the top windows as if he were either a double-glazing salesman, which I knew he wasn't, or he was casing the place for a future break in, which was a possibility, but not very likely, seeing as he was comfortably off, having had the good sense to marry a rich woman; and I have very little worth taking.

'So, you are in after all,' he drawled in that patrician manner of his that implied I'd kept him waiting rather longer than was strictly necessary.

'Sorry,' I said. 'You caught me updating the membership. Terrible chore but got to be done. You know how it is.'

Funny thing, but whenever a party member called I always felt obliged to make out I was hard at it, nose to the grindstone, even if I wasn't. Though why I should have felt intimidated in this respect by Charles, who has never lifted a finger to do a damn thing in his entire life, is quite beyond me. A deep-rooted sense of personal inadequacy is what Andrea would say. She's probably right. Charles said nothing. 'Well, I guess I'd better be getting back to it,' I said. 'The back room's unlocked.'

The back room was usually what Charles called round for. It housed a Gestetner, a malfunctioning photocopier, boxes of envelopes, a portable Olympia typewriter with a worn-out ribbon, numerous battleship-grey filing cabinets and other essentials for the Revolution. Quite what Charles did in there I had no idea, but it seemed to involve dismantling the photocopier, because when he left everything was usually covered in a fine black carcinogenic powder.

Today, however, Charles did not seem particularly anxious to enter the back room. He retreated a step or two along the crazy-paving pathway, took another sneaky glance up at the guttering and then stared at me as if he still wasn't quite sure he'd come to the right house.

'Actually, want a confidential word with your good-self. Won't detain you long.'

'Sure,' I said. 'Sure. I'll lead the way.'

So I led the way up the uncarpeted stairs thinking Charles must have called round to deliver me a lecture on the importance of keeping your gables properly maintained. I rent a couple of rooms and a kitchen over what is somewhat pompously termed the Docklands East Local Constituency Labour Party Administrative Headquarters. I moved in there after my marriage broke up. It was originally to be a temporary arrangement while I found a place of my own, but that was two years ago and the place of my own still hasn't materialized. The rooms are cramped and squalid but they do have the decided advantage that I only have to walk down the stairs to work. Andrea claimed that my failure to find a suitable place to live was indicative of my total inability to face up to the realities of my new situation. I don't dispute this. But it was also another very good reason for not taking any precipitous action on the job resignation front.

'Make yourself at home,' I said, indicating the bed and throwing an assorted collection of clothing into a heap on the floor.

Charles looked suspiciously, first at the bed and then at me and then at the bed again, as if he suspected that I was either trying to seduce him or playing some elaborate practical joke.

'It's a much better deal than the chair,' I said encouragingly. 'I'll put some coffee on.'

When I returned, Charles was sitting on the chair. He was a tall, heavily-built man with enormously long shanks so that, when he was seated, his knees tended to obtrude in front of his face, which was no bad thing. He had a great prow of a nose, numerous dewlaps of jowl and drooping, bloodshot eyes. Think of a cross between a piece of Stonehenge and a spaniel and you're getting pretty near the mark.

'Is this instant?' he asked haughtily.

' 'Fraid so. But then what do you expect on the exploitation rates I get paid. Sugar?'

Charles shook his head rapidly like he'd just been offered cyanide. He cleared his throat, fidgeted with his mug, cleared his throat again. I began to feel uneasy. What the hell did he want? Maybe Andrea was behind it. Maybe she'd sent him round to say that I would not, after all, be welcome at the potluck that evening and where was my resignation letter. It would be just like Andrea to spring a nasty surprise of that sort through a third party.

'I have a formal announcement to make,' said Charles.

I began to choke, dribbling coffee down my shirt front.

'It's important that it should not be taken the wrong way.'

'Too late, already have.' A spurt of coffee came back down my nose. I caught it neatly in the mug. An impressive bit of hand-eye co-ordination.

'What?' said Charles.

'Taken it the wrong way. Coffee down the wrong tube.' I gasped and giggled alternately.

Charles looked disapproving. 'If you could just stop being facetious for one moment. It is important, not just for myself but for the Party as a whole, that my decision is not misunderstood. And I thought as agent you should be the first to know. I have, after much careful weighing up of the arguments on both sides, come to the conclusion, albeit reluctantly, and it's no good you trying to persuade me otherwise Joseph, I have made up my mind that this is an appropriate time for me to take something of a political back seat.'

'Fair enough,' I said, greatly relieved that after all Charles' visit had nothing to do with Andrea.

Charles looked most put out. He had clearly been expecting me to beg him on bended knee to play his usual full and active role. Not that he'd ever done anything in the past except take a back seat.

'More coffee?'

Charles clamped his hand over his mug and shook his head vigorously.

'Rather on the bitter side, isn't it? Got it from the Oxfam shop. Supposed to be of Nicaraguan extract.'

'Of course, it's not the kind of decision one comes to lightly.'

'Certainly not. The politics of coffee-buying is a very tricky business.'

'I was referring to my future role in the Labour Party.'

'Ah yes.'

'What most concerns me is that there will be those who will deliberately misconstrue my standing down. They will say it is sour grapes. They will say I've dropped out because I was not chosen as candidate, when you and I and all fair-minded people know perfectly well that the truth is quite otherwise. I only ever allowed my name to go forward because I came under great pressure from a number of different quarters in the Party to do so. For myself, as you are only too well aware, I am quite without ambition to hold public office.'

As it so happened, I had always been somewhat puzzled as to what exactly Charles' motives had been in going to what was, for him, the considerable trouble of getting his name added to the short list of candidates, when there had never been the remotest possibility he would be selected. It was now apparent, however, that he had all along been playing a long and, for Charles, moderately subtle hand. He had clearly never been after the prize of the candidacy. What he had been staking out for himself was the far more congenial role of the martyred and slighted elder statesman.

16

'I wouldn't worry about it, Charles. I think most of the comrades will just be relieved you haven't gone over to the other side.'

Charles looked profoundly shocked. His dewlaps wobbled with indignation.

'Are there people in this party who really think that I, who have been a socialist all my life, who was one of the original Aldermaston 100, that I would stoop so low as to join a gang of opportunists?'

'No, of course not. Just a silly joke.'

'A joke in rather poor taste if you don't mind me saying so. Really Joseph, there are times when I feel this flippancy of yours clouds your judgement.'

'Sorry. Anyway, I'm sure no-one will think any the worse of you if you decide to lie low for a bit.'

'Lie low! Now you make me sound like some kind of underworld racketeer. I am drawing in my horns that is all. Taking a well-earned sabbatical. Recharging the spiritual batteries. I have sadly neglected my art these last years. I am an artist, Joseph, not one of your political animals. And I feel this deep personal need to get in touch with my real self again.'

Charles drank off the rest of his coffee and shuddered.

'Well, if there's anything I can do to help,' I said. I cleared the coffee mugs away in the hope of terminating the conversation. When Charles started on about getting in touch with his real self, I always felt this deep personal need to vomit.

Charles lurched to his feet. After this initial burst of energy, however, he seemed to lose momentum.

'As a matter of fact, there is a little something you could do for me,' he said coyly. 'I shall not be attending the potluck this evening.'

'But Charles, isn't it in your house?'

'That is correct. And I shall not renege on that commitment. Grove Lodge will be placed at the disposal of the Party for the duration. I have been blessed with a certain amount of good fortune in the material sense, and I think it incumbent upon those so favoured to utilize their advantages for the common good. Not that material things have ever meant very much to me. But if you could arrange for a couple of crates of Perrier and some wine to be delivered, I'd be grateful. I promised Celia I'd see to it, but I don't think I'll be returning until late.'

'Sure, no problem, will be done.' I was always accepting tedious little commissions of this nature with a show of enthusiasm, because I was always slightly relieved that they hadn't turned out to be even more tedious. Besides, I liked the idea of ingratiating myself with Celia.

Meanwhile Charles had come to another halt. He stood towering in the middle of the room, rocking back and forth inside his size twelve brogues, gesticulating at the floor with a look of deepening horror.

'Is that thing yours?'

'You mean the leather jacket? It's not mine exactly, but I suppose you could say I have a custodial responsibility for it.'

'You're not a closet Hell's Angel are you?'

'Oh no, nothing like that.'

'Only you never know where you are with people these days, do you? All this in and out of cupboards.'

I gradually manoeuvred him towards the front door. It was what I imagine manoeuvring a Henry Moore statue must feel like.

'Silly old fart,' I muttered once he was safely out of earshot. One good thing though – he hadn't raised the Alan Sayeed business. Obviously it had never crossed Charles' mind that I should resign because of a little domestic complication like that.

The only problem still outstanding was what to wear. My clothes typically have the kind of low-key qualities one associates with a brown hedge moth on a brown hedge. But tonight I felt something rather more flamboyant and assertive was required. So I tried on the black hat with the wide brim, the paramilitary dark glasses, the leather jacket with the skull and cross bones, the riding boots that didn't fit, the rainbow-coloured neckerchief, all trophies I had acquired from my long years of clearing up after jumble sales. None of them created quite the effect I was searching for. That insouciant touch of urban revolutionary esprit remained as elusive as ever.

3

The Ronaynes lived in a large Georgian house in a tranquil little backwater just a stone's throw from one of the borough's worst slums. In the circumstances, I was surprised more stones didn't get thrown straight through the front room windows. But the Good Lord looks after his own, so it seems, and the spasmodic summer riots repeatedly passed off without any apparent damage to the Ronayne fascia work.

The house was a fairish old distance from my place, so I took the Party van. I went the river route along by the docks, or London's answer to Venice as the estate agents liked to hype it. The nearest I've got to Venice is the San Remo Grill, but if the high density of rodents, the lousy sewage and the general stink of corruption and decay is anything to go by, then the comparison holds good, I went that way in the hope of spotting some new billboard announcing luxury apartments for impoverished but worthy citizens, easy terms, no deposit. I was out of luck.

On arrival I parked on the square with its private garden for residents only. The van's wing mirrors had been vandalized the previous week and the windows didn't open, so I used the aural technique of reversing till I hit something. Unfortunately, what I hit was Meryll's Lambretta. I straightened it out as best I could and sprang up the short flight of steps that led to the Ronayne portico. I pressed, with a tremble of anticipation, a twee little porcelain bell set in a brass dome, that put me in mind of one of Celia Ronayne's nipples. Not that I was in the habit of pressing, or doing anything else for that matter, to Celia's nipples. I had, however, once glimpsed them through a transparent silk blouse she had worn to a garden party the previous summer, and the experience had made a deep and lasting impression.

For a start it was such a quaint old-fashioned thing to do, appropriate perhaps to the Sixties, but hardly to be expected at a serious gathering of hard-nosed politicos under the thrall of Thatcherdom. And for seconds, Celia was just not the sort of woman you would have expected such behaviour of during any era, which made me wonder whether she was fully aware of quite how revealing the blouse really was. But surely a woman always checks that sort of thing in front of a mirror? And the absence of a bra must have been deliberate. I mean, it isn't the sort of item you just forget to put on, is it? Clearly I have no direct personal experience but I'd guess you'd feel the weight of them swinging about.

So there had to be another explanation than simple absent-mindedness. Perhaps Charles had accused her of not being sexy enough. Or she was trying to provoke him by flaunting herself. Or, and as far as I was concerned this was by far the most interesting of the various alternatives, she was trying to seduce a third party. I certainly got the impression that afternoon, as we stood together on the damp lawn in the fading pink light, discussing, as far as I can recall, the feminist novel, that she was paying me special attention. To this day I am convinced that I could observe her nipples lengthening as the shadows deepened. But whether this was entirely an effect of the sensual qualities of my conversation, or whether the chill wind whipping round from the back of the greenhouse also had something to do with it, I'm not too sure.

I realize I've gone on about Celia's breasts at some length. I hope I don't appear guilty of prurience. Andrea has always accused me of having a dirty-magazine mentality. But, in this instance, Celia's bra-lessness has not been gratuitously introduced. It happens to have a curious bearing on what happened later.

21

I pressed the bell a second time and focused my attention on a plum tree in the centre of the private garden that was just coming into white blossom, as if nature had contracted a sudden case of acute anaemia. Still no-one came. I tried the handle and discovered I could let myself in. The hallway was full of people milling about. I hadn't penetrated very far when I was brought up short by someone bawling out, 'Ticket.'

It was Meryll. She was seated behind a rather rococo-looking table piled up with raffle tickets, miscellaneous tins and the odd dog-eared socialist tract. She was wearing a green Barbour and a red beret and had a pair of iron spiral fire escapes dangling from her ear lobes.

'Got one somewhere,' I said, searching through my pockets. Meryll looked ostentatiously bored. I rechecked my pockets in the reverse direction. 'I think it must have fallen through one of these holes.'

I flapped my jacket open to display the parlous state of my pocket linings.

Meryll averted her eyes like she'd just been flashed. 'Oh for fuck's sake. I really can't stand men who put on the big pathos act just because they haven't got a little woman to service their every need any more.'

I paid for a second ticket and pressed on in to the main body of the house. I didn't take what Meryll said too personally. It was just her manner.

Going with the general drift, I shortly washed up in what Charles and Celia called their morning room. It had a fine moulded ceiling, tall south-facing windows and French doors which led on to a verandah. There were a large number of other guests, most of whom I'd never set eyes on before, but then there had been a large influx of new recruits during the previous few months. The main spread of the food was laid out on a polished elm table, which reminded me that I was still clutching my own little sacrificial offering. I was just looking around for somewhere to deposit it when Celia descended upon me as if from the heavens. She was wearing a grey linen dress, her usual rather severe spectacles and had her red hair tied back in a bun. She affected something of the style of a Soviet psychiatrist specializing in neurasthenic disorders. But then I've always had this weakness for authority figures. And she did also have high cheekbones, a long neck, pale skin, grey eyes, and a surprisingly sexy mouth.

'Joseph. How lovely to see you. And you've brought sausages. What an original idea. I don't think anyone's ever thought to bring sausages to one of our potlucks before. I'll just pop them on a salver. I do think presentation is half the battle, don't you?'

'That's what the Right always say when they want to water down our policies,' snorted Ted Clarke, simultaneously cramming a salmon tartlet into his mouth and spluttering large quantities of it out again.

Celia bristled and half turned away so as to exclude Clarke from further conversation, and also perhaps to protect herself from the astral shower of pastry crumbs that was now descending. She placed two fingers on my wrist in a gesture that was both intimate and authoritative. 'I do hope we can find a few minutes later on in the evening for a little chat. There's something I rather wanted your advice on. And I do so enjoy our tête-à-têtes.'

'Yes, yes, of course,' I said. 'So do I. Whenever you like.' Afterwards I regretted I couldn't have come across as rather more witty and masterful, instead of so eager and willing. Andrea once said of me that, where women are concerned, I have the finesse of a Labrador emerging from a muddy pond.

'It's about Charles,' whispered Celia. 'He's threatening to take up painting again.'

'Wives have complained of worse activities on the parts of their husbands,' I said.

'I realize that,' said Celia, removing her hand. 'But it's for his sake I'm worried. The truth is he just isn't any good. He'll never get a top West End dealer to handle him. Oh, I know it's not very loyal of me to say this, but we've been through it all before, Joseph. He'll end

23

up getting depressed. I just wish he'd stick to playing politics. Perhaps I shouldn't interfere, but I do feel it's all my fault.'

'I really don't see how you can blame yourself for your husband's artistic aspirations,' I said. Though I knew very well from past experience that Celia was quite capable of blaming herself for anything from the deterioration of British Rail to the malign character of her pet cat.

'Don't you?' she said, giving me a mournful look. 'Don't you? Wealth is a mixed blessing you know. But we can't talk now. Later. I'll just give these a bit of a face-lift.' She patted my hand again and whisked the sausages away to a back room somewhere for emergency plastic surgery.

'What the bugger was that lot? Bag of constipated dog turds?' Clarke was now busy snuffling his way through an enormous slice of strawberry gâteau.

'Chipolatas, actually,' I said.

'Looked a bit on the overdone side to me.'

'I think that's all a matter of taste, don't you? Anyway, what did you bring?'

'Me! Bugger all, comrade. Bugger all. I'm not a lackey of the bourgeoisie. Don't go along with your cosy supper party view of politics. If we're ever going to get any change in this sodding arse'ole of a cunt-ry of ours, it'll be through action on the factory floor, not arty-farty yuppy dinner parties.'

If Ronnie Mullins was the godfather of the Right, then Ted Clarke was certainly the guru of the Left. He had an almost legendary status among the younger generation of party activists, because he had actually been a shop steward at British Leyland, in the days when British Leyland was still Austin Rover. Made redundant by Michael Edwardes, he had gone on to do a degree at Ruskin College and was now a lecturer in Industrial Relations at one of the London polys. However, he had not allowed academic success to detract from his working-class credibility. He remained an old-fashioned, hard line vanguardist, with a pot belly, lank greasy hair and trousers that continually required hitching up.

'Is there any decent beer in this place? This stuff tastes like piss.' He poured a nearly full glass of white wine into a maidenhair fern.

'I don't quite understand why, feeling as you do, you bother to come along to these little gatherings.'

'To support Alan, the poor bugger. Once this mob of middle-class do-gooders sink their nails into his bum they'll have his balls for meat paste.' Clarke smirked.

I realized this was a not particularly subtle reference to my ex-wife's relationship with our newly-selected parliamentary candidate. I also realized I was meant to be outraged. Provoking outrage was a Ted Clarke speciality. But what I actually felt was a barely suppressed desire to laugh. You see, it had not struck me forcibly before, but if there was anyone in the Party who would find the Alan Sayeed-Andrea affair even more unacceptable than I did myself, it was Ted Clarke. Clarke and Andrea were both on the hard Left, of course. But while Andrea was a militant feminist, Clarke was a member of Militant. As such, he had no time for the women's movement, the peace movement, the environmental movement, etc., etc. 'All these trendy movements give me the shits,' was how he was fond of putting it. Andrea, for her part, regarded Clarke as a Neolithic chauvinist who didn't change his underclothes often enough.

'So, you're here as Alan's self-appointed minder are you?' I said.

'Just want to see he gets a fair crack of the whip. What are you doing? Wouldn't have expected to see you within a million miles of this place. Your old boss Ronnie Mullins sent you along to spy on us has he?'

'Me? I'm the Party Agent. It's my duty to be here.'

'I heard you were jacking it in.'

'Did you? I don't know who told you that. But I'm afraid you must have been misinformed.'

The hairs began to twitch inside Ted Clarke's nostrils,

a sure sign his passions were aroused. I'd known all along, of course, that he, like Andrea, would want me out the way, if for different reasons.

'You won't mind holding Alan's coat for him while he screws the wife then?'

I suppose, in retrospect, I should at that point have punched Clarke on the nose. It would have been the manly thing to do and Clarke's nose was a large bulbous affair providing an ample target. But punching noses has never been much my style. It would have caused a scene and I'm not over-fond of scenes. I get easily embarrassed. Besides, I have to admit I'm something of a physical coward.

'Andrea and I were divorced eighteen months ago,' I said. 'Her personal life is entirely her own affair. As for Alan's jacket, I don't think you need concern yourself on that score. There is a wardrobe in the bedroom plentifully furnished with coat hangers.'

I didn't wait around for Clarke's response, but made off smartly towards the drinks table.

There was quite a crowd at this end of the room and getting to the front was a pretty ruthless business. When my turn eventually came, I decided to make the best of it and so drank off three glasses of some sweet white german stuff in quick succession. It tasted horrible and I knew I'd regret it before the night was out, but the immediate effect was what was required. My exchange with Clarke had shaken my nerves somewhat. I was just backing off when I collided with Melrose Guthrie.

'Sorry, Melrose, didn't see you there in the crush.'

'My fault, dear boy. My fault entirely. I'm good for nothing these days except getting in the way of others. The unenviable fate of the old and lame.'

'Nonsense,' I said. 'You're a damn sight fitter than me and you know it.'

Melrose's blue eyes twinkled boyishly. He liked to be complimented on his extraordinary state of physical preservation. He was about seventy, a Quaker and a retired headmaster of a private progressive boarding school with firm ideas about diet and exercise. He was wearing his usual pair of khaki shorts and an open-neck check shirt.

'Can I tempt you to some of my home-made apple juice?' he whispered, indicating a thick murky substance in what looked like a recycled paraffin can.

'Later, later,' I said.

'Well, you know where it is. No need to ask. It's for the general good.'

'Most kind of you.'

Melrose then turned his beatific attention upon the room at large. 'I must say it is most encouraging to see so many of our people turning out in support of the new candidate. And I do think he is a first-class choice don't you. First-class. I know there are those who say he's a bit far to the left. Well, there are always those who will say that. Personally, I don't think a little leftward leaning is such a bad thing in a young man. I was a communist myself before the war. Of course, we all were in those days. But what really sets Alan head and shoulders above the rest is his manner. He has such an attractive manner. Don't you agree? He has your support, I hope?'

Melrose gave me a searching look, no doubt the sort of look he was in the habit of giving his pupils when they came before him on charges of subverting the moral values of the school.

'Support? Oh, yes. Yes, of course. He is the Party's choice, so naturally he has my full backing.'

'Good,' said Melrose. 'I'm glad of that. He's going to need all the support he can get, I fear.' He assumed an expression of grim foreboding but did not elaborate. 'By the way,' he added, with a sudden change of tack that was characteristic of him. 'Have you finished printing that little leaflet of mine yet?'

'Which leaflet?' I asked. Melrose was forever giving me little leaflets for printing.

'The one on leaf mulch.'

'Ah, yes. No. No, I haven't quite finished it yet. Afraid

the old Gestetner's been playing me up a bit lately.'

'No hurry, no hurry. I thought if you had finished I'd drop by and pick it up. But no hurry.'

'I'll have it done by the end of next week,' I said, 'And that's a promise.'

'I know how hard-pressed you are, my boy. And what stalwart work you have been doing. Ah, there's Eric. I must have a word with him about the Sunday stall. So nice talking to you again.'

I helped myself to another drink and then went in search of a lavatory. I tried the downstairs cloakroom first, only to discover that it had a 'Women Only' notice hung on the door, a pre-emptive strike by the feminists no doubt. Andrea was forever complaining about how women were discriminated against when it came to the allocation of urinal resources. I was not unduly discomposed. A residence such as the Ronaynes' had to possess at least five different lavatories tucked away in various nooks and crannies. And, truth is, I like an excuse for poking around in other people's houses.

I was halfway across the hall on my way towards the stairs when I was brought up short by Meryll again, this time thrusting a tin under my nose.

'We're holding a collection for the Walthamstow Eleven, in case you hadn't noticed.'

'The Walthamstow Eleven, eh?' I racked my brain. I'd heard of the Clay Cross Seven, of course, and the Alconbury Nine and the Brent Three. But for the life of me I couldn't place the Walthamstow Eleven. Still, it would never have done to have admitted ignorance of their sufferings so I slipped a few coins in. Meryll waited until I'd finished and then said, keeping the tin thrust firmly under my nose, 'We're asking those in work to make it a note.'

'Afraid I've only got a tenner,' I said.

'That'll do.'

'Yes, well I would and willingly, only I'm already feeling a bit the worse for wear and I was thinking I might need to get a taxi home.'

Meryll shrieked. 'For fuck's sake. Haven't you got legs? Just think for a moment what those women have gone through on our behalf. And you're not even prepared to hoof it a few yards down the fuckin' road. Your sort make me want to fuckin' throw up.' And Meryll went into her impressive imitation of someone gagging routine.

'Thinking about it, I guess I might be able to cadge a lift off someone,' I said. I shiftily stuffed the note in the tin, hoping no-one had witnessed my craven act of submission.

'Thanks,' snarled Meryll.

I made for the staircase. Halfway up the main sweep I ran into Jonathan and Julian crouching together. They were both postgraduates with short haircuts and Doc Martin boots and I could never for the life of me remember which was which, not that it really mattered. They were arguing about the relevance of Gramsci's prison notebooks for a future Labour government. I clambered past them using their heads as newel posts for which purpose they were surprisingly well-suited.

I was just starting down the landing when Charles emerged from a door on my right. He didn't look over-pleased to see me.

'Thought you weren't going to be here,' I said.

'I'm not here,' he said. 'And if anyone says anything to the contrary, you haven't seen me.'

'Fine,' I said. 'Fine. Oh, before you disappear, could you just direct me to the nearest loo?'

'Nearest what,' said Charles as if he was entirely unfamiliar with the term.

'Loo, can, john, bog, carzey, little boy's room, that sort of thing. Only the one downstairs is off limits, for us males at any rate.'

'You could try the last door on your left,' said Charles vaguely, as if he wasn't too sure of the topography of his own house. He then crept off in the other direction. The sight of Charles creeping was like an elephant walking a tightrope.

'Thanks awfully,' I called.

29

The last door on the left indeed turned out to be the very haven I was searching for. I shot the bolt and leant back against the cool, wooden panel. I savoured for an exquisite second the delicious anticipation of relief, secure in the knowledge that nothing could now come between me and the eau-de-nil double syphonic by Armitage Shanks. Secure. How deluded I was. This world admits to no such condition. The folly of human optimism has perhaps never been more brutally demonstrated. My hand had no sooner begun to locate my zip when there came a terrible rapping at the door. I froze. The banging was renewed with increased fervour, rapid, staccato, like the heel of an expensive shoe.

'It's no good you thinking you can hide away in there indefinitely, Joseph. Because you can't. I shall simply wait here until you come out. And I don't care how long it takes.'

It was Andrea, and she didn't sound in the best of moods.

'There's another one downstairs,' I said. 'Women only. Dry seat.'

'It's you I want not the bloody pisspot. Though by the sounds of you there isn't much to choose between the two.'

'Me! How can I help?' I said, reluctantly rezipping my trousers. It was no good. I would just have to postpone micturition. I have always suffered from this inhibition that prevents me from having an argument and passing water at the same time.

'I'm not talking through a shut door,' said Andrea.

'I don't see why not,' I said. 'We seem to be managing adequately so far.'

This was the sort of preliminary haggling about place, time, agenda, that always went on before one of our rows.

I took a quick glance out of the window. There was a soil-vent pipe tastefully wreathed with a wisteria and an anonymous-looking tree at a distance of about five yards. But I have no head for heights.

'All right,' said Andrea, in that precise, controlled voice of hers that always preceded the onset of screaming. 'If you don't mind having our sordid business shouted about so that the entire assembled company can hear every last dirty little word, that's fine by me.'

I promptly slid the bolt back. First round to Andrea. It had always been my contention that Andrea won all our arguments, not because of the superior morality of her position or even the ruthless logic of her discourse, but because she was always the one prepared to deploy nuclear weapons first.

'What was it you were wishing to discuss with me exactly?' I said. I tried for a cool distant tone. But it was difficult with Andrea standing there hand on hip, head thrown back, looking stunning. She was wearing a sharp, cream two-piece suit, combining femininity with efficiency. Her honey-coloured hair had been stylishly cut around those neat, well-controlled ears. And all in all she looked at least ten years younger than when we'd been married, which made me wonder whether in the past I hadn't infected her with my own dowdiness. Perhaps I really had destroyed her self-esteem, as she was always claiming, not through any deliberate strategy for domination on my part but simply by association. Right now she was positively glowing with health and confidence.

'You really are pathetic,' she said, looking me up and down.

'Would you care to elaborate a little?' I said.

'You promised me if Alan was chosen you'd give up the agent's job.'

'I promised you I'd think about it, which I have done.'

'Most people in your situation wouldn't have needed to think about it. They would have resigned as soon as Alan had been selected. They would have pissed off not just because everyone in the Party wants them to piss off, but out of some sense of dignity. But not you. Oh no, you must go on clinging to your pathetic little bit of power. You don't give a fuck about what is good for

31

just so long as Joseph Pink is not put to any ⌐ce.'
me in here?' I raised an index finger in the manner.
'May I just finish, if you don't very much mind.'

'Yes, of course.' I lowered the said finger.

'As I was saying, I did not actually expect you to do the decent thing and piss off out of it. That would have been asking too much. You've always taken a delight in making my life as awkward as you possibly can. But I did think you might show me the simple courtesy of informing me of your decision first, instead of leaving me to find out for myself, second-hand, in the most humiliating of circumstances.'

'You've been talking to Clarke.'

'Clarke has been making obscene utterances in my hearing, would be a more accurate description.'

'Yes, I'm sorry about that. But on a point of information, I did tell you I was coming to the Ronaynes.'

'So?'

'I thought you would realize that if I was putting in an appearance I obviously intended to stay on as the agent.'

'I don't play guessing games, Joseph. It's not my style. You might enjoy that sort of thing. You have a devious mentality. I happen to believe in straight talking.'

'Well, it was certainly my intention to inform you first.'

'Intentions are irrelevant. It's actions that count. Still, at least we both know where we stand now. No more of this charade of civilized behaviour. From now on it's gloves off. I think I shall prefer that. And by the way, that orange tie looks perfectly ridiculous with that shirt.' With which parting shot she turned and swept off down the stairs.

I was still reeling a little when, just to add insult to injury, some flame-haired youth rushed past me into the lavatory. From the way he had one hand cupped in front of his mouth, it looked as if he was intending to take up occupation for a fairish length of time. So I was back to

32

square one in my long march for a place to relieve my swollen bladder.

I was leaning against the balustrade considering my next move when, from the well of the hallway, there rose a buzz of excitement. Alan Sayeed had arrived. He thrust his way through the crowd like a man who meant business. He was wearing a shiny grey suit with a shortish Italian waiter style jacket which showed off his biceps and pectorals to good effect. His necktie was loosened and the top button of his shirt was undone. He was sweating slightly in the press of his supporters. His skin shone like a film actor's.

'Comrades, comrades. Thank you for your warm welcome. Thank you. I would have been here earlier, only at about quarter to eight this evening I discovered I hadn't got a clean shirt to my name and I thought, Christ, I can't make my first appearance as your candidate smelling like a Tory pig farmer,' (laughter) 'so I popped down the laundarola for a quick wash and tumble dry. And you know I'm really glad I did, because it turned out to be a really valuable experience. I don't know how many of you people use launderettes? Yes, I thought as much, not many. Well, I do use launderettes and what's more I make a solemn pledge to all of you here tonight, I shall go on using them just so long as the people I represent use them. I'm talking now about the pensioners, the students, the single-parent families, the blacks, the gays.' (Applause.) 'And when you think about it, the true socialist shouldn't be ashamed to wash his dirty linen in public, should he?' (More laughter.) 'Anyway, while I was there I got chatting to some of the old people and kids and workers, and we got on to the subject of the Labour Party and how let down they all felt by the Wilson-Callaghan years. Betrayed was the word used. Betrayed. Not a nice word is it? But I had to agree with them. You're all the same they said. Full of promises. Full of lies. That's the challenge, comrades. To get rid of the lies. To make socialism a reality. Believe me, if we fail our people this time, we might never be given another

chance. That's why we must insist on a radical pro-
gramme of reform, not a shopping list of compromises
with the ruling class.'

Rapturous applause faded out into a chorus of *The
Red Flag*. I can never listen to communal singing of any
sort without experiencing an uncontrollable surge of
emotion. The immediate consequence of this was a
doubly renewed desire to pee. The flame-haired youth
had still not emerged, and the melee in the hall was
blocking a rapid exit to the garden. There had to be an
alternative.

I opened a door at random. Within, a half-dressed
couple were thrashing about on the floor amid a pile of
guests' coats. The woman had straight platinum-blonde
hair with a thin gold chain around her left ankle. But it
was the expression in her eyes that, afterwards, I found
difficult to forget. She was staring at the ceiling with a
look of utter boredom, as if what was happening to her
body had nothing whatsoever to do with her. Her glance
strayed to me and I hastily closed the door. The man on
top of her had borne a marked similarity to Jack White,
the Assistant National Agent with special responsibility
for co-ordination. Jack had a reputation for being a bit of
a womanizer. Even so I was somewhat surprised at his
choice of locale. Of course, some people are supposed to
get an added frisson from that sort of thing. The sleight
of hand up the skirt during the pudding course. The
quick screw between railways stations. And so on. Personally, I can't see the attraction. It's not as if sex isn't a
nerve-wracking enough business under the best of conditions. Why go out of your way to make life difficult for
yourself?

I tried another door. It wasn't right either, but I felt
less inclined to rush straight out again. The room before
me had a gentility and refinement immediately sugges-
tive of Celia. The walls were painted the palest of pale
lavender, with a stencilled frieze. A white lace curtain
stirred as the air circulated through an open lower sash.
A bowl of potpourri stood on a polished chest of drawers.

I particularly noted that there was only a single divan bed with a patchwork quilt chastely turned back. So Celia and Charles had separate sleeping arrangements. Of course, that didn't necessarily mean anything more than that they lived in a house that was more than large enough to allow for such luxury.

On the bedside table, placed face down, was a copy of Barbara Pym's *Excellent Women*. Next to it was a small bottle of Temazepam pills and an alarm clock set for six-thirty. An early riser. There was also a desk against one wall and a cane chair with a cardigan neatly folded over the back of it. On the desk was a half-written letter to someone called Janine. It was written with a fountain pen, dark blue ink on light blue paper, a slightly wild upward-sloping script. Celia was apologizing to her correspondent for some selfishness, but quite what she had done wasn't immediately clear.

I turned my attention to a wardrobe built into an alcove. Celia's collection of clothes was not particularly extensive, but what she had was mainly good quality; Jaeger, Liberty, that style of thing. There was one ensemble, however, which immediately caught my eye as being anomalous. A short black leather miniskirt, a wide red leather belt, and the see-through blouse that I remembered from the garden party. All these items were neatly arranged on the one hanger. Beneath was a pair of red stilettos. What was this? Some sort of reliquary from her girlhood that she was reluctant to throw away? The clothes looked too new for that. A fancy-dress get-up for some vicars and tarts party? Hardly Celia's style. There were clearly depths to Celia's character that I knew nothing about, I was intrigued.

I crossed the room and opened a second cupboard door. Inside was a closet with a basin and a mirror above it. A single pink toothbrush stood in a glass tumbler like a rose. I removed the toothbrush and sniffed it. It smelt of peppermint. I slipped it into my pocket for my own future use. I wanted it as a love token. What could be more intimate than a toothbrush, the bristles of which had explored Celia's most secret cavities. I was rather drunk.

It was only as I was about to leave that a further idea occurred to me. The bowl. Why not the bowl? And once the thought had entered my consciousness it became totally compelling. I am not in the habit of peeing down other people's sinks, nor my own come to that. But I was desperate. And the alternative options, as they presented themselves to me at that moment, did not seem very favourable. And where, after all, was the harm. Urine is just about the most sterile substance known to mankind. And I would rinse the bowl thoroughly afterwards. And if I didn't find somewhere soon God knows what embarrassing events might come to pass.

However, I had no sooner taken the matter in hand than a complication occurred. I was not quite tall enough. I took a step or two backwards and considered an upwards trajectory. But what if I calculated the parabola wrongly? The pressure on my bladder was now such that I might well overshoot. And I had no desire to spoil the soft white carpet beneath my feet or leave a nasty stain on the pretty William Morris wallpaper which lined the inside of the closet. Then a solution presented itself. I fetched the cane chair and positioned myself upon it above the porcelain bowl shaped like a scallop shell. Perfect. I was in full flood hitting the plug hole with the uncanny accuracy of a first-class marksman when I noticed, in the mirror, Celia, standing in the doorway.

There were no histrionics, no recriminations. She just went on standing there being quietly appalled. Towards the end, shortly before she rushed from the room, she did just utter a little scream and raised her hand to her mouth as if she had just burped or committed some other mild indiscretion. But that was all.

4

I can remember very little about what happened after Celia's departure, apart from drinking a lot more wine than was good for me and eating an excessive quantity of chipolatas, more out of paternal pride than any real hunger. Somehow I must have got home, because that was where I found myself the following morning.

I was woken by a horrendous clattering and banging which started off inside my head, but which I gradually externalized as coming from down below. My first thought, naturally enough, was that the police had arrived to arrest me for indecent exposure. I would have to resign the agent's job now, of course. There could be no avoiding it. I could hardly drag the Party through an embarrassing series of court appearances. I just hoped that whatever they chose to do to me it would be quick and painless. However, when after several minutes they had still failed to burst through the bedroom door, I began to have doubts as to whether I'd got it right. Perhaps it wasn't the police. Perhaps it was the entire cast of The Ring of the Nibelung having an impromptu rehearsal in my understairs cupboard. I got out of bed. There was no need to dress because I had clearly dispensed with the formality of undressing the previous evening.

On descending I discovered Pam, wheezing horribly and hugging a large metal tubular container with a wire coming out of its base. It might have been an electronic waste-disposal unit or a portable silo or, just possibly, the bottom stage of a miniature Apollo rocket. Pam was

Meryll's flatmate, or do I mean house person? She was large and rather on the tubular side herself, with a gash of vivid red lipstick in the general area of her mouth. She put me in mind of an animated pillar box.

'Oh dear,' she said.

'Can I be of help?' I said.

'I think I can manage, thanks. I was just bringing round a few odds and ends of jumble.' She collided a second time with the wall, dislodging a large flake of plaster.

'Mind the fabric. I am sort of responsible for keeping this place in good internal order and repair.'

'Gosh, it's heavy,' said Pam, promptly dropping whatever it was, a tea urn perhaps or a Scandinavian-designed commode, on my foot. I winced manfully. Pam heaved a satisfied sigh.

'Well,' I said, after a pause to allow the pain to subside, 'are you going to enlighten me as to its nature?'

'It's a Baby Burco.'

'Really! Looks more like a Jumbo Burco to me. What do you do with it exactly?'

'You boil things in it.'

'Like babies, I suppose.'

'That's a very tasteless remark.'

'My apologies. I'm feeling a bit off-colour this morning.'

I lifted the lid. A smell not too dissimilar to rancid cauliflower water hit me right between the olfactory passages. I hastily replaced the lid again for fear of gagging on the spot.

'They're very useful,' said Pam.

'Oh, I can see that, all right. Should be just fine for putting the mulled wine in at the next Christmas bazaar.'

'You do nappies and things in them,' said Pam. 'I was thinking I might try and buy it myself.' She gave me a coy look which I didn't quite know how to interpret.

I helped her fetch in the rest of the items. The usual mountains of clothes, a set of aluminium saucepans, a rather risqué plaster statue of a woman with amputated arms, draped in a sheet in the classical manner, with bare breasts. I was surprised that had got past the sado-sexism censors. The hallway began to take on its familiar aspect of temporary refugee camp.

'You've done well,' I said, balancing the last paperback on top of the eight-foot-long radiogram, which no longer worked but which could easily convert into a de luxe rabbit hutch.

'Well, someone's got to do it, haven't they,' sighed Pam in her sacrificial victim voice. 'Oh dear. I just wish there was a bit more co-operative effort. The trouble is, it's always left to the same old few stalwarts. Meryll and me to be precise. Not that we mind. But we can't go on doing it all by ourselves for ever. I always thought socialism was about everyone shouldering their fair share of the burden. Oh dear.'

'Well, how about me making you a cup of coffee,' I said.

'I don't drink coffee any more.'

'Tea then. I think I've got some somewhere.'

'I don't drink tea either.'

'What's all this? You become a vegan or something?'

'If you must know, I'm trying to get pregnant.'

'Ah, I see.' I didn't see at all, but I didn't want to appear prying.

Once Pam had started, however, there was frequently no stopping her.

'Meryll says all stimulants are bad because they increase tension and tension is one of the main causes of lack of fertility.'

'Well, that makes sense.'

'It's really Meryll's idea that we should have a baby. She thinks it will help bring us closer together.'

I nodded. This was difficult territory.

'Meryll thinks once the baby is born it will be easier for us to have sex together.'

I turned the gas jet on too fast, blowing the match out. I was finding the combination of these intimate confessions and Pam's plodding nasal voice at this hour of the morning slightly surreal. Of course, being party agent had always been a little like being a priest. Even so it was difficult to know quite how to respond. Fortunately, Pam didn't seem to require too much in that way.

'At the moment, you see, we're not doing it. I have done it in the past with other women, but Meryll says she's not ready for that yet. She wants us to have a baby first to prove that we really care about each other. Oh dear, I expect this all really shocks you, doesn't it?' She looked at me combatively.

'Shock? Me? No, I'm not shocked. Why, should I be?'

'A lot of men feel threatened by the idea of women having babies without them. Makes them redundant, doesn't it? Do you mind if I have a glass of water before I start duplicating?' Pam stood up.

'No, of course not.' I reached for the tap.

Duplicating. My God, was she going to start here, right now, in my kitchen? I had this horrific vision of Pam replicating herself, by parthenogenesis, of course, all over the Marley lino tiles.

'If you'd just explain how the duplicating thing works,' said Pam.

This was going from bad to worse. Was she really wanting my advice on the mysteries of conception? Then it clicked.

'Oh, you mean the Gestetner?'

'Yes, the Gestetner duplicator thing, whatever you call it.'

It was just then that the phone went.

'Excuse me a moment will you.' I went through to the office.

'Joseph.'

'Andrea.'

'You're late.'

'Oh my God. I'm meant to be . . .'

'Exactly.'

'I'll be right over.'

'It's not very fair on Livingstone, you know. He builds

40

up these outings with you into big occasions. God knows why, but he does.'

'Yes, I'm sorry. I really am sorry. I'll be with you in five minutes.'

'You realize it's grounds for stopping your access altogether?'

'I'm coming now. Oh, and Andrea?'

'Yes.'

'Look, I've been thinking over what we were talking about yesterday, you know, about me giving up my job and everything, and I think perhaps on mature reflection you have got a point and it might be the best for everyone concerned if I chose this moment to sort of bow out.'

'Oh no you don't.'

'I don't? Why not? I thought that was what you wanted. I thought you'd be pleased.'

'I know your game, Joseph. You just want to off-load all the responsibility and guilt for making a decision on to someone else. You forget I know you of old. You've never had the guts to make up your own mind about a damned thing. You always need someone to blame. Well, I'm afraid I'm not prepared to play your scapegoat any more.'

'Let me get this right. You're now saying you want me to stay on as agent?'

'No. What I'm saying is that if you'd resigned straight off, like any decent person with any moral dignity, I would have thought better of you. But it's too late now. The moment is past. And I'm not prepared for you to go around bleating to everyone about how I pushed you into it.'

'But what if circumstances were to change?'

'In what way?'

'Well, talking hypothetically for the moment, what if I had done something that might possibly damage the Party?'

'What the hell are you on about? What sort of thing?'

'Never mind. I'll be with you in two ticks.'

41

I put the phone down. So Celia had said nothing. Or so far she had said nothing. There was still plenty of time, of course. She was probably consulting her solicitors at that very moment. After all, someone of Celia's background wouldn't just go mouthing off. But even so there was the slenderest of slender chances that she might just be too embarrassed to speak of it. It was the only hope I had.

I went back to Pam. She was standing with her arms folded like a woman who meant business.

'The duplicator.'

'Ah yes,' I said. 'Look, I'm not trying to be difficult about this or anything but what is it you wanted done?'

Pam looked suspicious. 'I suppose there's no harm in you knowing. A group of us, well Meryll and me mainly, have formed an action committee to mobilize mass support to put pressure on the police to re-open the case of the Walthamstow women. We want to circularize the membership.'

'Fine, fine, only it's a bit tricky just at the moment. I have to dash off you see. Why don't you leave me the master copy, I mean the important person copy, and I'll get it done for you later on.'

'I'd rather do it myself if it's all the same with you.'

'Sure. Sure. But it's a pig of a machine, no offence meant to the animal community, and I really don't mind doing it.'

'Of course you don't mind. Knowledge is power, isn't it? Something men have had a monopoly on for far too long. Well, if you're not going to show me I shall just have to find out for myself.'

It was quite uncanny how sometimes, just lately, Pam, who was usually pleasant and mild-mannered, managed to sound exactly like Meryll. It was as if she'd been programmed.

'Well, watch out for the ink,' I called. 'It squidges a bit.'

5

I took the Party van round to Andrea's. Strictly against the rules, but right then I feared the wrath of my ex-wife rather more than the punitive sanctions of the General Purposes Committee. Even so, I took the elementary precaution of parking in the next street, like a guilty lover. It would be just like Andrea to report me for misuse of Party assets if she was given half the chance.

Walking up the garden path overgrown with lilac, I experienced a pang of something rather more acute than nostalgia. Amputation was probably nearer the mark.

The door was opened by Alan Sayeed in white shirt and jeans, bare foot, tousle haired, grinning like a toothpaste advert.

'Joseph, how nice to see you. Come on in.'

Andrea was nowhere in sight.

'Is Livingstone ready?' I said. 'I'm taking him out. It's my access day.' It sounded like it was my turn to use the joint credit card.

'I'll rustle him up for you,' said Alan. 'But come on in.'

I had the alternative of standing on the doorstep like a lemon or suffering the humiliation of having Alan Sayeed welcome me into my own house. I infinitely preferred the short sharp business-like transactions I had with Andrea. At least they allowed me the luxury of self-righteous anger.

'I say that was quite a party we had last night, wasn't it? I thought you were on particularly good form.'

He led the way into the knocked-through sitting room with its varnished floors, Indian rugs, cast-iron tiled fireplace in pine surround, brass wall lamps. The place had undergone some considerable degree of gentrification since my departure. Andrea had a good job in housing welfare which enabled her to indulge her taste for Victoriana. I had never quite understood why Victorian values were out but the furnishings were OK. But then Andrea had always accused me of having the aesthetic sensibility of a loo seat cover salesman.

'Make yourself at home,' said Alan, which I felt was a bit tactless in the circumstances. He draped himself elegantly over the pink chesterfield sofa as if to illustrate just how relaxed and at home he felt himself to be. I could see why Andrea had swopped us. He toned so much better with the general colour scheme. Put me on a pink sofa and I would just look florid and sweaty.

'How do you mean, good form?' I said, suspiciously.

'What you had to say to Julian about the place for ideology. It was well said. I don't agree with you, but I admire your guts for saying it. How about a drink? Tea, coffee, hair of the dog?'

I shook my head. Thank God for that. For one awful moment I thought Alan might have been referring to the sink debacle.

'Where's Andrea?'

'She's just popped out for a bit. She goes to this assertion training group on Saturday mornings. Should be back before long.'

'She what!' I knew I should have kept my mouth shut, but the idea of Andrea requiring assertion training was like an alcoholic needing home-brewing lessons.

'You sound surprised,' said Alan.

'I just never noticed Andrea was particularly slow in coming forward,' I said, already regretting getting involved in this. Alan, however, clearly had no such inhibitions.

'No offence or anything, but I guess as her husband you had something of a vested interest in undermining her. Believe me, Andy is really deep down a very unsure of herself person. We're having to do a lot of work on that together. But we're making progress. Rome wasn't built in a day.' And he gave me one of those famous Sayeed charming smiles that old Melrose was always on about.

'If Livingstone's ready I'll get straight off,' I said.

'He's just getting me a few groceries from the corner shop,' said Alan. 'Shouldn't be long.'

I felt another surge of irritation. How dare he use my son as an errand boy. Wasn't he content with living in my house scot-free while I, poor sucker, was still obliged to pay fifty per cent of the sodding mortgage, without exploiting my flesh and blood to boot?

'By the way,' said Alan, 'I wanted to say to you how pleased I am that you've agreed to stay on as my agent. I know you've been coming under a bit of pressure from certain quarters lately to quit. But that's all been straightened out now. You shouldn't have any more problems on that score. The way I see it, I'm going to need all the professional expertise I can get in this constituency and no-one knows the ropes like you do. So, welcome aboard.'

Alan made an all-embracing gesture with his arms. I smiled weakly, the famous Joseph Pink sneer. So that explained Andrea's sudden change of tack on the telephone that morning. Alan had instructed her to lay off. But would Alan still be so glad to have me along when the Celia scandal broke. Phantom urinator strikes again. Labour Agent cavorts as fountain cherub. The rehearsal of various banner headlines upon a similar theme gave me a sort of perverse pleasure.

'I shall do what I can to help,' I said.

'Ah, the famed English love of understatement,' said Alan. 'You know bloody well that you're the best in the business. Here's to the partnership of Sayeed and Pink. Together we shall be unstoppable, believe me. But let me also make this clear right from the start, Joseph.' He dropped his voice and fixed me with those dark sincere eyes, clutching my shoulder as he did so. 'I'm not in the business of keeping the old system ticking over. It's no good providing more of the same. People want change. And if that means us getting out into the streets and showing the people what socialism really stands for, well then, so be it.'

Just then Livingstone came in trailing what looked like the entire weekend's groceries. He looked pale and worried. He nodded in my direction but didn't smile. He was wearing a dark grey suit with a white shirt and striped tie.

'There's two pounds, seventy pence change and the bills are in the bag,' he said seriously.

'Good boy,' said Alan, ruffling his hair.

'Are they the only clean clothes you've got?' I asked.

Livingstone said nothing. He stared at the ground and shuffled his feet.

'He's allowed to wear his suit at weekends,' said Alan. 'As a special concession.'

'Oh right. Well, that's fine.' I'd clearly put my foot in it again. 'Jolly smart you look, too. That's a really nice tie. So let's go shall we?'

6

'Well, what shall we do then?' The van was stuck in a traffic jam. A blue haze of petrol fumes gave the Commercial Road a faintly exotic quality. 'Any ideas?'

Livingstone shrugged.

'No ideas at all?'

'Not really.'

'You mean there's nothing in the whole wide world you can think of that you'd actually positively like to do?' I tried to sound good-humoured about it. I drummed my fingers on the steering wheel and hummed a few bars of an old Beatles song that always made me cringe when I heard it on the radio. Funny how it's the songs I most dislike that come easiest to me.

The traffic moved about six yards and then stopped again. Christ, what was I doing living in this godforsaken city anyway, with a mugging every two minutes and a rape every half-hour and a drugs problem and a race problem and a sewers problem and just about every other problem you'd care to name. This was no place to bring a kid up in. One of these days I was going to get the hell out of it. A smallholding in Wales or a croft in Scotland, that sort of thing. There was still a little bit of the hippy in me, even though I could never stop myself being as rude as hell about them. Of course, getting it organized was another question. It was a bit like cracking the existence of God problem. A matter for continual deferment.

'You promised me a surprise.' Livingstone spoke with just a hint of reproachfulness in his voice.

'Yes. Yes, I did. I haven't forgotten.' I did a rapid mental somersault. One of the disconcerting things about Livingstone was you thought nothing of what you said to him was going in, but then he'd come up with something which suggested that, not only had it gone in, but it was likely to be used as evidence in the case for the prosecution.

'What is it?' he said, with inquisitorial remorselessness.

'Well, what I thought is, we'll do something different for a change. We won't go back to the flat. We'll go somewhere exciting. Anywhere you like. The seaside. The Natural History Museum. London Zoo. A football match. How about it?'

Livingstone clammed up again.

'The choice is yours,' I said.

'I don't mind.'

'Well, I don't mind either.' I tried very hard not to be bad-tempered about it but this continual non-engagement, combined with the nil progress trafficwise, was making me edgy. Why couldn't Livingstone be rude and demanding like other children just for once?

'I'd quite like to go to Westminster Abbey,' he said eventually, in a small but determined voice.

'Where?'

'Westminster Abbey.'

'That's what I thought you said. Well, why not? Good idea. You've been doing it in history have you?'

'No.'

'So, why the interest?'

'I like looking at tombstones.'

'I see. Well, Westminster Abbey then. Great idea.'

I had always known calling him Livingstone was a mistake, but Andrea had insisted. She and the infamous Ken had both served as Lambeth councillors in the early days and I think she was infatuated with him. The problem was, Livers, poor kid, seemed to think he'd been named after the great African missionary, David Livingstone. He certainly had a morbidly religious streak.

We did a U-turn and sat in the same traffic jam, only going the other way. That took up most of the morning. We then spent an hour or so reading the inscriptions on the tombs. Livingstone seemed particularly interested in working out how old people were when they died.

Afterwards we went and had a spot of late lunch in the San Remo Grill, a cosmopolitan little café, in the Lower Dock area. It was situated on the corner of a narrow street in the shadow of a disused wharf where kids held acid house parties, dossers slept, graffiti artists worked and speculators came to dream. Greasy smells from the river mingled with the equally greasy smells from the kitchen. It was run by a Greek called Dimitrios. Quite why a Greek should run a café called the San Remo was as obscure as the gastronomic inspiration behind the menu.

Dimitrios greeted me in the doorway. He was plump, balding and aproned, with dark watery eyes like olives floating in brine.

'Ah, Jozeef, I'ave not zeen you in such a long time. This eez such a pleasant surprize. Come seet over here. And this is your son, yes. How tall he has grown. Ah, the wings of time. Come, it is the best table. The very best only for my old friend. Such a long time. Too long, too long.'

I allowed myself to be guided to a corner table with a check plastic tablecloth that bore no apparent distinction from the other tables, unless it was the tomato sauce bottle, shaped like a tomato, that was haemorrhaging badly from the neck. Dimitrios flicked a few traces left by previous diners on to the floor. I ordered the house speciality of risotto-ed chicken livers with chips. Livingstone seemed somewhat less than ravenously hungry. It was all I could do to get him to try an omelette. Having shouted the orders down a hatchway Dimitrios came and sat opposite us and sighed.

'Theez are sad times, yes, for the Party. I do not understand the British Peoples. The Labour has done so much for them. It has given them the free hospitales and the free schools and the welfare state that is the envy of the world, and all the good things. And now the Peoples kick the Party in the teeth. In Greece we would be so grateful for theez things.'

Dimitrios liked to talk politics. He told exciting stories of how he had been mixed up in the democratic struggle against the Colonels and how he had finally been forced to flee for his life. Andrea claimed he had an emigré story to suit the political complexion of anyone who came in through the door. She had only ever been through the door once to my knowledge, but she objected to Dimitrios because he was too obsequious, and to the food because it was too oily. Andrea liked her waiters to be rude to her because it showed they had the right kind of political awareness of their servile role.

Livingstone spent a long time cleaning his knife and fork on his handkerchief and then left most of his omelette because it had bits over it. I tried convincing him that the bits were a garnish of herbs but Livingstone wasn't taken in. They were bits. The pudding course wasn't much more successful. In the end I was reduced to making a ship out of a paper napkin and then converting it into a party hat in a last-ditch effort to liven things up. Origami happens to be one of my long suits. I was in the middle of trying the hat on, much to Livingstone's embarrassment, when the Mullins' red Mercedes drew up on the pavement.

Now the San Remo was hardly the sort of place I would have expected to bump into Ronnie and Lorraine. They were more Berni Steak House sort of people. But then it was a small world. And there was no accounting for taste. Ronnie was looking paunchy and affluent in a navy-blue blazer with a lot of gold cufflink showing. He went straight through into a back room like someone who was here for business rather than pleasure.

Lorraine, who was wearing a sensational leopard-skin backless one-piece jump suit thing, which was so tight you could almost see her stretch marks through it, sat herself down at a table near the door and ordered a long vodka and tonic from one of Dimitrios' many daughters. Dimitrios himself had disappeared after Ronnie flapping a tea towel and making squawking noises.

One thing you could definitely say about Lorraine was that she was a woman who had kept her figure. The skin might have turned a shade leathery, the bags under the eyes might need lifting, but her figure was still A1. Andrea always said she looked like a tart. I didn't exactly disagree with that verdict but I did sneakily admire the outrageousness of her get-ups. She had just lit up a cigarette when she spotted me. She came straight over.

'Joseph darling, this is a coincidence. But I've never known anyone actually eat here.' She pulled a face.

'It's sort of my local.'

'And this must be Livingstone. My goodness isn't he growing up into a handsome lad. Just like his daddy.' She wriggled her cigarette between her lips and gave me one of her predatory looks.

'Yes, it's amazing how fast they grow,' I said fatuously.

'Do you mind if I join you? Ronnie will be hours.' Lorraine sat herself down, crossed her legs, dangled an open-toed silver slingback with a purple painted toenail poking through.

'Be my guest,' I said.

Suddenly we both seemed to have run out of things to say to each other. I'd known Lorraine for years, of course, but we'd never exactly had what you'd call a real heart-to-heart. And right now, what with Ronnie having been dumped by the Party and everything, things were more than usually awkward.

'How's Ronnie taking it?' I said.

'Taking what?' said Lorraine.

'The de-selection business.'

'Oh that. I haven't actually asked him.'

'Ah, right.'

'To be frank with you, Joseph, politics really gets on my tits.' And as if to underline her meaning, Lorraine thrust hers out a little bit further. They were pretty thrust out in the first place.

'It does have its tedious aspect,' I agreed. Clearly I had got off on the wrong tack.

Lorraine transferred her attentions to a large ceiling fan that had ceased turning some years back. She frowned at it with a look of intense hatred. It was rather dusty, but even so I was surprised it should induce such opprobrium. I was about to take my leave when she leant across the table as if suddenly recollecting my presence.

'I hope you're not going to use Ronnie as an excuse for not coming to visit me?'

'Of course not,' I said.

'Only I get the impression you've been ignoring me lately.' Lorraine pouted.

I couldn't recall that I had ever been in the habit of paying Lorraine much attention, but I didn't want to cause offence.

'I've been a bit tied up these last few weeks,' I said.

Lorraine gave me a sideways look. 'Really! Now I would never have guessed you went in for that sort of thing, Joseph. Still, I'm a broad-minded lady.' She rolled her tongue around the word 'broad'.

I laughed politely. Lorraine really was a bit over the top. Besides, it was embarrassing with Livingstone sitting there, ears flapping. He might not say much but he took it all in.

'Does Ronnie know Dimitrios well?' I asked brightly, changing the subject.

'Business,' sighed Lorraine. 'Boring bloody business. Wouldn't mind so much if he was any good at it. But he hasn't got a clue, not a fucking clue. Still at least it keeps him out of the house.'

'Now you surprise me there. I was always of the opinion that Ronnie had an excellent track record in the commercial department. Not that I know the first thing about it myself, of course.'

'Do we have to talk about Ronnie?' snapped Lorraine, lighting up another cigarette. And then suddenly she came on with the pout and the slinky looks again and I felt a hand running up my thigh. 'I'm sure there are all sorts of more interesting things we could talk about.'

'Yes, I'm sure there are.'

I glanced at Livingstone. He appeared to be innocent of what was happening, but you could never be too certain where Livingstone was concerned. It wouldn't be beyond him to go home and tell Andrea how daddy spent the afternoon in a café groping this woman under the table. Of course, I was quite entitled to have affairs with other women if the chance came my way, which, incidentally, it didn't too often. And it wasn't Lorraine's reputation as a bit of an easy lay that was putting me off. On the simple level of lust I found her rather attractive. But there was such a thing as time and place. And, from the political point of view, Lorraine was a pretty delicate proposition right now. It might just be construed as fraternizing with the enemy. Besides which, and this was probably the most crucial factor, I didn't entirely trust her. I'd known her blow hot and cold before. I had the feeling she was up to something. When all was said and done, I'd been available for a number of years and she'd never made a play for me before this occasion, and I wasn't aware of having suddenly developed an irresistible sexual magnetism.

Fortunately, Ronnie re-emerged at this juncture. On seeing me with Lorraine he came across and clapped me on the back.

'Joey, my boy, how you doing? Coincidence, eh? I was going to give you a ding-a-ling tonight. There have been developments.'

He stood there with his hands in his pockets, swaggering a bit and looking terribly knowing until I was forced to say, 'What sort of developments?'

'Can't give you the details as yet. Under wraps. But I had a top-level meeting with our leader this afternoon and there will be a major announcement shortly. Yes, there's life in the old firm yet. Sayeed and his gang of wet behind the ears Trots thought they'd seen me out for the count. But, just between me and you, Joseph, I think they might have bitten off a bit more than they can chew. Ronnie Mullins doesn't give up that easy. I shall fight this one through the NEC, through the courts, through the European Commission, through the bloody UN itself if needs be. I'm not going to leave my people in the lurch.'

Lorraine yawned loudly. 'I'll wait in the car.' Halfway out of the restaurant she turned and said, 'And don't forget, Joseph. I shall be expecting you.'

Ronnie seemed quite unaffected both by her departure and the assignation.

'Won't keep you my sweet,' he called. And then, turning back to me, he steamrollered on. 'Where was I? Ah yes. Easiest thing in the world. Throw in the flannel. Go and live in the villa in Spain. I mean, let's face it, it's a thankless bloody task being in the Labour Party. You sweat your guts out for thirty years. You give your lifeblood. And what do they do? They turn round and kick you in the balls. But I can't just walk out on the people of Docklands. Not after thirty years. These are my people. I've grown up with them. I can't just sacrifice them to some black pansy jumping on the immigrant bandwagon. That's not my style. Loyalty. That's the name of the game in my book Joey boy. You've always been loyal to me and I appreciate that. I've always looked on us as a team. And I don't mind telling you I was, . . . I was moved pretty near to tears when old Jack White told me you were thinking of resigning over this whole sorry business. But what I want to say to you Joey is hang on in there. Don't quit yet. We might have lost a battle but we haven't lost the war. Stick it out my boy and we'll soon see the bastards off. Can't say any more than that at the moment. Under wraps. This your son is it?'

'Yes, yes he is.'

Livingstone was quietly arranging the cutlery into a geometric pattern. Ronnie Mullins looked at him pityingly.

'Terrible thing a broken marriage. Terrible thing. I've been very lucky with my Lorraine. She's stood by me through thick and thin. Be seeing you, Joey. Look after yourself.'

7

When I got back to the flat there was a note pinned to the Gestetner. It read: 'You can't stop the march of time by running in the opposite direction, MERYLL.' There were also large quantities of printing ink over the walls and floor.

I spent the best part of Sunday going over the place with some sort of petroleum solvent. By the time I'd finished, if you'd dropped a lighted match you'd have heard the explosion in Crystal Palace. Come to think of it, feeling the way I did, a quick bit of self-incineration wouldn't have been such a bad idea. I still had the monthly newsletter to write. Not exactly an alluring prospect. And with the Celia business hanging over my head like a hundred megawatt hangover I found it difficult to concentrate.

By late Monday afternoon I'd written about half a page. There are only so many ways you can say the Party is in a state of terminal debt and I'd said them all a thousand times before. I was just wondering whether some sort of BES flotation might not be the answer when a call came through from Walworth Road. Jack White wanted to see me at 6.30 sharp in the Marquis of Gransbury. Nothing more than that, but it didn't sound too good. I reckoned Celia must have broken silence at last and I was now up to face the firing squad. Well, at least it would get it over and done with.

I caught the bus. It wasn't quite the same as travelling in an open cart with the crowds jeering on, but it was probably a deal more uncomfortable. The driver seemed

56

intent on seeing how many OAPs he could spew out of the back whenever he took a corner.

When I arrived at the Gransbury Jack was already there, propped against the bar reading the racing pages of the *Evening Standard* and smoking one of his foul cigars. Despite the relative warmth of the weather he was wearing an old tweed overcoat with the collar turned up. His shock of white hair was brushed rakishly back and he was sporting one of his loosely tied red cravats. There was something of the nineteen-thirties communist dandy about Jack's appearance, but his politics had long ago atrophied into knee-jerk cynicism.

'And what sort of time do you call this?' he snorted as I approached.

'Had a long wait for the bus.'

'You were supposed to be here at five-thirty.'

'Six-thirty was the message I got.'

'Dear God! And you wonder why this Party is in the mess it is. It's like I've been saying to you for years. They wouldn't know how to organize a piss-up in a brewery, let alone an election.'

Jack ordered a beer for me and a G & T for himself and then discovered he hadn't got any cash on him. So I paid and we went and sat in a quiet corner. Quiet corners were something the Gransbury had plenty of. It was one of those cavernous mock-Tudor pubs with a wealth of fake oak beams, brass knickknacks and red plush seating. The most distinctive feature was the size of the car park which resembled a deserted airstrip.

'If you had arrived much later you would have missed the fun and games,' said Jack, wiping a line of moisture from his purplish lips on to his sleeve.

'What fun and games?' I said.

'The stripper, laddie, the stripper. A little visual diversion to get those tired old blood cells jigging again.'

'You mean this place has strippers now?'

'It's best to get here for the early performance if you want a good view.'

'Look Jack, this really isn't my scene.'

'What's the matter, laddie? Dear God, this is a service economy we live in nowadays. You have to go with the times. Besides, this young lady has as nice a pair of titties on her as you'll come across this side of the border. Name of Janine. So sit back and enjoy yourself, laddie. I won't tell the wife. Besides you haven't got one any more.' He subsided into a fit of coughing.

The name of Janine rang a bell. I recalled that the half-finished letter in Celia's bedroom had been addressed to a Janine.

Just then a tape of band music started up and a pale thin girl with straight platinum-blonde hair and long skinny legs and arms started gyrating around and taking her clothes off. She was on a small raised platform, adorned with a jug of mauve plastic tulips that looked as if they could do with a good clean. The platform was so close to our table you could almost reach out and touch her. The pub was near enough empty. Those that were present mainly stood around, talking and watching in a half-hearted sort of way. The odd jeering remark was greeted with a great deal of belly laughter and beer slurped on to the floor. The girl was dressed in a maid's outfit, complete with small white mobcap and frilly apron. When she revealed her breasts a big cheer went up. They were surprisingly large, considering how thin the rest of her was, and cone-shaped, as if they had been pumped up with silicone. She wasn't a very good dancer and had difficulty keeping time with the music. I recognized her straight away as the girl I had seen on the floor of the Ronaynes' coat room, with Jack. She had the same distant glazed expression in her eyes, as if none of what was taking place was really happening to her.

'And what would you say to the chance of shafting that juicy little bit of rump,' said Jack lubriciously.

Motes of dust oscillated in a shaft of sunlight.

Janine had turned her back on us and adopted a crouching position, swaying from left to right and groaning as she wriggled her stockings down.

'All human desire is subject to the same laws of entropy,' I said, wondering exactly what Jack's game was in bringing me here. Was it simply a bit of macho one-upmanship, like a man's desire to show off his recently acquired Rubens to a fellow collector, or was there some more devious purpose?

Jack looked at me patronizingly.

'Dear God, what the hell has entropy got to do with it. But you must notice a difference, being back in the marketplace after all these years.'

'Marketplace? I don't quite follow.'

'I mean, laddie, when you want a woman nowadays you've got to get out there and pull her, haven't you? Not like being married, is it? To my way of thinking, marriage is a bit like the welfare state. Sex on wheels three times a week. It might be tepid and stodgy but at least it comes at regular intervals. Don't misunderstand me now. Marriage has its place. I might get wed myself one day. When I take my pension. But it must have come as a bit of a shock to the old system. All those years of cosily getting your leg over and suddenly you find yourself back in the real world, competing with the rest of us red-blooded males. You soon find out whether you can still deliver the goods. Get an eyeful of that, laddie. Not bad, eh?'

Janine was now totally naked apart from a few square inches of cloth covering her pubis, not enough to blow your nose on even. She was cupping her breasts in her hands and offering them round the audience. One joker flicked his cigarette ash over them much to the amusement of his fellow drinkers. Jack nudged me.

'Be honest with yourself. You'd like to get her into bed wouldn't you?'

'Look, is that what you asked me here for, some sort of sexual therapy? Because if so . . .'

'Easy does it. Easy does it. Hold your horses. You're awful touchy tonight, Joseph.'

'I'd just rather we got down to business. I take it you had some reason for dragging me all this way?'

'Suit yourself. Just trying to cheer you up, laddie. Thought you'd been looking a bit hangdog lately.'

Janine tripped off into a back room somewhere to desultory applause. Jack stared into the bowl of his glass like it was a crystal ball.

'You might not believe this, Joseph, but I've stood up for you. It hasn't always been easy. There are special problems down in Docklands I've told the Committee. Joseph is doing a good job in a difficult situation. Oh yes, I've argued your case, even at risk sometimes to my own position.'

'I'm grateful.'

'But there are limits.'

'Sure.'

'And those limits are getting mighty close, laddie.'

'They've sacked me, is that what you're trying to say?'

'Sacked! Who's talking about sacked. The Labour Party doesn't sack people, Joseph. You know better than that. We're the Party of full employment.'

'So what are you getting at?'

'Have you seen the evening paper?'

'No.'

'I think perhaps you'd better take a look,' Jack tossed it over.

I flinched. So Celia had gone to the press had she. She wasn't going to be satisfied with just ruining my career. She wanted public humiliation. I refolded the paper so that the front page was outermost. It took some time because Jack had a way of turning papers inside out and upside down which suggested he'd just eaten his chips out of them. When I finally got there it was some moments more before I took the headline in.

'OVER MY DEAD BODY, says Labour Leader.' The article went on: 'Newly selected, prospective Labour candidate Alan Sayeed, who is to stand in the Docklands East Constituency, a safe Labour seat at present held by Ronnie Mullins MP, was condemned on both sides of the House yesterday. The Labour Leader said, in response to Conservative questioning, that there will be an enquiry at national level into how Sayeed came to be selected and if necessary the whole process would be re-run ... Sayeed, a member of the hard Left, has been quoted as saying that he believes in the need for extra parliamentary activity to bring about a revolution in this country . . .'

And so on.

Of course, I knew sooner or later Jack would be wanting to see me about the Mullins/Sayeed re-selection furore. I had been expecting a call for some time. It was just that the Celia business had clouded my mind.

'Mullins must have leaned very hard to get him to come out with a statement like that,' I said, when the full significance of the article had finally sunk in.

Jack removed the wet stub of a cigar from his coronary-coloured lips and thrust his face unpleasantly close to mine. 'Mullins threatened to defect to the Tories if Sayeed wasn't ditched. Our leader has at last discovered where his balls are and told the Loonie Left where to get off.'

'But why start with Sayeed? Docklands East is a safe seat. Alan won't lose it.'

'Dear God! Of course he wouldn't. You could run a bare-arsed monkey in your patch of Docklands and the electorate would still vote it in, providing it was on the Labour ticket. But that's not the point. You have to consider the effect on the morale of the rest of the country. The image of the Party with the public. The wider context.'

'But the Left aren't going to just lie down and let this happen. They're going to fight it all the way. And you seem to be forgetting the Left control Docklands East.'

'That's where you come in, laddie.'

'How do you mean?'

'I would be guilty of something rather less than total honesty, Joseph, if I didn't tell you that there are those in the upper echelons of our organization who are not over-pleased about what's been going on down in Docklands East and, to put it bluntly, hold you to blame. Well, you can see their point of view. They haven't been paying you a wage all these years for you to sit on your posterior and let the Party be taken over by the Trotskyite rabble.'

'You mean they want a scapegoat.'

'It's like the paper says. There's to be an internal inquiry. The selection process is to be rerun from square one. What it doesn't say, of course, is this time Mullins is to come out winner.'

'So that's the deal?'

'That's the deal.'

'It can't be done.'

'Come along now, Joseph. You know better than that. Who was it said politics is the art of the impossible?'

'This was the cleanest selection I've ever been involved in. Party cards were checked. Delegates' credentials scrutinized. You have a rerun and Sayeed will just get selected again, probably with a bigger majority. He has wide-ranging support throughout all the sections. He's tapped into something called 'idealism'. I'm not saying it's a good thing, but it's happened and it isn't very susceptible to manipulation. Besides it's not just Sayeed you're up against. He's backed by Ted Clarke and Clarke has total control of the organizational base. It'll be like banging your head against a brick wall.'

'Not my head Joseph, yours.'

'Whoever's head it is, it still can't be done.'

'There are ways and means, Joseph.'

'Such as?'

'You could try calling in the Electricians and Plumbers.'

'A fix, is that what you're asking me for?'

'I've explained the overall strategy, Joseph. Mullins in, Sayeed out. The detail, laddie, is down to you. And now, if you'll excuse me, I have a little behind the scenes business to attend to.'

8

The Election Victory Campaign Committee was quick to react to Alan's denunciation by the Party leadership. An emergency meeting was called for the following evening. Small meetings of this nature were usually held in the downstairs room of the Local Constituency Party Administrative Headquarters but, on this occasion, Andrea complained that the smell of petroleum was giving her a headache and suggested we adjourn to my bedsitter. As I only occupied it as a concession from the Party anyway, I could hardly argue, but I was deeply suspicious of her motives. She obviously wanted to snoop. I hastily pulled the yellowing candlewick bedspread over the equally yellowing sheets and removed the worst of the coffee cups, the ones that had mould growing in them. I didn't want her claiming it was an unsafe environment for a ten-year-old.

The Committee consisted of Jonathan and Julian, Andrea, Meryll, Ted Clarke, Melrose, Alan, of course, and myself as clerk, not an elected member. It was quite a squash.

'Well, this is jolly, isn't it?' said Melrose. 'Takes me back to my early CP days. We used to pack nearly a hundred of us into this cellar in Putney.'

He squatted on the floor between the chest of drawers and the wastepaper bin. The latter just happened to be full of unfinished letters from me to Celia in which I had attempted to explain that the unfortunate event of the other evening should be regarded as a freak of nature in common with hot water spouts and flying fish and that in no way was it intended as a comment on a relationship that I had come to value more and more for its moments of selfless tenderness, so rare in the exploitative society in which we were both doomed to live out our declining years, etc, etc. I was worried that Melrose might start rummaging around in the contents of the bin and even read passages out loud under the misapprehension that he'd got the agenda in front of him. The old buffer was notoriously fond of going through garbage cans, builders' skips, waste tips, any pile of old rubbish, just so long as it had been thrown out by someone else. But the meeting was already under way so there was precious little I could do about it now.

Alan was the last to arrive and the first to speak. He perched himself balletically on top of my Olivetti portable. 'Sorry about the delay, comrades, but I was just down the supermarket getting in a few groceries. Yes, even your candidate has to do menial chores like buying in the cornflakes now and again. I regard it as a wonderful opportunity for keeping in touch with our grass roots. Believe me comrades . . .'

'If I may interrupt,' said Clarke, interrupting, 'we're here to decide what we're going to do about the arse'ole leadership, not discuss this week's bargain offer.'

'I was just coming to that,' said Alan, looking a trifle hurt.

'I think Comrade Clarke has made a very good point,' said Julian or it might have been Jonathan. 'The leadership of this party has systematically betrayed the aspirations of the working classes since Ramsay MacDonald sold out in 1931. It's up to us to decide now whether we're going to let it happen again. This is an historic moment.' And he made a note in his diary, presumably for the sake of posterity.

'Exactly,' said Alan.

'The question for us as socialists is how are we going to respond to this attack upon our legitimate claim to determine our own lives?' said Meryll. 'Are we going to

64

stand up and fight and be seen to fight for the principles we believe in?'

'I don't believe you selected me as your future candidate,' said Alan, 'to become a lackey of the bourgoisie.' He smiled around the assembled company.

'I suggest we write to the arse'ole leadership making it quite clear to them that whatever they decide, we are not going to be intimidated by their tactics and that Alan will stay as our candidate.'

Having delivered himself of this opinion Clarke farted roundly into my pillow, presumably as a protest against the self-indulgence of having a pillow when two-thirds of the world had to make do without.

'I take it that is the unanimous feeling of the meeting,' said Alan, quite cocky and bouncy again after his initial put-down.

There was a murmur of approval. And it could have all ended amicably there if Andrea hadn't intervened.

'I think writing letters is a total waste of time,' she pronounced from a position of lofty superiority on top of the filing cabinet. She was looking immaculate in a new peach-coloured blouse and a black pencil skirt, legs crossed, tights sheer: seamless beauty. All eyes turned in her direction.

Clarke delivered himself of another broadside into my pillow. 'What's your idea then? A Girl Guides' pin-sticking session?' But this was not sufficient to regain the initiative.

Andrea smiled serenely. 'There are currently over fifteen hundred people in this borough being harassed for rent arrears. I propose we give the leadership a practical demonstration of just what we mean by extra-parliamentary activity by passing a resolution in council wiping out those arrears. We must use what power bases we have control of to build support amongst our natural allies.'

There was a moment's silence. It was a suggestion of quite breathtaking audacity. There would, without doubt, be a national furore. Alan looked fidgety. Clarke was furious. He snorted and grunted and ground his shoe back and forth into my carpet, like a bull about to stampede or possibly, and the thought was not a pleasant one, like a man trying to remove some dog shit from his heel.

I thought it was perhaps appropriate to say something myself at this juncture.

'It is not my place to comment either way on the merits or defects of the particular course of action that has just been put forward by our esteemed comrade. However, I feel I should point out on a simply technical level that what is being proposed here might not be strictly legal and, therefore, it might be a good idea to take professional advice before committing ourselves to a final decision one way or the other.'

'How pathetically gutless,' said Andrea, tossing her hair back and tilting the perfect plane of her nose in my direction.

'I was merely advocating a little caution,' I said.

'Caution is for those who are frightened of the future,' said Andrea.

Alan pouted like a spoilt boy who, having been asked along to recite his party piece, kept finding himself upstaged. But Andrea had got the meeting on a roller coaster and there was no jumping off now.

'The judiciary are a tool of the Establishment,' said Jonathan.

'We can't allow ourselves to be intimidated by the law,' said Julian.

'It will certainly put the cat among the pigeons,' chortled Melrose.

'And it's consistent with the tactics already adopted by the Walthamstow women,' shrieked Meryll.

So Andrea's resolution was carried without being put to the vote. Of course, there were still various formalities to be gone through, such as getting the Management Committee to agree. But all the key members on the Management were already present so that wouldn't prove an obstacle.

The meeting broke up in a general air of euphoria. Only Clarke seemed somewhat less than ecstatic. 'That smart-arsed wife of yours is a pain up the bum,' he muttered on departure. 'Pity you don't keep her on a tighter leash.'

'Ex-wife,' I corrected, but he was already out of ear-shot.

Andrea stayed behind after the others for a few private words with me.

'I think I should inform you that I shall be applying to the courts for an injunction.'

'For what!' I said, thinking this might have something to do with the proposed rent amnesty, but failing to quite see the connection.

'To stop your access to Livingstone.'

'But I thought we had just agreed that the judiciary was a tool of the ruling class? Besides, you're always complaining that I don't fulfil my fair share of the parental responsibilities. An injuction preventing access isn't exactly going to help that any.'

'I've decided the disadvantages outweigh any possible advantages.'

'So what's this all about?'

'How can you honestly stand there and ask me what it's all about. This pretence at innocence, Joseph, just makes me angrier.'

'You've been talking to Celia.'

'No, I haven't been talking to Celia. Why should I have been talking to Celia, for God's sake? I can't stand her. As far as I'm concerned Celia is an over-privileged, self-obsessed, bitch.'

'Well, if it's the business with Lorraine you're on about, there's really nothing in it.'

'I'm not talking about Celia or Lorraine or any of your other fancy women. I couldn't care less about them. What I object to is your brainwashing my child into a set of vicious sexist beliefs.'

'Sorry, I don't quite follow.'

'You took him to Westminster Abbey, didn't you?'

'Yes, but . . .'

'Well I happen to think Christianity is paternalistic crap. And why is it only men who get buried in Westminster Abbey? I'd rather my child wasn't encouraged in patriarchal ways of thinking, thanks very much. You only do it to undermine me.'

'But it was Livingstone's suggestion.'

'And you think that's an excuse. You don't think that as an adult you might be expected to behave a little more responsibly? And this place of yours. Look at it. It's so squalid. No child should have to experience it, not even for an afternoon. It smells of something quite indescribably foul.' She wrinkled her pretty little snub nose and moved towards the door. 'Oh, and by the way, I almost forgot to tell you. Those socks look perfectly ridiculous with those trousers. No-one in their right mind would wear lime-green socks and certainly not with a pair of dirty corduroys which are too short in the leg.'

I began to get that battered feeling I so often had when talking with Andrea. And just to rub it in, I'd been right about the dog shit on the bottom of Clarke's shoe.

9

Around tennish the following morning I was standing in my bay window staring across the street, for no particular reason other than I didn't know what to do about the Sayeed/Mullins cock up, didn't even really know which side I was on, and staring out of windows was as good a way of passing the time as anything else I knew. The woman who lived opposite had put a box of geraniums out on her sill and the petals impacted on my jaded retinas like drops of blood. I'd complimented her the other day on the beautiful show they made. She had replied that she'd only put them out because the smell of the leaves in the house made her husband sneeze. She sounded resentful about me getting the benefit of them.

I was about to turn away when I happened to notice a rather seedy-looking character, with a brown trilby pulled down over his face and a lot of flashy camera dangling from his neck, hanging around behind the privet. It gave me quite a turn. How long had he been there and what the hell was he up to? He was wearing one of those pale fawn sub-military raincoats with belt and epaulettes, and from the size of the telescopic lens it looked like he might also have a serious virility problem. What he appeared to be up to was taking photographs of the front of the building. Now the administrative headquarters of the local constituency Labour Party is not exactly *Homes and Gardens* stuff. Nor is it, as yet, a major place of homage for pilgrims of the Left. So there had to be another explanation. The press perhaps, after the monster who had desecrated Celia's sink. I felt a bit queasy as I imagined hordes of reporters beseiging me for the juicy details. Did I have a lifelong history of acts of public defecation? What childhood trauma had first triggered these displays of infantile behaviour? Was it my predilection for perverse practices that had caused my long-suffering wife to divorce me? And so on. I was vaguely considering whether I shouldn't rush out into the street and smash the bastard's lenses when he lowered the camera and I recognized the haughty features of Charles Ronayne. I hardly had the time to start feeling puzzled before the downstairs' phone began to ring. I made a dash for it and was going well when I fell over the Baby Burco, badly bruising my right shin. Even so I carried on, gamely ignoring the intense spurt of pain, reaching the phone the exact second it stopped. What was it about phones that made me go to such extraordinary lengths to answer them when they invariably meant bad news?

Feeling cross with myself, I diverted to the kitchen and rolled up my trouser leg to examine the damage. My shin was almost luminously white beneath the tiny black hairs waving around like the fronds of a sea urchin in a state of panic. And a long slick of blood had just about reached my sock. Still, it didn't look like an immediate transfusion job. I was in the middle of rinsing the dishcloth under the cold water tap when the phone went again. I had the distinct impression I was being messed about by some supernatural agency with a penchant for call boxes.

'Docklands East Labour Party.'

'Joseph, at last I've got hold of you.'

'Hello, who's that speaking please?'

'It's me, Lorraine, of course.'

'Oh, hello Lorraine.'

'You mean you don't even recognize my voice any more?'

'Sorry.'

'Well, I'm deeply hurt. I thought I was special for you, Joseph.'

'Tone deaf I'm afraid.'

70

As a matter of fact Lorraine's voice sounded decidedly odd, sort of languid and echoey.

'How can I help?' I added as something of an after-thought.

'Well, I was sort of wondering whether you'd do me this big favour.' She put a lot of husky emphasis on the word 'big'.

'Well, that sort of depends what it is,' I said.

'Oh, I hate cautious men.'

'Better safe than sorry.'

'Better sorry than bored out of your head.'

'You might have a point there.'

There was a pause during which I thought I detected faint splashing sounds. I wondered whether I'd left the cold tap running in the kitchen. In which case there could be a major flooding problem since the overflow was blocked with the detritus of a thousand meals.

'I feel depressed,' drawled Lorraine, apropros of nothing in particular, 'terribly bored and depressed.'

So, it was therapy she was after was it. In which case she'd come to the right person. The one thing I was good at was the sympathetic ear role.

'I suppose the present situation vis-à-vis the inquiry and everything must be a bit unsettling for you and Ronnie,' I said. 'It's unsettling for everyone. I think we'll all feel better when it's over and we know where we are.'

'I know where I fucking am, thanks very much. I'm inside this fucking house and it's driving me up the fucking wall. It's a tip. One great big fucking horrible tip.'

'I see. Well, these things are all relative, you know.' Lorraine Mullins lived in a new, six-bedroomed estate house with a cleaner who came in six mornings a week. 'It always looks like a palace to me.'

'It's a shit hole. I know a shit hole when I'm in one and this is a shit hole. Everything I touch feels tacky. You know that feeling? Like all the furniture's got chewing gum on the underneath of it.'

'My furniture is held together with chewing gum,' I

71

said. 'It's structural. So naturally I probably feel differently from you about it.'

Lorraine began to giggle. I felt pleased. At last I'd found someone who was appreciative of my sense of humour. Unfortunately the giggling went on rather longer than was really appropriate. It wasn't that funny. I was also beginning to wonder what all this was leading up to. The offer of a part-time position at the end of a vacuum perhaps. And what were these splashing noises, louder than ever now. Soda hitting the sides of a whisky glass? Hardly. But she did sound pretty pissed.

'So what's this big favour?' I said.

'Favour?' Lorraine sounded like she'd never heard of the word.

'You were talking about a big favour you wanted doing.'

'Oh that. It's nothing really. I've just been chucking a load of tack out, that's all, and I thought you could use it for your next jumble sale.'

'That's a very kind thought,' I said. Perhaps I didn't quite manage to keep the disappointment out of my voice.

'You want it or not?' said Lorraine, suddenly coming on La Grande Dame.

'I never turn down the offer of good-quality jumble,' I said. 'But you couldn't hang on to it for a few days could you? Only the hall's a bit crowded at the moment.'

'Look, if you don't want it, I'll burn it.'

'Oh, I want it. I definitely want it. Perhaps if you popped it over tomorrow afternoon? I dare say I could squeeze it in somewhere. What sort of volume are we talking about?'

'Too much for the car. Can't you bring the van round?'

'Well, yes, I suppose that's feasible. Tomorrow afternoon then?'

'Tomorrow is therapist day. I get the jitters before and I'm shagged out after.'

'Thursday?'

'Thursdays are no good.'

'Well, when do you suggest?'

Lorraine suggested nothing. Instead, there was the sound of an underwater explosion followed by much crackling. My first thought was that the Home Office tappers had pulled the wrong plug. Then Lorraine's voice came back on.

'Joseph, Joseph, are you still there?'

'Yes. What was that?'

'I just dropped the phone in the bath.'

'In the bath!'

'Oh Joseph, I do believe you're shocked.'

'No, no not at all.'

'Some men would find the idea of my lying here, starkers, chatting to them, very, well, titillating.' Her tongue relished the word 'titillating'. She made it sound like some new form of nipple fetishism.

'But isn't there a danger of getting electrocuted?'

'Joseph, telephones don't run on electricity.'

'I've never been too sure how they do work. It's all magic to me I'm afraid.'

'So why don't you come straight over, before my water gets cold, and I'll give you a few lessons in basic physics.'

I'd no sooner hung up when the doorbell rang, a long imperious summons. My immediate thought was that Lorraine must have changed her mind. In her eagerness she must have jumped in the Merc and driven straight round and was at this very moment panting on my doorstep with that long pointed tongue of hers lolling sideways. Of course, if I'd cared to think about it, it was a logistical impossibility, but I didn't care to think about it. I just ran recklessly down the stairs. In the event it was Charles Ronayne.

' 'Bout bloody time,' he said, even though his finger must still have been hot from pressing the button.

He pushed straight past me. He was frowning so hard his eyebrows didn't just meet, they crossed over. He'd obviously popped round to avenge the dishonour I'd done his wife.

'Come in,' I said. 'Any time. Feel free. Barge away.'

But mild sarcasms of this kind were entirely lost on Charles. He was far too busy trampling over my sensibilities and dirty laundry, which was liberally distributed along the landing, to pick up on any slight nuance of irritation that I might wish to convey. But then again I had seriously insulted his wife. Perhaps he felt justified in dispensing with the normal courtesies.

I caught up with him in my room. He had already deposited his camera equipment on my occasional table, occasional because more often than not it was in use as a Maggie Thatcher dartboard around the fêtes of East London, which explained its somewhat pocked appearance.

'I can explain everything,' I said.

Charles made a dismissive gesture with his hand. 'Forget it. I'm not one to harbour grievances. It's just when one has a lot on one's plate as I have one doesn't like to waste time unnecessarily.' He proceeded to pace the floor, size up my bed from different angles, measure the light, and adopt heroically anguished postures.

There was something here that didn't quite add up. I decided the time had come to bite the bullet.

'Charles, did Celia send you round here? Because if she did . . .'

Charles drew himself up to his full height and looked at me down the chute of his great nose.

'My dear fellow, I am not in the habit of running errands for my womenfolk.'

'You mean Celia didn't send you round here?'

'Certainly not.' Charles suddenly got down on his hands and knees, lifted the skirts of the candlewick bedspread and peered underneath.

'If it's porno mags you're after, I'm afraid you're out of luck.'

Charles scowled. 'Your sense of humour, Joseph, leaves a lot to be desired. Can this bed be got out of here, on a temporary basis?'

'I expect so,' I said. 'But before you entirely rearrange

the furnishings, would you mind telling me what all this is in aid of?'

'Your photograph,' said Charles, as if my question was childishly absurd. 'This wall would make a useful background. But the bed spoils the simplicity.'

'You want to photograph me!'

'That's right. That's what I just said.'

'I just wish you'd given me some warning. I would have got my hair fixed.'

'I'm not in the glamour business,' said Charles. 'Get hold of the other end can you.'

'But Charles, do we really have to move the bed? Why not snap me in situ, as it were. The agent reclining. That kind of thing.'

'Out of the question. The bed must go. I want austerity. I demand austerity.' He threatened to come on all prima donna.

'OK,' I said. 'OK, if you absolutely insist. We'll move the bed.' Sometimes capitulation was the quickest route to freedom.

'Straight back,' said Charles. 'Lift from the thighs. From the thighs, Joseph. You'll do yourself a mischief like that.'

'Sod the thighs,' I said. 'Just mind the dado.'

Between us we manhandled my sleeping arrangements onto the mezzanine. On returning into the now bedless bedsit I determined to press Charles for further details.

'Is this by way of a personal fan thing or have you been commissioned by the *Sunday Times*; you know, Joseph Pink a shit hole of his own?'

Charles gave me his Mona Lisa smile. 'Not really prepared to go into those kinds of detail. Not sure you'd understand even if I did. Let's just say that by helping me in this you will be making a small but not altogether negligible contribution to altering the world's perception of reality. That is after all the function of true art, is it not? Get your clothes off can you. I haven't got all day.'

'My clothes off?'

75

'That's right. Is there a problem? You're not ashamed of your body are you?'

'Not ashamed exactly.'

'Perfectly natural things, bodies.'

'Yes, of course.'

'At my public school we used to swim in the nude. It's stood me in very good stead.'

'I didn't go to a public school, Charles.'

'No need to go through the rest of your life with a chip on your shoulder about it.'

'But that's just it. I'm hump shouldered, with a concave chest, bow legs and sagging buttocks. I'm just not full-frontal material.'

'It is for those very qualities I selected you,' said Charles.

Jesus, I thought. This guy is weird to the point where weirdness begins to get a bad name for itself.

'Sorry Charles. You've picked the wrong chap. Mug shot is one thing. Life class is something else. I get goose pimples. And I've just remembered I'm supposed to be in a meeting with the NEC. Must dash. Drop the latch when you leave. See you.'

I had entirely forgotten about Lorraine in her bath. If I left her there much longer she'd probably die of exposure.

10

There was in fact something just a touch shabby about the Mullins' residence. Not that there was any obvious shortage of cash. On the contrary, there was a most conspicuous abundance of the stuff lying about: a black Porsche in the integral garage with roll over door, antique carriage lamps stuck on every available corner, bits of kitsch statuary on the lawns. But there was still this underlying air of neglect. One of the gates to the driveway was off its hinges. The roses had not been dead-headed from the previous autumn. There was a nasty rust stain from a piece of broken guttering. A plastic-covered wrought iron chair lay on its back on the patio.

I clanged the bell rope that hung in the porch. Lorraine answered the door on the chain and blinked.

'I haven't got my lenses in,' she said. She was wearing a long white silk gown, rather loosely tied.

'The bell's quaint,' I said.

'I hate it,' said Lorraine. 'Ronnie picked it up cheap from some demolition job he had his finger in. It gives me a headache whenever anyone comes round. You took your time.'

'I ran into Charles on the way over,' I said, not quite accurately.

'Good,' said Lorraine. 'I hope it was fatal. He's such a prat.'

We had made it as far as the hallway. Lorraine was leaning back against the door jamb, arms folded beneath her breasts, which were fine in their way, though perhaps they hung down just a little too low. Still, it never did to be too perfectionist about such things. Muscle tone apart, I wasn't sure whether she was being sultry or was simply overcome by inertia at the sight of me. There was a faintly cloying smell, as of overripe melons or rotting floorboards, coming from somewhere.

'Well, if you'd just point out what's to go, I'll get on with loading up,' I said, rubbing my hands together like some kind of parody of the jovial tradesman. Andrea once accused me of having the sycophantic manners of a greengrocer. Trade was the ultimate dirty word in Andrea's vocabulary.

'Don't you want a little drink of something first?' Lorraine drawled without much enthusiasm.

'Oh, a cup of tea is always welcome, thanks very much.'

Lorraine slouched into the kitchen. I followed. It was a vast room with acres of expensive fitted work – surface entirely covered in dirty dishes.

'Ronnie says I've debilitated my nervous system through drinking too much tea.' Lorraine retied the gown cord, but still failed to cover herself up very adequately.

'I think that's a bit unlikely,' I said, thinking it sounded highly probable that if it wasn't tea she'd debilitated it with, it was something else.

'He doesn't understand how I have this need to put hot things inside me the whole time.' Lorraine smirked in my direction. There was an innuendo here that I was meant to pick up on. I picked up on it all right, but I didn't know what to do with it. It was a hot potato and I fumbled the catch.

'I consider tea to be the most refreshing of drinks,' I said, boring myself even as I said it.

Fortunately Lorraine wasn't listening. She was too busy sniffing like a demented bloodhound.

'Can you smell something off in here?'

I sniffed.

'No, I don't think so.' The rotten melon smell was

78

considerably stronger in the kitchen, but I didn't consider it polite to admit I was aware of it.

Lorraine sniffed again.

I surreptitiously lowered my nose towards my right armpit. Nothing noticeable. But then you could never be too sure where your own bodily odours were concerned. And I did tend to sweat when feeling nervous.

'It's probably the bin,' said Lorraine. 'Hasn't been emptied for days. Ronnie can deal with it when he gets home.'

'I've got catarrh,' I said. 'Can't smell a thing.'

'Is there any bit of you still in working order?'

Lorraine wriggled her lips at me. She had a greedy mouth. I was reminded of a nature film I'd once seen on the feeding habits of pike.

'I do feel a touch atrophied around the extremities,' I said, which was a good deal better than my tea remark, or so I thought, but Lorraine didn't appear to take it on board. She was already off on a new tack, or reverting to an old one.

'Ronnie and me have got this war going on.'

'Oh yes?'

'I am refusing to do anything around the house until he gets a new cleaner.'

'What happened to the last one?'

'I sacked her.'

'Why was that?'

'She was a slut.'

'I see.'

'Anyway, I hate having other people hanging round the place spying on me, prying into my life.'

'Fair enough.'

'Let's go through into the lounge. I shall puke on this smell if I have to put up with it much longer.'

So we went into the lounge. Lorraine flung herself on to a sofa in the Hollywood manner, one arm curled above her head, one knee slightly drawn up. 'You don't mind if I leave the curtains drawn? I like to pretend the outside world doesn't exist.'

'Yes, life can be a pretty depressing business, can't it,' I said chummily.

'So why don't you come and sit nearer to me,' drawled Lorraine, and she patted the cushion next to her. 'We could try cheering each other up a bit.'

I was astute enough to realize that this was one of those critical moments in my life, the like of which had only occurred half a dozen or so times in the past, but which had been cropping up with increasing frequency of late. I had hardly got over the trauma of having to decide whether or not to quit the agent's job and here I was being confronted with the offer of a little hanky-panky with the sitting MP's wife. I'd realized what I was getting myself into, of course, before I put the phone down, but very much further along this road and there could be no turning back.

Let it be frankly stated I am no Lothario, whoever he was. Nor was I in love, which is an excuse for almost any kind of bad behaviour. I wasn't even emotionally involved, or at least I didn't think so. But I was, and this was the nub of it, more than a little flattered by the invitation. And what the hell? What had I to lose? My reputation. Well, there wasn't much of that left. And once the Celia story got around I'd be hard put to it to persuade anyone of the opposite sex into bed with me. And the bottom line was I was just plain curious to find out what was going to happen.

I crossed the room and knelt down by the sofa, my head about on a level with Lorraine's navel. She bent towards me and we kissed. I noted the taste of alcohol and it wasn't even tea time. I loosened the girdle of her gown and glimpsed her pale, slender legs, freshly shaved, surmounted by a dark and surprisingly extensive triangle of pubic hair. A man could get lost in that jungle and never come out alive I thought. I looked back towards her face. I was more at home with faces. Her mouth was slack at the corners, vulnerable, appealing. A trail of saliva ran from the left-hand side. I thought of snails.

'Talk to me, Joseph,' she whispered.

'What about?' I said.

'Do you find me attractive?'

'Yes, of course.'

'What do you like about me?'

'All sorts of things.'

'What things?'

'Well, your breasts are very beautiful.'

'How Joseph, how?'

'They're very full and silky.'

We continued to negotiate each other's bodies. It was a clumsy business, but we were courteous and helpful with each other. Quite unexpectedly Lorraine began to groan.

'Talk to me more, Joseph. More. I want more.'

My mind went blank. I'd never been very strong on the literary side of love. 'Your breasts remind me of melons, large ripe melons.'

'Not mush, Joseph. I can do without mush. You want me to shake them for you, yes? You want to bury your fucker in them, right? You want to shoot your hot stuff all over them, right?'

'Right,' I said.

'Get those trousers off then. I'm not fucking with any man who looks like he's running in a three-legged race.'

So I removed my trousers. As a a matter of fact I was glad of the opportunity to stretch a bit, because I'd just got cramp in my right leg. I was halfway through folding them along the crease lines when Lorraine grabbed me from behind.

'I knew you had a big one. I like them big and hard. I like them big and smooth and hard. Let me be your sex slave, Joseph. I want you to fuck me all angles. Fuck me inside out. Fuck me to pieces, Joseph. Fuck me to pieces.'

Lorraine shouted a litany of obscenities at the top of her voice. Thank God the house was detached I thought. I was just getting into the linguistic swing of it when Lorraine broke off.

'The damn thing isn't long enough.'

81

'It's a question of perspective,' I said, feeling a little deflated after all the build-up.

'Not your prick, you idiot. It's the couch I'm talking about.'

'Oh right. Perhaps we should go upstairs?' I'd got cramp again. This time in both legs. I'd never been that wild about sofas, not even as a teenager.

'Not upstairs. The marital bedroom has the wrong associations for me. I want you to screw me right here on the floor,' said Lorraine. 'But first you'd better slip on your little plastic pixie hood.'

Plastic pixie hood. I was just ever so slightly gobsmacked. What was I getting myself into here? Garden gnome fetishism. Noddy worship. Then it struck me like a slap in the face with a wet fish. Aids. Condoms. You just didn't go around waving your willy, willy-nilly any more.

'I'm afraid I've er . . .'

'Fucking typical,' said Lorraine. She slunk across the room to her handbag and tossed me a pack of twelve.

'I hope you're not expecting to get through all these this afternoon,' I said, laying my cards on the table as it were.

'I never have expectations,' said Lorraine. 'Come on, let me roll it on for you.'

She went about it in an efficient and business-like manner.

'Just like stuffing sausage meat into skins,' she whispered romantically.

'They always make me feel like I'm going to suffocate,' I said.

'Don't tell me you breathe through your dong,' said Lorraine. 'What is it, some kind of periscope?'

I laughed uneasily as we lowered ourselves on to the luxurious Persian carpet. We hadn't been there more than a couple of minutes when Lorraine sat bolt upright.

'Talk to me, Joseph. Why won't you talk to me more?'

I re-racked my brains for something to say. Lorraine, however, once more came to my rescue.

'You want to shove your great big gun right up inside me, yes?'

'Yes.'

'You want to force it into me till I scream for mercy, yes?'

'Yes, yes.'

'You want to pump me full of white hot shot till I'm out of my head?'

'Oh, yes please.'

I wasn't at all sure this was entirely the kind of conversation my feminist friends would approve of. There did seem to be a certain obsession with images of violent penetration. On the other hand, was it up to me to be prescriptive about these things?

It all seemed to be going pretty well in the circumstances, which to my mind were far from ideal, when Lorraine, while transferring her foot from my right buttock to my left shoulder, caught her purple painted toenail on my damaged shin. I let out a shriek of pain and pulled off rather abruptly.

'What's wrong,' said Lorraine.

'I'm bleeding,' I said.

'Christ! I thought it was only women who were supposed to bleed. For God's sake don't drip on the carpet. Ronnie will kill me.'

'Have you got any tissues?' I said.

Lorraine handed me a box.

'I'm such a clumsy cow,' she said. 'Such a fucking clumsy cow.'

'It wasn't your fault,' I said. 'I did the worst of it this morning on the Baby Burco. I should have put a plaster on it.'

I put my arm around her shoulder in a comradely manner. 'Shall we?'

'Shall we what?'

'Continue.'

'Oh, I think we'd better call it a day. I don't want you bleeding to death on me.'

'Another time?'

'Yes sure.' Lorraine sounded about as enthusiastic as someone making an appointment with her dentist.

'I was really enjoying it,' I said. 'I don't want you to think . . .'

Lorraine shuddered. 'Please, no inquests. They make me feel like a corpse.'

'Sorry.'

'And stop apologizing will you. I can't stand men who apologize the whole time.'

'Right.'

Lorraine wrapped herself in her gown and sank back on the sofa. 'Mind if I smoke?' she said.

'No, of course not.'

She looked like a poster you might come across on the surgery wall warning against the dangers of postcoital depression.

'You can't see my pants anywhere can you?' I said.

'They're on the telly.'

'Thanks.'

I got dressed. I felt better for getting some clothes on.

'I do find you beautiful. It's difficult the first time. Strange place. Unfamiliar habits. You know what I mean?'

'There's really no need to keep making excuses, Joseph. We screwed up. End of story. What does it matter? It's no big deal. You're not the first.'

I stroked her hair. The odd thing was I really did fancy her a lot at that moment.

'Right, well, I guess I'd better get this jumble loaded and be on my way.'

'Joseph.'

'Yes.'

'I want you to help me.'

'Yes, of course.'

'You see, I'm in trouble. I mean serious trouble.' Lorraine was hunched forward staring at me with an intensity I found unnerving. What the hell did she mean. What sort of trouble. Pregnant? Hardly. Short of cash? Even less likely. And there was certainly no point in

84

looking to me if that were the case. These rapid reflections were interrupted by the sound of tyres on gravel.

'Oh God, that's all we needed. Ronnie's back early. Here, start loading this.'

Lorraine thrust a large earthenware pot into my hands shaped like a hospital urine bottle that she had grabbed off a nearby nest of tables. At which point Ronnie came charging in looking red in the face and sweaty.

'Hello sweetheart, back early.'

'So I see.' Lorraine grimaced as he kissed her noisily and possessively full on the lips.

'And Joey, my boy. Good to see you. But what brings you into these parts? Thought you'd be busy rounding up the loyalists.'

'I'm just collecting a bit of jumble,' I said, wishing I could disappear into a handy black hole.

'You're not referring to my James Wilson as a bit of jumble I hope,' said Ronnie, blustering a bit.

'Your what?' I said.

'I asked Joseph to dump it for me,' said Lorraine. 'I can't stand it in the house a minute longer. It gives me the creeps.'

'But, my sweet, I bought it for your birthday. You haven't forgotten surely.'

'That doesn't mean I have to like it, does it?'

'No, but it's a collector's item. It's worth three times what I paid for it.'

'You bought it for me and I'm giving it to the jumble. If you want it you can go and buy it back from the jumble. You'll probably get it cheap.' Lorraine flounced out.

While this little domestic altercation was taking place, I was left standing there holding the baby, or the James Wilson, and feeling pretty awkward. After Lorraine's departure, Ronnie turned to me, and spoke in his confidential man-to-man mode.

'It's probably the time of the month. Got to humour them haven't you. If you could just put it to one side I'll give you a couple of quid for it before the sale. It's worth nearly half a grand so don't drop it, there's a good chap. And by the way . . .' He lowered his voice and pulled his conspiratorial face. 'How's the inquiry going?'

'Fine, just fine,' I said, backing towards the door. I didn't like to tell him right then that he hadn't got a hope.

'That's the game, Joey boy. We'll teach those Leftie poofters a trick or two.' And he took an amiable punch at my shoulder.

11

Jack White's office floor was stacked with piles of reports, working papers, memoranda, draft proposals, all in cardboard boxes, among which little paths ran like the burrows in a rabbit warren. He had this theory that there were never any new ideas in the Labour Party, it was simply a matter of recycling the old ones. So if you hung on to all the old bumph long enough, its day would come again. Trouble was his retrieval system wasn't quite up to his theory. When I arrived he was snuffling around from one box to the next like an old sow who had mislaid her favourite runt.

'Oh, it's you. Thought you were someone rather more interesting. 'He gave me a brief glance and returned to his rooting activities.

'You asked to see me.'

'Did I? So I did. Well park your bum, laddie. Those copies of *The Way Forward* are moderately comfortable. Always assuming you haven't got piles. Have you got piles?'

'Not that I'm aware'

I perched on the edge of *The Way Forward*. It was like sitting on the edge of a landslide. Jack picked up an old copy of *Horse and Hound*, stared at it a moment or two and then threw it down again.

'I never knew we subscribed to that particular publication,' I said. I knew very well the Party only took *Horse and Hound* because Jack liked to read the bloodstock articles.

'Got to keep a weather eye on what the other side is thinking,' said Jack. 'All part of the intelligence network.' He drooped a lid in what I took to be a wink, though it might have just been an hereditary defect.

It was hot in the office. It had been even hotter on the journey over. About an hour beforehand I had received this urgent message that my presence was required at once at Walworth Road for an impromptu top-level policy meeting. There didn't seem much urgency about it now I'd arrived.

'Hot enough for you, is it?' Jack terminated his search, mopped his brow on a spotted handkerchief, and collapsed back into a swivel office chair.

'Actually, I can do without this weather,' I said.

'Really! Can't get enough of it myself. All those dolly birds going around with next to nothing on. And in that dawn 'twas bliss to be alive. Who was it said that? Shakespeare?'

'Wordsworth.'

'There you are. Even an old fart like Wordsworth got a hard on in weather like this.'

'I think he was referring to the French Revolution.'

'Was he, by God. What a pervert. Ah, Susan my love. It's always a delight to see you. We were just discussing how this weather brought out the best in you young things.'

Susan, one of the secretaries, dumped another yard or so of briefings unceremoniously on Jack's desk.

'Were you,' she said without enthusiasm.

'I don't think I've seen that top before, have I?' Jack continued, quite unabashed by the initial cool. What he lacked in subtlety, he certainly made up for in persistence.

'I've had it for yonks,' said Susan.

'Have you indeed. I've definitely never seen it before or I would have remembered. Very charming. Not everyone who could get away with it. But it suits your sylph-like figure, my dear.'

'Well I've had it for yonks,' repeated Susan.

'Lovely colour. Such a subtle shade.'

'If you must know, I got it from Marks but I doubt whether they carry it in your size.' Susan smirked.

Jack laughed. 'Alas, too true. And even if they did, I fear I would not grace it quite as you do. But Susan, my love, you wouldn't do me just this small wee favour would you and make an old man happy for life.' He waggled his eyebrows in a roguish manner. I was beginning to wonder for who's benefit this whole pantomime was intended.

'All depends doesn't it,' said Susan, sullenly chewing the inside of her cheek.

'Pop the kettle on, there's a sweet lassie.'

'I'm not paid to make you tea.'

'I know you're not and I wouldn't ask but, as you can see, poor Joseph here looks more like a wet rag than a wet dream and if he doesn't get a little infusion of something soon I fear I'll have to give him mouth to mouth.'

Susan sniggered. 'Well, I'll see what I can do but I'm not making any promises.'

'You're very good to us, my dear.'

She threw me a filthy look, which in the circumstances I felt I hardly deserved, and left.

Jack turned back to me. 'Sad case. Treated like dirt by her West Indian boyfriend. Knocks her about by all accounts. String of other women. Turns up at two in the morning when he feels like a quick bang and then she doesn't set eyes on him for a week.' Jack leant forward across his desk and lowered his voice. 'You know where the likes of you and me so often go wrong with our females, Joseph?'

'No,' I said, under the dismal apprehension that I was shortly to be enlightened.

'We think they'll respond to qualities like kindness, patience, steadfastness, sensitivity. And they don't. Not a bit of it. But I'll let you into a trade secret. I'll tell you what really gets a woman wetting her knickers with desire.'

'What,' I said, gloomily, thinking a heart bypass was probably the only hope for someone of Jack's complexion.

'Power. Naked brute power. In my experience, Joseph, women have a nose for it. They sniff it out. Oh, I don't just mean money. Though that can help. But there has to be that streak of ruthlessness. The mean bastard who knows what he wants and will stop at nothing until he's got it. He's the one who scores. Our trouble, laddie, is we're often just too damned nice.' He stubbed his cigar out in a mug commemorating the Great Miner's Strike of 1983–1984.

'Is that what you asked me over for? A bit of under the table counselling on how to lay one's secretary?'

Jack looked hurt. He swivelled briefly on his chair, first one way then the other. 'Okay laddie. If that's how you want it, fine by me. From now on I shall dispense with the niceties. I was trying to break it to you gently. Clearly I was wasting my time.'

'Break what gently?' I asked. 'Have I just won the wimp of the year award or something?'

'You'll see. You'll see.' Jack began opening and closing drawers with increasing ill-humour and muttering darkly about where the damn thing could have got to and how if one of the cleaners had had it there would be no end of a row. Eventually he got up from the desk, threaded his way to the door and bawled, 'Susan!' down the corridor several times with increasing volume. He then returned to the desk, placed his elbows on the blotter, interlocked his fingers and rested his chin on his knuckles.

'While we're waiting for Susan to arrive, perhaps you'd like to give me an update on how your inquiry is going. As you are no doubt aware the leadership wants results and wants them fast. So what have you got for me?' His voice was heavy with schoolmasterly sarcasm.

'Nothing,' I said.

'Nothing,' repeated Jack, with theatrical astonishment.

'Correct.'

'Doubtless you recall the words of Lenin. Nothing will come of nothing.'

'Lear actually.'

'Lenin, Lear, one communist is much like another in

90

my book. The point I'm making, Joseph, is, isn't it time you pulled your frigging finger out?'

I sighed. 'I told you at the start, the selection process was clean. All I've established is that three members attended meetings when they were dead and a couple of union delegates voted from defunct branches. But that was on Mullins' account, not Sayeed's. There were no conspiracies. No deliberate attempts at falsification. Nothing that adds up to declaring the result null and void, or that will make a significant difference next time round.'

Jack pulled ruminatively on the beak of his nose. 'You realize if this goes badly it's not just your job that's on the line. It could have repercussions all the way up. It could even affect my own position. I'm an old man, Joseph, an old man who no longer enjoys the best of health. It's too late for me to get on my bike.'

'I don't see why it should affect you,' I said.

'Well, I'm telling you, Joseph, there are those in this Party, and they constitute a powerful grouping, who consider allowing a Pakistani ponce to take over Docklands East was an act of gross negligence on someone's part.'

'There have always been those in this Party who want to point the finger. The language of betrayals and traitors is part and parcel of the Labour mythology.'

'Oh is it? Well it's all very well for you to sit there all high and mighty and pretend to be above it all. But I'm telling you, laddie, I'm not prepared to stand idly by and take the flack for this one. I collect a nice pension in a few years and I'm not putting that at risk for you or Sayeed or the Virgin Bloody Mary. Ah Susan. A most timely reappearance. My dear, there was a brown paper bag with a magazine inside it lying on my desk which seems to have disappeared into thin air. You are not familiar with its whereabouts are you my dear?'

'Is this it?' Susan held up such a bag as had been described by one corner, as if it was a dead skunk. It had been lying in a box labelled: Worker Participation in the Decision Making Process.

Susan departed for the second time. 'Don't forget our tea,' called Jack. There was no response. 'She's a damned efficient girl that one. Got a good brain on her as well as a fine pair of titties. But down to business. I realize this is going to be painful for you, Joseph,' Jack spoke with relish, 'but if you're in the politics game then you know as well as I do there's no room for personal feelings.'

'Just get to the point,' I said.

Jack removed the magazine and passed it across the desk. It was about five months out of date and was intended as an information forum for homosexual men.

'Very interesting,' I said. 'But I don't quite get the bottom line, if you'll excuse the pun.'

'Dear God, it stinks,' said Jack. 'It's an obscenity from cover to cover. But try taking a look at the article on "Gay Communes in Crete".'

'I'm not in the market for a Mediterranean holiday, thanks.'

'Just read the frigging thing will you.'

I reluctantly picked the magazine up off the desk again and turned to the aforementioned article. It was by Alan Sayeed.

'I realize in your situation it can't be very pleasant coming across something like that,' said Jack. 'Bad enough business your wife running off with another chappie. Finding out the other man is a raving queer must be a bloody sight worse. Maybe starts you thinking about what she ever saw in yourself, doesn't it? But personal feelings apart, Joseph, you must see that that scurrilous little rag you have in your hands is political dynamite.'

'Where did you get it from?' I said.

'I don't see it matters where I got it from. Let's just say I have my sources. The point is we don't sit on our bums all day in this department doing sweet FA. Oh no, we've got our ears to the ground all right. We've got our fingers on the pulse. And personal feelings apart, this little can of worms might just save you your arse.'

'I don't quite follow?'

'Bloody obvious isn't it? The papers get one sniff of

this and Sayeed's political career is finished.'

'And you'd give it to them?'

'I'd give him the option of going quietly first.'

'It won't work.'

'And why not?'

'Because you seem to have overlooked one rather important factor.'

Jack flushed with irritation. 'You don't want the public embarrassment, is that what you're saying, laddie? Because this is one of those occasions when the greater good of that Party must needs take precedence over individual considerations.'

'As a matter of fact I couldn't care less about that aspect. But you seem to have forgotten we're in the business of selecting a Labour candidate, not electing a Labour MP, and they are two very different activities with different ground rules. Now, if you wanted to damage Sayeed's standing with the general public then sure, go ahead and print. But it won't stop him getting selected. Just the opposite. It will be one more minority bandwagon he'll have managed to climb on to. He'll become the champion of gay rights as well as of the blacks. The delegates will love it. You'll guarantee him an even bigger majority than he got last time.'

Jack snorted to himself. 'Dear God, you're not telling me our people are prepared to select a self-confessed fairy to represent them?'

'I don't think they see it quite like that, and actually there's nothing in that article that makes it obvious Sayeed is a homosexual or a bisexual or a hermaphrodite or a whatever. It's merely a piece of reportage. But yes, any association with the gay movement will improve his standing among the Party activists.'

Jack floundered. He was uncomprehending, a man out of his element, a beached whale. He was furious not just that his plan was perhaps not as well founded as he had originally thought, but because the personal triumph over me that he had been anticipating with such relish had somehow backfired.

'So what do you bloody well suggest?' he spluttered. 'One thing is for sure. We're not going to stop Sayeed by sitting on our backsides and counting old age pensioners' membership cards.'

'I'm not sure we can do anything to stop him, but, as it so happens, the Sayeed camp have decided to abort themselves.'

'In plain language please. I'm a simple man with simple views.'

'The Left have decided, in response to our leader's recent pronouncements, to pass an emergency resolution through the Council that will wipe out all existing rent arrears. If they succeed they will almost certainly be committing an illegal act which will enable the NEC to step in and disqualify Sayeed as a candidate.'

'But the Left haven't got an overall majority on the Council have they? So they won't succeed in getting it through. That's why they feel free to make these crazy gestures. It's all piss in the wind, Joseph.'

'But what if the Right decide to abstain on the issue and leave the Left enough rope to hang themselves with?'

Jack allowed his left eyelid to droop again. He lit up another cigar. 'You mean we nobble the Mullins' group in advance of the vote?'

'It's not for me to suggest any interference with the established democratic procedures. Councillors must be left to decide for themselves according to their perception of what is in the local interest. But I can see no reason why certain selected members shouldn't be apprized beforehand as to the desirability or otherwise of their allowing this motion to be passed.'

Jack pondered. 'There might be something in what you say. It'll have to be looked into in more detail, of course. I'll need to get my back-room boys involved. But there might just be something in it. Leave this one to me, Joseph. And whatever is decided, you can rest assured your name won't be mentioned.'

It was only as I was returning from Jack's office that I

began to reflect on what I had done. Alan Sayeed was the legitimately selected candidate of the local Party and I was his agent and as such I owed him my loyalty. And yet I was guilty of colluding with Jack White in a plot for Alan's downfall. Worse than that, the particular strategy agreed on was of my own suggestion. Who's side was I on?

Of course, I could argue that Jack White was my superior and as such I had no choice but to carry out his instructions. But that was a miserable excuse. Alternatively, I could claim that I was taking a lofty view of the political scene and that the retention of Mullins as MP was in the long-term interests of the working classes. But I rather doubted that. No, I suspected my real motive was rather less noble. Perhaps Andrea had been right all along. Perhaps I should have resigned at the outset rather than stayed on to play Judas.

12

I had reached the junction of Victoria Road and the High Street when I heard loud hooting noises. I presumed there was some altercation taking place between two or more commuters and so didn't pay much attention to the details. There had been several cases recently of shootings, knifings and miscellaneous acts of violence perpetrated by frustrated drivers who felt themselves to have been misused. It didn't do to get too involved.

It was only when I became aware of my name being shouted that I also noticed Lorraine leaning out of the nearside window of the red Mercedes, attracting rather a lot of ribald attention from some nearby scaffolding workers. Her attractions were not exactly of the subtle kind. I hadn't seen her since the James Wilson jumble debacle and would rather have avoided the occasion now. A session with Jack White was not the ideal prelude, nor was an East London traffic jam the perfect setting. However, short of cutting her dead, which is not my style, there was no avoiding some kind of acknowledgement.

So I waved.

'Get in,' shouted Lorraine, continuing to drive half on the pavement, half in the road, and threatening serious damage to the local council's arboreal policy.

'I only live just down the next street, thanks.'

'Get in will you,' she repeated.

'It's only a couple of hundred yards, honestly.'

'I know where you fucking live. Just get in.'

Put like that I felt I had no choice but to comply.

She promptly swung the Merc into the outside lane and took off towards Epping Forest. As always, I was most impressed by her personal decor. She was wearing tight jeans, one of those off-the-shoulder jumpers that threatened to fall down completely every time she took a corner, but somehow never quite did, and a pair of large silver hoop earrings. Her hair was pushed back with a pair of tortoiseshell combs, with one or two loose dark strands escaping across her cheeks creating that softened, slightly blurred, effect of a woman who has only recently got out of bed.

We were about two miles past my flat before a word was spoken.

'I thought you might have rung,' said Lorraine.

'I've been meaning to,' I said.

'I've just been rather low on your list of priorities, is that it?' Lorraine looked at me over a bare shoulder as we sped across a zebra crossing, pedestrians hurling themselves towards the pavements like a backwash from a speedboat.

'I wasn't too sure how an approach on my part would be received,' I said. 'By the way, I don't live in this direction.'

'Jesus, one minute you're tearing the pants off me on my own lounge floor like you've just had an overdose of rhino horn and the next you don't want to know.'

'It wasn't that I didn't want to know. I just wasn't too sure what the next correct move was. I'm afraid I'm not very familiar with the etiquette of adultery.'

'Adultery!' Lorraine shrieked and let go of the steering wheel for about quarter of a mile, not that it seemed to make much difference to our direction of travel, if anything we followed a straighter line. She then shrieked again. 'Adultery! Fucking Ada, are you out of the ark? Is that really the way you see it? You think Ronnie owns me? You don't think I have the right to do what I like with my own body? I bet you were surprised I didn't have a brand mark on my arse. A big R burnt into my hide.'

'I think we've taken a wrong turning,' I said.

'More than a wrong turning. This is the end of the road, Joseph. I want you to know I do what I like, where I like, with who I like and I don't have to ask anyone's permission. Not yours, not Ronnie's, not anyone's, get it?'

'I was meaning this is not the direction I live in.'

'Sit back and relax will you! You never been this far away from home before? Jesus, if I lived in that dump of yours I'd be only too glad to get away from it for a while.'

We were now deep into suburbia. The houses got larger and the spaces wider. The sun was shining and the brightness hurt my eyes. I was used to that opaque protective filter of dust you got in the centre. People who lived out this far probably all got skin cancer.

After about twenty minutes we turned off on to a side road which wound its way upwards for a mile or two through a sort of scrubland of stunted gorse bushes and elder trees. Eventually we swung off on to a bit of muddy trackway and came to a halt at the edge of a golf course.

Lorraine switched the engine off. The car sighed. Lorraine sighed and slid lower down the seat.

'I didn't know you were keen on golf,' I said.

'I'm not,' said Lorraine. 'A bunch of overweight men trying to get their silly little white balls into smelly little holes. Not for me thanks.'

'So what are we doing here, if it's not a rude question?'

'I come here when I want to get away from things. When I want a bit of peace and quiet.' She smiled across at me. She was certainly a woman of quickly changing moods.

'I see.'

'Matter of fact, I brought you along here because I thought it would be a good place for us to have a serious talk.'

Lorraine leaned towards me. The jumper slipped off on the left side revealing the penumbra of a nipple.

'Well, fire away,' I said. 'Fire away. I'm all ears.' I assumed a breezy business-like manner.

Lorraine straightened up and gave me a sideways look. 'They do stick out a bit.'

'What do?' I said.

'Your ears, Joseph darling. Though I dare say there are other bits of you I could get to stick out if I tried really hard.'

She stared at my crutch and ran her tongue around her lips. I crossed my legs virgin-style. Lorraine laughed a deep throaty laugh and then cut off and assumed a more thoughtful expression. She tapped her purple painted nails on the walnut fascia dashboard.

'Okay. Relax. I'm not going to eat you. Look, I'll come straight to the point. Thing is Joseph, I need your help. I need it badly. Well? What'd you say?'

'I'll do what I can,' I said. 'But first you'll have to tell me what the problem is.'

'You've heard of Stentor Properties?'

'Of course.'

'And you know Ronnie has had dealings with Stentor over some of these Docklands redevelopment schemes?'

'Yes.'

'Well, there's been a lot of bad-mouthing about how Ronnie has had these backhanders. You must have heard something of it?'

'There are always rumours.'

It was actually widely accepted in Labour Party circles that Ronnie had received a fat payoff from Stentor for smoothing planning procedures.

'Those rumours aren't true,' said Lorraine with unexpected ferocity. 'James Stentor is far too mean a shit for hand-outs of any kind, back or front. Do you know him?'

'No, I've never had that pleasure.'

'He's a real bastard. Anyway, the point is Ronnie has never received a penny over the Docklands business. OK, there might have been one or two business lunches and the odd evening out but that's just normal entertainment. It's not the same as a bribe is it? Well is it?'

'I wouldn't have said so.'

99

'Trouble is Ronnie's a bit simple. Oh, I know he puts on this hard tough-guy act but underneath all that he's just a big softie. He can't seem to see that Stentor is just using him and that sooner or later he's going to drop him in a pile of shit.'

'I see. Or rather I don't quite see. So long as Ronnie keeps his fingers clean what particular pile of shit can Stentor drop him into?'

Lorraine put a hand on my knee and squeezed it.

'Promise you'll never mention a word of this to anyone else.'

'Promise.'

'Well, Ronnie is not as discreet as he could be. There've been a few letters between him and Stentor. Nothing criminal. Just thank yous for past favours and talk about co-operation in the future and all that crap. OK, you and I know that adds up to nothing more than a freebie at some crummy steak bar, but would the rest of the world see it the same way? Here, take a look yourself. I've got them with me.'

Lorraine reached over to the back seat for a black attaché case. As she did her jumper rode up her midriff revealing an interesting dorsal curve that I wouldn't have minded exploring the extremities of a little further. She adjusted herself and removed a brown Manila folder which she handed me. Inside were a number of letters between Stentor and Ronnie. The contents, while never explicit, were not particularly edifying either.

'Well, what do you think?' asked Lorraine.

'Could be embarrassing if they got into the wrong hands.'

'Exactly.'

'I still don't quite see where I fit in?'

Lorraine was playing incy-wincy spider up my thigh. I had the uneasy feeling any second she was going to pounce on my flies.

'I expect you'll think I'm being interfering, but my idea was if someone Ronnie really respected told him these letters had come into their possession, and that they could prove very awkward for him, he might take some notice. If I talk to him about it he'll just think I'm a silly woman poking her nose into things she doesn't understand.'

'Does Ronnie really respect me?'

'Of course he does. You shouldn't be so modest, Joseph. There are a lot of people in this Party who have a very high regard for you.'

Lorraine nuzzled softly against me. She certainly knew a thing or two about the art of flattery.

'And where do I tell him I got the letters from?'

'Does it matter? Tell him they came through the letter-box one day. The fact you've got hold of them at all should make him piss his pants and perhaps then he'll put a stop to all this messing with Stentor. I don't want him getting in any deeper than he already is, Joseph. Well, will you do it? For me?'

'I don't know,' I said.

'OK, I get the message.' Lorraine pulled away. 'You can't be fucked. I'd much rather you came straight out and said it.'

'I'm just not sure I could handle it how you would want it handled.'

'You don't want to get involved. The male philosophy of life. A woman is OK for a quick screw but if she starts making any demands, drop her. I don't know why I ever thought you'd be any different from every other bastard.'

'I'll have a go,' I said. 'I'll do it. Just don't hold me responsible for how it turns out. That's all I ask.'

Lorraine turned towards me. 'You sure? I don't want it said I twisted your arm. Or any other part of your anatomy.' She screwed her eyes up and wriggled her mouth in that lewd way she had.

'Sure I'm sure. It's in a good cause, isn't it? Trying to persuade a man that he should stick to the straight and narrow.'

Lorraine leant towards me and put her arms round my neck. I noticed the skin around her own neck was deeply creased in a series of concentric circles. Jack White always said that was a sure sign of a woman who went well in bed. I wouldn't know about that. But I had noticed how of late I had become increasingly attracted to the blemishes and ruckles in a woman's skin rather than the blandly polished surfaces of youth. Perhaps age would bring its compensations.

Lorraine's tongue flickered like a lizard's. 'How long ago was it that you last made love in the back of a car?'

'I can't remember,' I said, not liking to admit that I had never made love in the back of a car. In my adolescence I had had to make do with bus shelters.

'How about rediscovering the thrill,' said Lorraine.

'What now,' I said. 'With all these golfers bobbing in and out of view. We'd probably get done for indecent exposure. I don't think that would do Ronnie much good.'

There was one particular chap viciously swinging a club that I didn't much like the look of. He seemed to have lost a ball in a gorse thicket near to where we were parked. He was wearing a ridiculous plaid hat with a pompom and kept savagely glancing in our direction every time he took a swipe at the undergrowth. He also had a number of scars over his face which made me wonder whether he didn't perhaps make a habit of tangling with gorse bushes or similar bits of predatory nature.

'Not now you idiot. But soon.' Lorraine started the engine up and reversed back on to the lane, adjusting her hair in the mirror as she performed this somewhat complex manoeuvre. 'I'll give you a ring and pick you up. We can play Buddy Holly tapes. I'll wear one of those pleated skirts, the sort you can get your hand up easily. In fact, why don't we drive to the coast? You can put your hand inside my knickers and feel me while I drive at a hundred miles per hour, overtaking everything in sight. I like speed. In fact, I'd really like to fuck in an aeroplane.'

'The lights are red,' I screamed.

Lorraine hit the brakes and slurred to a halt.

'I saw them,' she said. 'I saw them miles back. No point in slowing down before you have to.'

Lorraine dropped me on the roundabout and handed me the brown folder as I got out of the car.

'Don't forget these,' she said.

'No,' I said.

'Oh, by the way.'

'Yes?' I was halfway out of the door. Traffic was slurring and skidding on all sides.

'I knew there was something else I was meaning to say to you.'

'What is it?'

'Your friend Charles Ronayne. Is he some kind of porno freak?'

'Not that I was aware of. Look, I think I'd better get out before we cause an accident.'

'Just a minute,' said Lorraine, placing a restraining hand on my arm. 'He came to see me the other day.'

'Really?'

'He wanted to photograph me in the nude. Said it was for some kind of artistic project he was working on. I mean who does he think he's kidding?'

'He is an artist,' I said. I didn't like the way this conversation was tending. And I also didn't like the way cars kept hurtling at us like this was the Dodgems. 'I take it you refused.'

Lorraine smirked. 'As a matter of fact I let him have a few snaps. Well, pathetic old codger. I couldn't see the harm. And being married to that Celia bitch can't exactly be fun, can it?'

'I really must go,' I said.

'See you,' she said, moving off while my foot was still caught in the seat belt. 'What d'you say to Brighton?'

'I like Brighton.'

She blew me a kiss as the Mercedes accelerated away.

13

The Scarborough Conference for local government councillors on how to resist the Tory cuts had been scheduled as far back as the previous February, and there was no ducking out of it now. I was slated to drive the minibus. I didn't mind the driving. Indeed there had been times when I had seriously considered long-distance haulage as an alternative to the agent's job. But the delegate list left something to be desired. Meryll and Pam were down for starters, as were Jonathan and Julian, Ted Clarke and Alan. But the real problem from my point of view was Celia. We hadn't spoken since the unfortunate peeing down the sink episode.

I rang Andrea and asked her whether she'd like to swap with me. At first she seemed quite amenable to the idea. She was just back from a session with her acupuncturist, which usually put her in a good mood. It was only when I suggested that she and Alan could probably do with a weekend away together, that it might even be fun, that things turned nasty. I promptly got an earful about how her relationship with Alan was not dependant on self-indulgent hedonism thanks very much, how if she had gone it would have been because she considered it to be in the interests of the community she represented, and how I had no business trying to interfere in her private life anyway. That was the end of that.

Celia turned up at the embarkation point wearing a long grey mac, which gave her a forlorn wistful quality, and carrying a neat travelling holdall. She sat by herself at the back out of view of my rear mirror. At the Granada services she disappeared to the Ladies and then joined Pam and Meryll for a coffee. Hardly soul mates I would have thought. Once or twice I saw her sneaking surreptitious glances in my direction, but there was nothing in her expression to build any hopes on, rather the opposite.

The hotel was a large Victorian Gothic pile slap on the seafront. It had seen better days. The furnishings were Cyril Lord mated with Parker Knoll and the coupling was of none too recent a date. The entire place was deserted, apart from a surprising number of pale gaunt youths with Mohican haircuts wandering up and down the long dark corridors like lost souls. DHSS claimants I guessed.

I retired early, feeling exhausted after the drive, besides I had no particular wish to listen to Jonathan and Julian discussing Jean Genet's prison novels punctuated only by the occasional fart ricocheting from between Ted Clarke's massy thighs. Clarke was still being grouchy about the rent amnesty idea, which he regarded as a seriously flawed tactic and for which he seemed to hold me personally to blame, presumably through my association with Andrea. I could understand why he felt badly about it. Clarke, more than anyone, had nurtured Alan's career. He clearly had big ambitions for the young Pakistani from Crouch End. If the rent amnesty plot went wrong, and chances were it would, then all that slow and painful groundwork would be wasted.

I was in the middle of cleaning my teeth with the Oral B Special that I had stolen from Celia's closet when there came a timid knocking at my door. I jumped to the obvious conclusion and my heart beat faster. Celia in black leather miniskirt and silk blouse slashed to the waist. It had to be. What was it Andrea had once said about how we could get anything in this world provided we wanted it badly enough? Well, I wanted it badly enough. I slipped back the lock.

It was Pam in a chunky fisherman's rib sweater, baggy cords and a pair of rather muddy walking boots. 'Can I have a word?' she mouthed.

'Sure. Come in.'

Pam came in and sat down on my bed and bounced on it and patted at it. I sat on the one upright chair.

'Isn't it wonderful,' she said.

'Yes,' I said, thinking the springing was pretty average for a boarding house, but not liking to quibble.

'We've just been for a walk up on the hill. It was so beautiful. You felt you could breathe.' Pam swelled up with a series of deep breaths to demonstrate what she meant. I was a bit worried she might over do it and go into a trance or a fit or something and then what would I do.

'Yes, it can be very invigorating up here,' I said.

Pam leant towards me a look of intense passion shining in her eyes. Her cheeks were glowing. Her hair was windswept. I'd never seen her looking so well. She reminded me of a Girl Guide I had once known who had confided in me that babies came out of rabbit holes and offered to show me one. I had turned her down, which looking back on it was probably a wise decision.

'I think Meryll's ready to do it,' said Pam.

'Do what?' I said.

'It,' repeated Pam through gritted teeth.

'Oh, right,' I said.

'I love her,' said Pam. 'I'm going crazy with love for her. Oh, I know I shouldn't lust after her body so much but I can't seem to help myself. You see, coming back tonight, we walked with our arms around each other and I licked the wax from her ear and it tasted like honey. I'd do anything for her. Anything she asked. Just anything.'

I'm out of my depth here, I thought to myself.

'I hope you don't mind me talking to you like this?' said Pam.

'No, of course not,' I said.

106

'You're the only person I know who understands what I'm going through.'

'Yes,' I said.

'Meryll told me, you see.'

'Told you what?'

'Told me you used to fancy her. It's OK. I won't mention it to anyone else. I know how awful it must have been for you. To love and to know that there was never any possibility of your love being returned.'

I was a bit fazed by this latest disclosure. So when Pam asked whether I'd agree to swap rooms, because there was a double in mine and they only had twin singles in their's, I hastily agreed.

'It'll seem more natural,' said Pam.

So I trogged off with my carriers, one in each hand like some kind of bag person, to Pam and Meryll's room. Meryll wasn't to be seen, for which I was thankful. Just a handful of adolescents sitting over the stairs drinking lager from cans.

I had not been in bed for more than fifteen minutes when there came a further knocking. This had to be Celia, I thought. Except how did Celia know that I had changed rooms? I thought of her stumbling on Meryll and Pam and could not resist a sly smile to myself. I opened the door. It was Meryll in a trench coat with a plastic shower hat pulled down over her ears.

'It's pretty obvious why you were so keen on a swap,' she said.

'I beg your pardon,' I said.

'The noise through the partition. It's disgusting. If there's one thing that really gets up my nose it's the noise heterosexuals make when they copulate. All that sucking and squelching and squealing and grunting. Worse than pigs in an abattoir. Ugh!' She shuddered expressively.

So I packed my things a second time and went back to my previous room. On the way I passed Pam with a duvet wrapped round her, looking awfully glum.

I don't know how long I'd been asleep when I was

107

woken by a sort of scratching noise. I turned over. The scratching was repeated and this time Alan's voice was recognizable.

'Joseph, we've got to talk.'

I stumbled out of bed and opened the door yet again, thinking there wasn't really much point in my closing it. I'd be better off sleeping in the foyer with twenty-four hour a day continuous access to insomniacs, fornicators, suicides, shift workers, and miscellaneous passers by. Alan was standing there wearing a pair of striped pyjama trousers with a pink towel flung casually over his shoulder. His torso was naked and muscular, gleaming with droplets where he had failed to dry himself properly.

'What's up,' I said. 'Hotel on fire or something?'

Alan grinned a little sheepishly and came further into my room leaving a trail of wet footprints on the grey lino.

'I thought I'd better warn you, Joseph.'

'Warn me? What about? The bath need rinsing does it. The plug hole blocked with hair. No problems. I've stuck my arm down more drain holes than you've had hot showers.'

Alan took no notice of this little bit of hyperbole. He seemed more interested in studying his profile in the wardrobe mirror, first one way then the other. Having apparently satisfied himself that he was still as good-looking as ever, he turned his solemn brown eyes in my direction.

'It's to do with the rent amnesty.'

'What about it?' I said, flopping back on to the bed and almost dislocating my spine as I did so.

'I'm afraid if it got through Council it could end up hurting you and Andy very badly.'

'Oh, I don't know too much about that. I've got rent arrears of my own. What's good for the goose is good for the gander.'

'Joseph, be serious a moment will you. Have you any idea of the implications of what we're getting ourselves into? Andrea sees this amnesty idea as a great revolutionary gesture. And so it is. But what if the gesture became a reality. OK, usually we can rely on the Right to block extreme resolutions of this nature. But what if some malicious bastard organized the Right to abstain on this issue. What then?'

I was beginning to feel a little uncomfortable about the way this conversation was developing. Had rumours got out that the Right had been nobbled in advance of the vote? Certainly Alan was showing more political astuteness than I'd previously given him credit for.

'If the Right abstain,' I said. 'Then you will achieve your objective. The rent amnesty will go through council. Where's the problem?'

'Joseph, you're being naive. You know damn well what will happen.'

'There'll be a financial shortfall.'

'And the District Auditor will be called in.'

The District Auditor. Alan gave the phrase the same kind of emphasis usually reserved for the Mafia or the Ku Klux Klan.

'We're not talking fifty-pound fines and a ticking off from the judge here, Joseph. We're talking major bankruptcy. We're talking houses being repossessed and women and children thrown out on to the streets. We're talking total annihilation.'

Now I was feeling distinctly uneasy. I had to admit the District Auditor had not been in the forefront of my mind when I had suggested to Jack White in his nasty little office that the rent amnesty might be exploited to finish off Alan's political career. The trouble with plots of this kind is they had a way of backfiring on you.

'If you remember correctly,' I said, 'I was the one at the Campaign Meeting who suggested it might be a good idea to take legal advice before rushing into this amnesty business.'

'OK. OK.' Alan threw his hands into the air. 'I'm not blaming you personally for this situation. I know you did your best. But you must see now if the DA is going to get involved it's critical you persuade Andy to back off, before it's too late.'

'I'm not sure I can do that,' I said.

Alan threw the towel at the wall, swung the chair round and straddled it.

'Look Joseph, I'm not asking you to do this to save my own political neck. If that was all that was at stake here, I'd say, to hell with it, let's go ahead and the DA can get stuffed. But it's Andrea I'm thinking of. Andrea and Livingstone. Andrea is a councillor. She'll be right in the firing line.'

'But what makes you think Andrea will listen to me? She's far more likely to listen to you.'

Alan lay his arms along the back of the chair and rested his forehead on his arms like he was preparing himself for the block.

'I realize Andrea and I have a very close under-standing. But if I start laying it on the line with her about the rent amnesty then I'll lose all political credibility with the Left of the Party. And I can't risk that at the moment. Especially not with this sodding inquiry still going on.'

'Whereas everyone knows I'm a funk, so coming from me it will seem perfectly in character, is that it?'

'Exactly. No, not exactly. Look, damn it Joseph, you still own thirty per cent of the equity in that house.'

'Thirty per cent. I always thought it was fifty.'

Alan looked embarrassed. 'Oh I don't know the details. Andy told me thirty per cent. But perhaps she got it wrong. The point is you have a legitimate reason for tell-ing her to back off.'

There was a call box in the foyer. The first couple of times I couldn't get my coin to stick. It just went straight through like the damn machine had the shits. I knew the problem. I felt them coming on myself. Andrea was not going to be pleased about a call from me at this time of night. But there were bigger things at stake than Andrea's good humour. She wasn't going to be overjoyed

110

about having her roof sold over her head. I tried a 50p piece and this time it lodged.

'Andrea?'

'Yes.'

'It's me.'

'Who?'

'Me, Joseph.'

'Jesus Christ, I thought you were one of those heavy breathers. Joseph, have you any idea what the bloody time is?'

'About two a.m. My watch could be five minutes slow.'

'I know it's two a.m. you moron. And I was asleep. Some of us have got to work tomorrow.'

'Yes, I'm sorry. I wouldn't have rung this late. Only it's urgent I talk to you.'

'What's happened?'

'Well, nothing as yet. It's more a matter of what might happen.'

'Is Alan OK?'

'Alan's fine.'

'Joseph, stop pissing around. I take it you had something more in mind than a bedtime story?'

'The District Auditor?'

'What?'

'The District Auditor is going to be called in. Hang on. I've got another coin somewhere. Don't go away, Andrea. You still there?'

'Yes.'

'He has these enormous powers.'

'So.'

'He can hold councillors liable for every penny of rent that isn't collected. That means the house will have to be sold, the furniture, everything. You could end up having to squat in the committee rooms along with me.'

Silence.

'Andrea, you still there?'

'Joseph, you have to be bullshitting.'

'Wish I was.'

'They could even take my house away from me?'

111

'Yes.'

'Livingstone and me would be thrown on to the streets?'

'Yes.'

'This is outrageous.'

'Yes.'

'Would you stop saying yes the whole time like a bloody sheep.'

'Yes, I mean right.'

'If the District Auditor can be called in to overthrow decisions the government doesn't like, then it's an end to local democracy.'

'Absolutely.'

'Well, why the hell didn't you say something along these lines at the original meeting?'

'I guess I wasn't thinking too clearly.'

'You're a bloody moron.'

'You've already made that point.'

'So what do I do now?'

'Well, it's not too late. You could still vote the other way.'

'You're suggesting I should betray a great ideal for the sake of my own material welfare?'

'Well, yes, I suppose I am.'

'Joseph, you're just the pits.'

'It's not going to be an easy decision, I realize that.'

'It's OK for you. You're not on the line like I am.'

'Fifty per cent of that house is mine remember.'

'Thirty.'

'I thought it was fifty.'

'Thirty.'

'Well, anyway, the point is a lot of the others who voted for this motion aren't on the line at all. Take Jonathan and Julian for example. They haven't got any assets worth speaking of. And besides they've got rich parents who will bail them out of any trouble.'

'Yes, and it's OK for Meryll, the ugly old boot. She isn't even a councillor. She can vote for what she bloody well likes and get away scot-free. Seems to me I'm one of

112

the few who actually stands to lose something by all this.'

'Quite.'

'I've worked for years to get this house together, Joseph.'

'And very nice it looks too.'

'And I don't see why some horrible little District Auditor should get his filthy hands on it.'

'And there's also Livingstone to think of. He's already had enough disruptions in his life.'

'Joseph, I hate you.'

'I'm sorry, what have I said wrong now?'

'Just everything to do with you has always been bad news.'

'But Andrea, I didn't invent District Auditors. I'm just the messenger.'

There was no reply only a monotone, signalling disconnection.

14

Celia was punctilious about turning up at the scheduled meetings and taking copious notes, at least I presumed that was what she was doing. Alternatively she might have been scribbling passionate letters to an absent lover who liked her to wear black leather miniskirts.

The meetings themselves ran their predictable course. It was agreed that although Thatcher had again won the election with an overwhelming majority, this was only because the Labour Party had failed to put before the people a radical enough alternative. The rest of the sessions were taken up with establishing just what these radical new initiatives should be. Ideas varied from special grants for lesbian workshops to the total banning of the sale of animal flesh.

It was only on the last evening that I was presented with an opportunity for talking with Celia. Most of the delegates were attending an impromptu satirical review. Jonathan and Julian were doing their Nigel Lawson and Sir Geoffrey Howe eunuchs sketch. I couldn't stomach the idea and so decided to give it a miss. Celia clearly had the same thought because I ran into her in the hotel lounge. She was sitting in the spacious bay window overlooking the concrete esplanade. My initial instinct was to turn on my heel, but before I had time to move a muscle Celia had looked up and smiled.

Encouraged, I went and sat near to her but, I hoped, not oppressively near. She was wearing a navy cardigan and a navy skirt. She seemed huddled into herself. She was reading a biography of Barbara Pym in hardback.

'Always freezing on the east coast isn't it? Even in the middle of summer it's freezing. No wonder the tourist industry is dying on its feet. No way Scarborough is ever going to compete with the sunny Med, is there?'

Celia said nothing. I began to panic. Perhaps I had misinterpreted her glance. Perhaps she was about to swipe me round the face with the book which was open before her but which she wasn't reading. When I panic I tend to talk very fast about the first thing that comes into my head.

'We always had our family holiday on the east coast. Bit further south, Cromer. Just as bloody cold. Me and my sister, she was a year younger than me, we used to take our shoes and socks off and stand on the rocks as the tide came in. The game was to see who could stay on the rock longest. One day my sister fell and gashed her head open. She had bright blonde hair and the blood soaked through it in seconds. I had to drag her out of the water. I thought she was dead but she was only unconscious for a bit. She was taken to the hospital by this nice old couple with a sausage dog and had eight stitches. When my mother found out she slapped me round the face and called me a wicked boy. Soon after that my father and mother split up and for a long time I thought it was all because of the game which I had invented and which had gone so badly wrong. It was only years later my sister told me that the reason it took so long to find my mother was because she was busy screwing the hotel manager while my father was off sea-fishing. Funny how things work out isn't it?'

Celia placed her book face down. 'What an awful story.'

'Yes, I suppose it is rather awful. Sorry, am I interrupting your reading?'

'No,' said Celia. 'No, not at all.' She crossed her long slender legs and fixed her gaze on the tip of her navy shoe that dangled precariously from the toes of her right foot. 'We can't go on hiding away from each other

115

for ever can we? There are some things that have to be faced, no matter how unpleasant.'

She turned to face me. I felt suitably unpleasant. And yet how beautiful and serene were those large grey eyes of hers.

'Celia. I don't know why I got into all that about my childhood and everything. Looking for sympathy is what Andrea would say. What I really want to do is apologize. I realize no words can possibly make amends for my disgraceful behaviour. But please believe me I never intended to cause you the slightest offence.'

'I think it's me who should be doing the apologizing,' said Celia.

'You. Why you? I don't see how you can hold yourself responsible because I got horribly drunk and behaved in a foul manner.' There were some peanuts on the table. I grabbed a handful and then offered the bowl to Celia. She shook her head. I took another handful.

'To begin with,' said Celia, 'I admit I was hurt by your behaviour. If it had been Ted Clarke then I would have not given it a second thought. It would have been par for the course. But you, Joseph. I suppose I had come to look on you as a special friend and I do not make friends easily.'

'But it wasn't intentional,' I blurted. 'Don't you see I was not really responsible for my actions? It was one of those absurd accidents of life.'

'All our actions, even the most trivial, have a significance,' said Celia.

'Oh I don't think so. Not mine at any rate. My life has been a series of random disasters.'

'Our motives are perhaps not always obvious to ourselves,' said Celia. 'But I do believe there is a meaning to everything we do. No, listen to me please. When my anger died away I realized that you weren't just pissing down my sink. What you were in fact doing was pissing on me. Yes, on me, on my whole life style, my privileged upbringing, my wealth, my accent, everything I stand for.'

116

'But that's nonsense,' I said. 'I love you. I love you Celia.'

For a moment I could hardly believe that I had said it. The words had just slipped out and disappeared like stones dropped into a deep well. Perhaps I had committed an indiscretion even greater than my original one. Celia stirred her coffee in a slow meditative manner, hardly breaking the surface with the spoon. Her face was quite impassive, her lids lowered, her gaze fixed on the dangling shoe.

'I don't blame you for what you did, Joseph. I am a weak self-centred woman who cannot give up the privileges that I have grown so attached to. My quiet garden, my nice furniture, my holidays abroad. I cannot survive without these things. Believe me, I have tried.'

'You're too hard on yourself,' I said. 'We are all fond of our creature comforts.'

'To the extent that we would let others die rather than put ourselves to any inconvenience?'

'We must all feel some guilt about the thousands who are starving.'

'I'm not talking about the starving,' said Celia. 'Though God knows that is bad enough. I'm talking about someone I knew, that I was fond of, that I was vain enough to think I could help, who ended up dying in the corner of a dirty subway from a massive overdose straight into the bloodstream.'

'I see.'

'No, you don't see. The point is she had asked me only a week beforehand whether she could come and live with me. And I had turned her down. Oh, I had made some weak excuse about how Charles wouldn't like it. But that wasn't the real reason. The real reason was I couldn't face the idea of her messing up my house. Leaving syringes on the worktops. Failing to rinse the bath. Just being there. You see that's the sort of person I really am.'

'It still doesn't make it your fault,' I said.

'No,' sighed Celia. She leant her head back upon the

117

embroidered antimacassar. 'It wasn't my fault. And I'm not so conceited as to think that if I had allowed her to come and live with me it would have made it all right for her. She would have probably ended up killing herself anyway. All I'm saying is when the chips are down I can be as big a bastard as the next person. I don't really like myself very much Joseph. I don't really like what's inside here. And now if you don't mind I think I'm going to retire early. I'm glad we've cleared the air between us. I feel better for it.'

I jumped up and in doing so knocked her shoe clean off her foot. I quickly grovelled on the floor for it and helped relocate it on the questing toes. 'I'm terribly sorry. How very clumsy of me. 'I allowed my hand to remain just a moment on the curve of her instep.

'I'm afraid I'm no Cinderella,' she said and left the room.

The morning of our departure I woke earlier than usual. I got out of bed and drew back the yellow diamond-patterned curtains. A mist was rolling in off the sea. The most polluted triangle of ocean in the world, or so I had read in an article somewhere. The esplanade was wet and slimy looking. A ship's horn sounded mournfully across the dark flat water. A gull hauled into the wind and yelped. I was about to let the curtain drop when I noticed Clarke and Alan talking together near the back of the minibus.

At breakfast Alan said to me, 'We are thinking of calling in at the Walthamstow picket on the way back. It's just a short detour round the M25. And I believe it's important we should show our solidarity with oppressed women whenever the opportunity occurs. And when you think about it, Joseph, this could be a turning point in history we're living through. Something to tell our grandchildren.'

I pushed my fried tomatoes to one side. They were of the tinned variety and made me think of clots of blood. I wasn't too keen on justifying my role in history to my grandchildren. On the other hand, a detour to Walthamstow might have its advantages, particularly if it meant we failed to get back for the rent amnesty vote on time.

'Good idea,' I said. 'It's not very far out of our way. Excellent idea.'

15

Half way back down the motorway the drizzle turned into a downpour and the windscreen became a constant slurry of mud and slime. Driving, never a very exact science as far as I was concerned, turned into something more akin to sledging along the bottom of the Thames Estuary. Every now and again the dog-eared wiper gave up the ghost altogether and I had to jump out and tweak it back into life. But the real pain didn't start until Meryll exhumed her acoustic guitar from its portable black coffin and suggested we cheer ourselves up with a little communal singing. I was pretty sure I wasn't the only one to groan, but the loyal Pam chimed in with, 'That would be really lovely Meryll.' And this, despite her disappointments on the earwax front. Before you could say Rosa Luxemburg, we were deep into, Where Have All The Flowers Gone? and We Shall Overcome and other mawkish numbers from the Sixties, which was puzzling because Meryll and Pam could hardly have been more than a twinkle in the eye when Bob Dylan and Joan Baez were making out. Some sort of cultural necrophilia had to be at work here. Anyway, it came as a blessed relief when the sound of wailing police sirens finally drowned the both of them.

I wound down my window. A uniformed sergeant stuck his head in. He had a face like a Scottish mountain side. Rain was cascading down the deep runnels of his cheeks.

'Can I see your papers, Sir?'

'Papers,' blustered Clarke, from just behind my right

ear lobe. 'What does he think this is, a fascist state? Tell the fucker we still have freedom of movement in this country. It's not South Africa, yet.'

'I think he only wants to see my licence,' I said.

'Show him your arse'ole until he produces a search warrant,' said Clarke. Which was all very well, but I was doing the upfront negotiating here.

'I might as well show him my licence,' I said. 'After all it's the cleanest thing about me.' In the circumstances I thought this was a pretty good joke, the sort of throwaway line that helps reduce tension in a crisis. The sergeant didn't seem too amused, however. But then again I guess if you have a face like a granite cliff you tend to be a touch on the implacable side.

I started rummaging in my carriers for the necessary documentation. I had just about everything anyone could possibly need in transit with me. Spare pair of socks. Special Xmas edition of *Marxism Today*. Tube of superglue. Bottle of Alka Seltzer. I even had the Stentor letters tucked away inside a pair of long johns, in case the weather turned inclement – the long johns that is, not the letters. The letters were an oversight. I must have picked them up by mistake thinking they were the conference briefing papers. But no damned driving licence.

'I must have mislaid it,' I said. 'It's probably in my Gateway carrier. I tend to keep my top security items in there. The handles are stronger.'

The sergeant looked unimpressed by this little titbit of classified information, shortly to appear in my forthcoming guide, *How To Survive Without A Suitcase*.

'Kindly produce it along with your MOT and insurance certificates at your local police station within the next forty-eight-hours. And now if you wouldn't mind vacating your vehicle while the constable here carries out a few routine road-safety checks.'

'If there's anything wrong with this bus,' said Clarke, 'it's the responsibility of the cowboys who hired it. It's time these racketeers were brought under some kind of centralized control. What we need is a properly unified, state subsidized, transport system in this cunt-ry.'

'Go easy,' I whispered behind cupped hand. 'I hired it from the Community Co-op.'

'Wherever it came from,' said the sergeant, who obviously had ears fitted with radio antennae, 'it's still the responsibility of the driver to see that any vehicle he drives complies with the requirements of the 1972 Road Safety Act.' His nose had just turned into a most impressive waterfall, probably the highest uninterrupted drop this side of Hardrow Force.

'Oh for God's sake let's just do as he asks and get it over and done with shall we,' said Celia, standing up and getting out of the back. The rest soon followed her initiative.

The constable, who had a brick-red complexion, and who also happened to be built like a brick wall, now proceeded to rock the minibus violently on its springs from side to side, as if intent on rolling it down the embankment and into the ditch below. Failing to achieve this, he walked round in a clockwise direction kicking savagely at the tyres. Finally, he got underneath the vehicle and wrenched off the entire exhaust system so that it hung loose from the chassis. 'Metal fatigue,' he announced triumphantly, as he re-emerged. Meanwhile the sergeant went through the interior throwing out crowbars, spanners, lengths of lead piping, screwdrivers and, rather curiously, an extraordinarily large number of used condoms. He held each one between thumb and forefinger and dropped them into a pile on the ground, with an expression of growing distaste.

'I said all along there was a funny fishy smell,' said Pam.

'Well, I can assure you, Sergeant, they're nothing to do with us,' said Meryll, grabbing hold of Pam's arm, to make it quite clear just who she meant by 'us'.

'I didn't say they were, dear, did I?' said the sergeant.

'And the name's Ms Shrike,' snapped Meryll, outraged.

'We'll take down personal details later, dear, thank you,' said the sergeant.

'If you don't address me in a proper manner I shall make a formal complaint,' shrieked Meryll.

The sergeant looked puzzled. 'So, let's get this straight shall we. If these ... er ... johnnies ... er ... prophylactics are not yours, madam, who would you say, among your number, they might belong to?'

'I have absolutely no idea,' said Meryll. 'But you could try asking Agent Pink. He's more likely to use that sort of thing than I am.' Meryll glanced witheringly in my direction.

'Me!' I said, thinking Agent Pink from Meryll's lips sounded like a rather worse version of Agent Orange. 'I'm afraid you greatly overrate my prowess, Meryll, if you think I could get through that lot even in a long weekend. But perhaps the previous hirers left them behind. It was the woodcraft folk, I think. They went on their annual picnic to Polesden Lacey last weekend.'

'Don't be ridiculous,' said Meryll. 'They were only elfins.'

'Elfins?' said the sergeant.

It was beginning to look like we were settling down for a prolonged session of accusation and counter-accusation, when Celia spoke out in a clear voice.

'If you must know, they're mine. I entertained about twenty sailors last night in my hotel bedroom. And I like to keep a little memento of each one. Is there a law against it?'

The sergeant looked at the constable and the constable looked at the sergeant. Both were obviously nonplussed. If there wasn't a law against it there quite clearly should be. The sergeant decided on a new line of approach.

'Perhaps you would kindly tell us where you are travelling to and for what purpose?'

'We're on our way to support the Walthamstow Eleven,' chipped in Meryll, though she was not the one who had been spoken to.

'I told you they looked like football hooligans, Sarge,' said the constable. 'Soon as we set eyes on them I said they were football hooligans. Also explains all the weaponry.'

Meryll could hardly contain her derision. 'Football hooligans. I can assure you, Constable, we are all fully paid up members of the Docklands East Labour Party. And we're on our way to a picket in order to show our solidarity with those heroic women who have suffered such a gross miscarriage of justice.'

'A picket, eh,' said the sergeant.

'That's right,' said Meryll. 'We intend to stop all movement in and out of Walthamstow town centre. Non-violent direct action.' She spat the words in his face.

'In that case I'm arresting you all, as I have reason to believe that you intend to cause a breach of the peace. I should also formally warn you that anything you say will be taken down and may be used in evidence against you. I suggest you collect your belongings from the bus. Constable, radio for a secure riot vehicle to shovel this lot into.'

'We must exercise our right to silence, comrades,' shouted Clarke, crooking his left knee, flexing his right buttock and giving vent to an ear-splitting fart.

So we settled down on the hard shoulder, sitting on our suitcases, those of us who had them, in the pouring rain, like the survivors of a road accident.

In the back of the riot van Meryll became slightly hysterical. She kicked and banged against the partition and shouted, 'I refuse to be strip searched. Do you fuckin' hear? If any one of you bastards lays a fuckin' finger on me I shall take you to the European Court of Human Rights. Do you fuckin' hear what I'm saying? The struggle will go on. You can't destroy the spirit of a people for ever. I refuse to be strip searched.'

She worked herself up into quite a state, Pam put a comforting arm round her. 'Don't worry, love. Whatever they do to you, they will have to do to me as well. We'll go through this together.' It was generously said, but Meryll didn't seem to find it very reassuring. She just banged more loudly.

I was seated next to Alan. He glanced at his watch. 'Guess that puts the kibosh on any chance we might have had of getting to the rent amnesty vote.' He didn't sound too cut up about it.

After arrival at the station our possessions were removed, checked, catalogued and signed for in triplicate. After this lengthy procedure had been gone through the police didn't seem to know quite what to do with us. A number of hurried conversations took place, phone calls were made, senior officers were consulted and eventually we were shown into a long narrow room that had the appearance of being a converted corridor. There was a bank of two-tone brown filing cabinets along one side with wooden benches facing them.

'They only put lino on the floors because it's easier to wash the blood off,' said Clarke, as the door was slammed shut on us.

'Oh dear, don't put ideas into their heads,' said Pam, who was busy trying to get Meryll to swallow some aspirin. Meryll had got a headache. I wasn't exactly surprised after all the row she'd been making in the van. She refused to take the aspirin because drugs were a capitalist panacea. But since arriving at the station she'd gone as quiet as a mouse.

It proved to be rather hot in the confines of the corridor, the kind of dry heat that causes the skin to prickle. Or perhaps that was just an effect of the body empathizing with the cacti plants grouped together on a small, high windowsill.

Clarke kept jumping up and down, pressing the call buzzer and demanding to speak to his solicitor. At one point he was taken into another room. On his return he claimed to have been roughly handled, but he looked no more dishevelled than he usually did.

'They're never going to let us go if you keep shooting your mouth off every five minutes,' complained Meryll,

and while this seemed a bit ripe coming from Meryll, it
fairly summed up the general mood by this stage.

Eventually, after a delay of three and a half hours, our
possessions were returned to us and we were released,
without any charges being made or any explanations
offered.

16

'So, the revolutionaries of the Left have made a cock up of it again.' Jack snorted down his nose and ran his hands back through his mane of white hair. It was a theatrical gesture. Jack was full of them. He would have made a good second-rate rep actor in some seedy coastal resort. Scarborough, for instance. 'I dare say when the communards finally get off their backsides and build their barricades they will collapse on top of them and kill the lot. Roll on the day. Save me a job of work.' More snorts of laughter.

I didn't quite understand what was going on. I'd expected the usual quantities of cynical comment re the mislaid plans of mice and men, but Jack was taking the news of the rent amnesty debacle rather better than I had expected. It was suspicious.

We were in the lounge bar of the Gransbury. It was about two-thirty. The place had the desolate stale feel about it of unwashed ashtrays and spilt beer.

'I don't think it's quite as simple as that,' I said.

'Sounds simple enough to me,' said Jack. 'Sounds positively cretinous. The Trotskyite rabble organize a palace coup. We go out of our way to make things easy for them. We even arrange for the Right to abstain on the vote. And then the comrades fail to turn up for the action. If it wasn't so bloody funny it would make you weep. Fortunately I've been blessed with a sense of humour.'

'Do we really have to go over it all in this kind of detail,' I said. 'It's not very productive at this stage.'

127

'Questions are going to be asked,' said Jack, suddenly coming on all self-righteous. 'Questions are going to be asked and I'm going to have to provide the answers. This whole episode is a major bloody embarrassment. You seem to be forgetting that I promised the leadership that Sayeed would commit political harikari.'

'OK, OK, I'll go through it again for you. We were prevented from getting back for the vote on the rent amnesty because we were under arrest in Chingford.'

Jack threw his hands in the air. 'Incredible. Simply incredible. And why may I ask was half the Labour Party of Docklands East under arrest in Chingford, of all the godforsaken places?'

'We were on our way to the Walthamstow picket.'

'Dear God! So, while you were charging round the countryside playing at the Red Brigade, the whole master plan for ditching Sayeed went down the Swanee. What a shambles. What a pathetic bloody shambles. And these are the people who think they should be entrusted with running the country. They couldn't organize a piss-up in a brewery. Fortunately, however, most fortunately for you Joseph, I took the precaution of having a fall-back plan. Just in case Messrs Pink and Co failed to bring home the bacon.'

Jack sat back self-satisfied and enigmatic. He clearly wanted me to ask the obvious question. So I asked it.

'What fall-back plan?'

Jack assumed his wiser and older man expression that involved a furrowing of the brow and a drooping of the eyelids.

'I'm afraid I couldn't tell you about this before, Joseph. It wouldn't have been professional of me. And also it could have placed you in a very difficult position vis-à-vis, well vis-à-vis just about everyone. But the truth of the matter is we never really expected Sayeed to lose the re-selection process. The inquiry was decided on purely as a delaying tactic.'

'You mean Ronnie has been taken for a ride?'

'I wouldn't put it exactly like that. I'd say rather he

missed the bus. Our strategy has been quite straight-forward. The first priority was to stop any possibility of a large-scale defection. If Mullins went others might follow. That meant buying Mullins' loyalty for a while with promises of ditching Sayeed. Mullins took the bait and broke off his talks with the Tories. Naturally they felt a little let down by their new convert, and have now gone ahead and selected their own home grown, blue eyed boy to fight Docklands when the time comes. So you see, poor old Ronnie's gone past his sell by date and we're into a whole different ball game.'

'But even if Mullins has lost his chance of joining the Tories, the leadership is still rather boxed in over Sayeed. You can't have forgotten the famous "over my dead body" speech.'

'You worry too much Joseph. Sayeed is small fry. By the time the General Election comes around no one will even remember his name. One of the great advantages of the British voter is that he has a memory span of approximately six weeks.'

'And what if Mullins chooses to resign straight away and create a by-election?'

Jack pulled on his cigar and waved a hand in a dismissive gesture.

'Where could he go?'

'The Democrats perhaps.'

'Don't be absurd Joseph. The Democrats are nowhere in your stretch of Docklands. This isn't Tower Hamlets we're talking about. You're too far down river for that kind of political fish to have a chance of survival. Democrats need cleaner water.'

'Well, how about Independent Labour then?'

Jack blew a cloud of smoke in my face. 'Not a cat in hell's chance. Dear God, do you think I haven't considered this. Mullins is a Party hack. He hasn't got what it takes to run a one-man show. When you've been in this game as long as I have Joseph, you get a gut feeling for which way a man is going to jump. Besides, as I've said before, you could run a bare-arsed monkey in Docklands

East and so long as it was on the official Labour ticket it would romp home. Come to think of it, bare-arsed monkey isn't a bad description of our candidate. Another half, laddie?'

I had actually been drinking pints, but the offer of a half from Jack was not something to be lightly turned down, so I accepted. Jack dragged himself to his feet and tacked his vertiginous way across to the bar. An obsequious young man with slicked down black hair and a neatly trimmed moustache asked him for his order.

'Where's my wee friend with the big titties then?' asked Jack, lubriciously smacking his lips. 'She usually waggles her pretty little butt for us on a Tuesday doesn't she?'

'You mean Janine,' said the barman.

'That is indeed the young lady I am enquiring after.'

'She's dead, Sir,' said the barman, ringing up his till.

Jack reeled a bit. Little bubbles of froth appeared at the left corner of his mouth.

'You're joking,' he said.

'Deadly serious,' said the barman, polishing up a glass. 'Janine, I'm afraid, has snuffed it.'

'But she . . . I saw her only last week.'

The barman shrugged. 'That's the way the cookie crumbles. Here today, gone tomorrow. Can I get you something?'

'A dram of Scotch wouldn't go amiss. Dear God, tell you the truth I feel a bit shaken.'

'Knew her well, did you, Sir?'

'Yes. No. No, not well. Seen her around a few times that was all. Lovely girl. Lovely. How er . . . what did she . . . was it an accident?'

'According to the post mortem, she asphyxiated on her own vomit.'

'Dear God.' Jack lurched on to a bar stool, clutched at his drink, tossed it back, ordered another.

'Not a very nice way to go is it,' said the barman with a certain relish. 'Matter of fact she was found in a subway quite close to here. Rolled in a blanket. Some kids discovered her. She was a user of course. Crack, smack, coke, dope, uppers, downers. Anything she could lay her hands on. Usual story, too much of too many. Cocktail that went wrong.'

'Why do they do it?' said Jack. 'Dear God, why do they do it? I don't understand. There was a girl who had everything going for her. Young, beautiful, lovely figure. And she goes and does something like that. It makes you wonder what this world is coming to.'

'I did hear,' said the barman, leaning over his pumps in a confidential manner. 'That she'd been interfered with. After she was dead.'

'What . . . I don't . . . I can't . . .' Jack spluttered into incoherence, got off the stool and made for the swing doors, one arm stuck out in front of him, his coat belt trailing. He didn't look too good.

17

I took the tube back to Docklands and then made a detour via the newly landscaped park area, partly because I didn't want to get on with writing up the minutes of the last Management Meeting and partly because after that business in the pub I felt in need of a little fresh air and tranquillity. So I strolled among the sad-faced mothers and the vandalized saplings, attempting to compose my thoughts. It was a muddy damp place with strategic stockpiles of rubber tyres and ropes twisted into nooses, to amuse the children.

I was beginning to wonder whether it possessed quite those qualities of peace and calm I was searching for when a plump man lurched out from behind a thorn bush. My first thought was that I had disturbed one of those voyeurs that hang around the park's periphery and make a nuisance of themselves with binoculars. On hot evenings they can outnumber the courting couples by about ten to one. But it was a dull grey afternoon and besides the clothes were all wrong. Black satin boxer shorts, pink running vest and white towelling headband could well indicate fetishistic tendencies, but they weren't exactly standard dirty old man gear.

The body heaved painfully closer and the blurred edges of Ronnie Mullins came into focus. I could hardly believe my eyes. Ronnie was just about the last person on God's earth I would have suspected of jogging.

'So, how you doing?' Ronnie slapped me playfully on the rump and then promptly doubled up like I'd just punched him in the stomach, though I had not so much as laid a finger on him. It was some seconds before I realized that he was attempting to touch his toes.

'I'm OK,' I said. 'And yourself?'

'Great. Great. Never felt better.' He straightened up and staggered a bit. 'Say, why don't you and me have a work out together one of these lunch times. Nothing too heavy. Break you in easy.'

'I'm not much of an athlete,' I said. I slowed my pace. Ronnie had started off again but he was lifting his knees so high into the air he didn't seem to be making much horizontal progress.

'Don't you believe it, Joey boy,' said Ronnie. 'You'll soon shape up. You'll surprise yourself. I've only been in training a few weeks and I feel like a new man. There, you see that?'

'What?'

'Squirrel.'

'More likely a rat,' I said.

'Can't beat nature can you,' said Ronnie. 'Talking of which, a little dicky bird told me that your Paki poofter is getting the nomination after all. You heard anything along those lines?'

'I'm not really privy to that sort of decision making,' I said.

'Course you're not. Don't worry son. I know you're just a small spoke in a big wheel. I don't hold it against you the way things have turned out. You did your best, course you did. But I can't help feeling betrayed by some of the big boys. After all the years I've put into this game. And then they drop you like a hot shit. Not right is it. Not right. Not right at all.'

We had ground to a total standstill again, this time beneath the shade of the gas works. The heavily oxidized cylinders merely served to heighten the violent pinkness of Ronnie's cheeks.

'Tell you what though,' said Ronnie, brightening.

'What,' I said.

'They're not going to get away with it. Because I've got a little bombshell of my own that's due to go off in just about thirty-six hours time.' Ronnie consulted his gold Rolex watch.

'What sort of bombshell?' I said.

'Hush hush,' said Ronnie, pulling a significant face. 'Look, there goes another. See its tail.'

'Definitely a rat,' I said. 'I'll be in touch.'

We had reached, with some difficulty, the ice cream hut which acted as a hub for a number of different paths. I was determined that our routes should from this point onwards diverge. Ronnie unfortunately had other ideas.

'Not so fast, not so fast. I want you to understand this, Joey. No-one goes kneeing Ronnie Mullins in the nuts and walks away smiling. Don't mean you personally, son, you know that. We're old mates. But some of the company you've been keeping lately. Let's just say one or two of them might end up regretting what they've got themselves into. See, Joey boy, I've got some friends in some very influential places. And this isn't the end of the road. Oh no, not by a long chalk.'

'It's the end of my road,' I said. 'I turn off here.'

18

I ground away at the typewriter until about nine-thirty
and then made my way along to the San Remo for something to eat. Dimitrios greeted me with his usual mixture
of effusiveness and melancholy.

'Ah Jozeef, my dearest friend. Where you bin hiding
all theez weeks? I bin so worried about you. I say to my
Reni, I say to her only this morning, it is not like Jozeef, it
is not like him to neglect his old comrades. Something is
wrong. He'z in trouble. But theez are bad days, yes, I
think. The Party is always fighting itself like a mad dog
chasing its tail. No not there, not there. Too draughty. I
keep this table for my very special guests.'

Dimitrios sat me down at my usual table, next to the
door that led to the Gents. Whenever anyone passed that
way a strong odour of urine mingled with Jeyes Fluid
wafted through.

'It was only last Thursday I was here,' I protested.

Dimitrios raised his eyes to the heavens, a mannerism
he also adopted when reckoning up bills.

'Last Thursday. That soon? So much bin happening. I
bin so worried about you. We have a little chat, you and
me. Man to man. You know what I mean. But first, what
you eat? You try today's speciality. Chicken livers in a
sauce of my very own recipe nestling on a bed of rice,
with chips.'

'I think I'll just have the bolognese, thanks,' I said.

'Chicken livers, very good. Special offer.'

'The bolognese will do me fine.'

'With chips?'

'OK, with chips.' I was a believer in compromise.

'And a carafe of the house wine?'

'Yes, why not.' In for a penny in for a pound.

Dimitrios went and shouted my order down the hatchway and then came back and sat down opposite me, his thick arms bare to the elbow, laid out on the table like a pair of meaty hams. If it wasn't for the apron you might easily have mistaken him for an all-in wrestler. He placed a carafe of retsina between us that looked like it could well be a mixture of Jeyes Fluid and urine. I poured two glasses.

'OK Jozeef. I won't beat it about the mulberry bush. I come straight to the points. My Reni, she have very sharp eyes. She miss nothing. She is a good girl.'

Dimitrios gave me that sad, slightly resentful look of his and took a long slug of the foul wine.

'Look Dimitrios, if I owe you anything, just tell me what it is and I'll settle up. I'd be the first to admit I've been very forgetful lately. My mind has been so full of other matters it is quite possible I just walked out without paying. If so I'm very sorry.'

Dimitrios banged on the table. 'Jozeef. How can you think I talk about money. We are friends, yes? Money does not come in it where friends are concerned. Everything I have is yours, you know that. Everything. But I have a warning for you. You must listen to me Jozeef. Sex is a dangerous net and many good men have got their fishes caught in it.'

Reni, the daughter with the sharp eyes, slouched across with a plate of bolognese and chips and plonked it down in front of me. She had long black hair and a sultry manner.

'So what's the problem?' I said. I desperately trawled my mind for some past misdemeanour. Could I inadvertently at some point have compromised Reni's chastity? Dimitrios did rather have the look of a vengeful godfather about him, ready to challenge the enemy to physical combat in order to preserve the family honour. In which case was it entirely wise for me to be consuming all this spaghetti? If I was going to be punched I preferred to be punched on an empty stomach.

'You know Mrs Mullins, yes,' said Dimitrios darkly.

'Lorraine? Yes, of course I know her. Known her for years.'

'You good friends with her.'

'We rub along.'

'No point lying, Jozeef. My Reni she have very sharp eyes. She miss nothing. She says you very good friends.'

'OK, so we're good friends. So what?'

'Mrs Mullins, she is a very bad woman.'

'Really?'

'Yes, she really very bad. You take Dimitrios' advice. You not go near her with a barge.'

'And how come you know all this?'

Dimitrios looked around him as if he was frightened of being overheard and then poured himself another glass of my retsina, for which I was grateful, because I was a bit worried it would turn me blind before I got to the bottom of the carafe.

'You heard of James Stentor?'

'Stentor Properties? Yes, I've heard of him.'

'Very powerful, very rich man.'

'I would imagine so.'

'My Reni she does cleaning for him in the afternoons.'

'Small world, eh?'

'Mr Stentor he has beautiful furniture. All antiques you know. Very old, very fine. My Reni she loves to polish them.'

'Well that's nice. But I don't quite see where I fit into all this.'

'Wait, wait, I tell you everything.' Dimitrios was beginning to get that melancholy far-away look that came over him when he told stories of how he fought the Greek fascists in the mountains and how the British let him down. He dropped his voice. 'Sometimes, in the afternoons, Mr Stentor he has special visitors. Mrs Mullins, she is very special visitor. They go to the

137

bedroom together while my Reni is still doing the floors. You understand my meaning?'

'I pretty much get the general drift,' I said, wearily.

'My Reni she hears everything. Mrs Mullins she shouts a lot when she fucks. She shouts her head off. Reni get very embarrassed.'

'I can imagine.'

'But then, two weeks ago, Mrs Mullins and Stentor have big fight. He says he doesn't want to see her any more. She goes mad. Says he has treated her like dirt. Says he owes her much money because he has broken all his promises. And if he doesn't pay her the money she will destroy him. She runs round the house without clothes smashing all the beautiful furniture.'

'I see.'

'Mrs Mullins very wicked, very dangerous woman. So you understand now why I warn you against her. My Reni she says Mrs Mullins comes in here and does things with you under the table while her husband is in the back room with me talking business. I not like gossip, Jozeef. Gossip is for the old ladies. But you must be careful. And now you have treacle tart and custard and forget all your love troubles.'

'I think I'll give the treacle tart a miss, thanks all the same.'

'But my dear friend, you must not pine away. You must keep your body and heart together. Women they are not worth the candle. And the treacle tart is on the house.'

'That's very kind of you, but really I must be off.'

Dimitrios looked deeply hurt.

'Oh, by the way,' I said, 'what was the business you and Ronnie were talking about?'

'A little private matter,' said Dimitrios, dismissively. He took a cloth from his apron pocket and began vigorously rubbing up the grease on a table top.

I took the hint and left.

19

On getting back to my flat I went to the kitchen and
made myself some cocoa. It was comforting warming
my hands on the mug and sipping the thick sticky
sweetness of it, and right then my need for comfort was
pretty high up the Richter scale. Not only had I permanently fouled up any possibility of a relationship with
Celia. I'd also made a complete fool of myself over
Lorraine. How could I, a worldly-wise, heavily divorced,
hard-bitten, party hack, have been so gullible as to
believe Lorraine had really given me those papers for
me to help keep her husband on the straight and narrow?
Much more likely she was simply out to get her own back
on Stentor. She probably wanted me to blow the whole
murky story and didn't care too much who got hurt in the
process, Stentor, Ronnie, or myself.

I was slumped on my bed mulling over the entire
sorry business when Lorraine's face appeared at the
window. A streak of hair cut across her eyes and her
nose was pressed white and flat. I closed my eyes and
then opened them again but she was still there. What's
more she was hammering at the window with her fist,
causing the pane to rattle and mouthing obscenities. It
was then I knew I must have flipped. The strain of the
past few weeks must simply have got too much. I mean,
not only was it a pretty odd thing for anyone to be doing
at that time of night, but the window was nearly twenty
feet above the ground.

I put my cocoa down and crossed to where the vision
was still agitating. I drew up the lower sash, not without

difficulty, because the wood had warped over the years.

'About fucking time,' said Lorraine. 'I thought you were never going to get off your bum.'

She was standing on an aluminium ladder wearing a pair of most inappropriate flip-flops, very tight elasticated jeans and a check shirt tied up under her breasts as if she was making a parcel of them. She climbed in through the now open window, handing me a gold cigarette lighter and a packet of Benson & Hedges first. I took her hand to steady her. It struck me as a rather courtly gesture. Her breasts wobbled inside their packaging as she thudded to the floor.

'That's a rather unusual means of gaining entry,' I said.

Lorraine gave me a sideways look. 'I'm sure there's nothing I can teach you about unusual means of gaining entry.'

Oh no, I thought to myself. No more funny business. No more fornicating on ladders twenty feet above the ground. I was through with all that for definite this time.

'So, what can I do for you?' I said, coolly.

'You could try getting your door-bell fixed for starters,' said Lorraine. 'And failing that you could get a deaf aid.'

She slouched into my latest jumble sale acquisition, a chair that looked like one of those they have in old people's homes, with a high straight back and a removable seat with a commode underneath. She lit up a cigarette, inhaled deeply, and then let out a long slow plume of smoke.

'You don't mind, do you,' she said.

I shook my head. 'Tell me, do you always carry a ladder around with you for the unforseen eventuality like a door-bell being broken?'

'The ladder was already there, you dummy,' said Lorraine.

'Was it? I never noticed it. But then I'm afraid I'm

140

not very observant.' I went across to the window a second time. Sure enough, someone had started white-washing the front. 'The Maintenance Committee must have decided to refurbish the fabric of the building. Not before time, I might say. But you'd think they'd put the ladder away when they'd finished, wouldn't you. It could encourage intruders.'

'So, you worried about being raped are you?' said Lorraine. 'Anyway, it's not the Maintenance Committee. It's Charles Ronayne.'

'Charles! What the hell is he doing up the front of the building?'

'Don't ask me. He's crazy isn't he. Would never surprise me what wall he started crawling up. Why don't you try asking Celia? You're pretty friendly with her by all accounts. Sit down, Joseph, you're making me feel nervous pacing up and down like that.'

I sat down on the edge of the bed, placing my hands between my knees and pressing my knees tight together.

'So, to what do I owe this unexpected pleasure?'

'Have you spoken to Ronnie yet about those papers I gave you?'

'No, I'm afraid a suitable opportunity hasn't occurred. In fact, on reflection, I'm not at all sure I'm the right person for the job.'

I fully expected Lorraine to throw a tantrum. But her reaction was quite the opposite. She looked relieved.

'That's OK. As a matter of fact it's just as well. You see the situation has changed rather. Ronnie and me have had a long talk and he's agreed to have nothing further to do with Stentor. So, there's no need for you to get involved after all. Tell you the truth, it was really daft of me to give those papers to you. Of course, I know I can trust you. But . . .'

'You'd like them back, is that it?'

'In a nutshell, yes.'

'I'll fetch them.'

I stood up. Lorraine also stood up, blocking my path.

'Joseph, you're not sore with me are you?'

She ran her fingers back through my hair and lay her weight against me, so that if I moved suddenly she'd probably topple over. She seemed more than usually precarious with her breasts cantilevered like that.

'Why should I be sore?' I asked.

'I don't know. No reason. Unless it's because Ronnie and me have patched it up. But he's still only my husband, Joseph. It doesn't change anything between us.'

'Why didn't you tell me you and Stentor had been having an affair?'

Lorraine pulled off. She sighed and grimaced and sighed again and threw her hands in the air.

'I suppose you've been talking to that cow Reni.'

'I don't see it matters much who I've been talking to. You don't deny it?'

'No, I don't deny it. Why should I? So James Stentor and me have fucked a few times. So what. I never presented myself to you as a vestal bloody virgin.'

'And is it also OK to ask a friend to do you a good turn when really you're just setting him up as the fall guy in a devious little plot to hurt a third party?'

'I'm sorry Joseph. I'm not one of your intellectuals. I don't quite follow your logic.'

'You gave me those papers because you wanted me to blow the whistle on Stentor, end of story. I was an awful fool ever to think anything else.'

Lorraine pushed her fingers into the tight hip pockets of her jeans, closed her eyes a moment and gritted her teeth.

'You don't think too much of me, do you Joseph?'

I made no response.

'OK, I agree the idea of you talking to Ronnie about those letters was a lousy one. I'm not too bright. I didn't think it through. I've had second thoughts now and it would be best if we dropped the whole thing. But, please Joseph, I might be a hopeless slut but I wasn't trying to dump on you.' She stubbed her cigarette out on the bottom of her flip-flop, nearly falling over as she

142

did so. 'Oh what the hell. Who gives a fuck what you think. Just give me the letters back and I'll get out of your life.'

I went to fetch them. I checked the Co-op carrier bag which I had taken to Scarborough with me. They weren't there. Which meant they had to be in the Safeway's carrier. I found the conference papers in something of a muddle. I found my long johns. But I couldn't find the Stentor letters. I tipped the contents out on to the floor in order to go through them more carefully. I still couldn't find them. I went back to the Co-op carrier. Nothing. I went through the conference papers a third time, systematically, piece by piece. My efforts were rewarded. I located the brown Manila folder which the letters had originally been in. It was now tucked inside a file called Positive Discrimination within the Local Government Sector. But my relief was short-lived. The folder was empty. When my possessions had been returned to me by the police, I had been so relieved to be getting out of their custody, I hadn't thought to check that they were all still there. Besides, the letters hadn't been individually itemized. On my inventory they'd just written down: 'Papers, Various'. I would have had no proof that anything had gone missing.

I went back to Lorraine who was fiddling with her eyelashes in the mantelpiece mirror.

'You're not going to believe this,' I said.

'What?' said Lorraine, still staring in the mirror, pushing her cheek out with her tongue.

'The letters are missing.'

Lorraine turned around. To say she looked dumb-founded would be a major understatement. Her mouth dropped so low she was lucky she didn't dislocate her jaw.

'Joseph, what are you trying to tell me?'

'I took the wrong carrier to Scarborough. It had your letters in it. I know I had them because they were in with my underwear. On the way back we were stopped

143

by the police. They went through everything. The folder's still there, but the letters are gone. They must have kept them for some reason.'

Lorraine didn't look too amused.

'You bastard. You sneaky little bastard. OK Joseph. You want to play dirty, I'll play dirty. I don't believe your police story. I don't believe it for a minute. But if you think you can put the squeeze on me or James or Ronnie then you're very, very wrong.'

20

The morning after Lorraine's visit I had to attend a meeting on leaflet distribution. This mainly consisted of a heated debate between Jonathan and Julian on whether the monthly newsletter should be put inside envelopes or whether the message should be thrust naked through the letter box. Julian was very much against any use of glossy advertising techniques. 'You can't sell socialism as a brand product,' he kept saying. 'The content would be lost in the packaging.' Jonathan on the other hand felt that so long as the packaging had its own integrity it was quite acceptable. Consequently, he suggested the use of brown envelopes would be preferable to white because brown was a more racially sensitive colour. When I made the point that the more fundamental problem was lack of manpower to stuff newsletters into envelopes in the first place, I was bawled out by Meryll for my inadvertent but remonstrably careless use of the word man in this context: 'Wasn't it time the male hegemony over our language was smashed.' In the end the meeting was adjourned without anything more having been decided than the time and the place of the next meeting.

I got back to the committee rooms feeling moderately suicidal, a state of mind which was not alleviated any by the sight of Charles clinging to the guttering. He was wearing a cream boiler suit about the size of a parachute and a cream panama hat, and he appeared to be whitewashing the front of the building. I knew, of course, that Celia had been anxious to find him some occupation to stop him brooding. I just wished she had signed him up for retraining as a deep-sea trawlerman or still better an astronaut. However, I could hardly complain.

'Good of you to touch it up a bit,' I shouted up to him. 'You never know when an election might be called. Just as well to be prepared.'

Charles descended a rung or two and looked at me like I was a jumped up earthworm.

'I'm not touching it up, to employ your own vulgar phrase. I'm sealing the brickwork, so that the detail doesn't flake off.'

'Just so long as it looks a bit smarter,' I said. 'What colour are you thinking of doing it?'

Charles made a series of guttural noises deep at the back of his throat and muttered something about allegory of depravity.

'My goodness, the names they dream up these days. Allegory of Depravity. What's that, a deep puce?'

Charles quaked and heaved and shook in such a manner I began to fear for the rung he was balancing on. 'Oh you can sneer, if you like. The world is full of sneerers and scoffers. The Clever Dicks who think they know all the answers. But perhaps you won't find it so funny when I have finished.

'Can't wait. I take it you've got approval for all this from the Maintenance Committee.'

Charles howled with derisive laughter. 'Maintenance Committee. And what do Maintenance Committees know about these matters, pray? You seem to forget Joseph, it's not approval I seek. It is truth that I am in pursuit of.'

'Fair enough,' I said. I went inside. I was glad to get away from Charles and his Old Testament style, doomladen gesturing. But the scene of primaeval chaos that immediately confronted me just seemed like more of the same in a different shape. Stacks of books were strewn everywhere. The radiogram was on its side. The statue of the naked woman had been decapitated. The Baby

146

Burco had had its lid stove in. I ran up the stairs and into the front room. It was the same story. All the drawers hung open with their contents spilling out as if they had been ritually disembowelled. I went back down the stairs and outside again to where Charles was still busily dabbing away at the brickwork.

'Any idea what's been going on in there?'

'Are you addressing me?'

'Someone has turned the place upside down.'

'And you're implying that I'm responsible, is that it?'

'No, of course not. I just thought . . .'

'Quite extraordinary, isn't it? It is always the artistic community who are the first to be persecuted when things go wrong. Go ahead. Hurl abuse. Throw stones. Make me the scapegoat for all the world's ills. I am used to such treatment. I have come to understand that speaking the truth is no guarantee of universal popularity. Quite the opposite.'

'Charles, I'm sorry if I snapped at you. I just thought you might have seen something that's all. Some stranger poking around?'

'Not that I recall.'

'Well, thanks anyway.'

'You think I have nothing better to do, I suppose, than observe the to-ings and fro-ings of every Tom, Dick and Henrietta with a Free Mandela badge pinned to their lapel?'

'Forget it. Sorry to have troubled you.'

'You could try asking Pam.'

'Pam?'

'She's in the office.'

I went to the office. Sure enough, Pam was slumped on a tubular metal and canvas chair looking depressed. She was wearing her dirty white lambswool coat done up to the neck and applying a rather sordid looking tissue to her already inflamed nostrils. The floor was strewn with files. There was a draught as I entered which made a sound through the papers as of tiny trapped birds beating their wings against glass.

'It was like this when I arrived,' said Pam guiltily.

'Mindless vandalism,' I said. 'This is the fourth time this year.'

The committee rooms were frequently broken into, fire-bombed, spray-canned and blitzed with bottles. Today's events were quite restrained in comparison.

'Seems like they were looking for something,' said Pam with a sleuth-like sniff.

'Possibility.' The thought hadn't immediately occurred to me. But perhaps it wasn't Charles in a rage, or even the National Front. Perhaps it was friends of Lorraine's looking for the Stentor letters. She had certainly given every impression of not believing a word of my Chingford Police story. I stooped down and began collecting up the scattered papers and dumping them into a heap.

'I would help,' said Pam, 'but Meryll said I should try and relax.'

'That's OK,' I said. And then added, as an unpleasant afterthought struck me, 'Is Meryll about somewhere?'

'She'll be back in a minute. She's just popped down the road to get some more milk.'

Pam already had half a tumbler of milk in front of her and most of a pint bottle next to that.

'So what is this? Dairy promotion week?'

Pam smiled and looked embarrassed. I couldn't fathom the look at all.

'We've got our first SIG, meeting starting soon.' She whispered the initials.

'SIG meeting?' I also whispered. It was infectious. But the letters didn't immediately mean too much to me. I speculated with Signals Intelligence Group or Socialist Insurgents, perhaps. Neither seemed to exactly fit the bill. 'So, what's all this SIGs business then?'

Pam looked quickly around as if to check there was no third party present. She then looked back at me with those small trusting pink eyes of hers.

'I'm not really supposed to tell anyone, but seeing as

148

you sort of live here it might be best if you knew, only promise you'll keep it to yourself.'

'Cross my heart and hope to die,' I said.

'Self-Insemination Group,' mouthed Pam.

'Of course. Of course. Self-insemination. Why didn't I think of that. Never was any good at crosswords. So how does it work? If that's not an intrusive question.'

'There's nothing sexual about it, if that's what you're getting at.' Pam pulled her coat more tightly around her.

'Oh, I realize that,' I said. 'I'm just interested in the organizational side.'

'Meryll will be back in a moment. She deals with all that.' Pam drank another couple of gulps of milk and shuddered.

But I wasn't to be that easily put off. There were some things in life any man worth his salt should get to know about and self-insemination groups was quite clearly one of them.

'For instance, why are you meeting here? I mean, why not arrange it in the comfort of your own flat? Don't get me wrong or anything. You're very welcome. But it's not exactly romantic, is it?'

'It's not meant to be romantic.'

'No, I suppose not. What I meant was private. It's not very private.'

'Oh dear.' Pam was obviously torn between the need for discretion and a desire to enlighten the ignorant. In the end her proselytizing instincts won out. 'Well, if you must know, you need to have a neutral address so the sperm donors don't know who the women are and the women don't know the donors. That way the women don't run any risks with regards paternity claims from men who change their mind and start wanting to poke their noses in where they're not wanted. Only Meryll, she's the convenor, knows the identity of both parties.' She spoke in tones of dogged seriousness, like she was explaining the birds and the bees to a five-year-old.

'So you do it blindfold do you?'

'We don't do it at all. We use jam jars and one of these syringes.'

Pam removed a large plastic object from a Snoopy pencil case. I cringed a bit at the sight of it. It wasn't exactly my idea of an erotic aid.

'Wouldn't it be simpler to use frozen?'

'You get better results with fresh.'

'I expect you like it organically grown as well don't you?'

Pam bristled. 'Isn't it amazing how, when men feel threatened, they always have to sneer.'

This was the second time in the last fifteen minutes that I had been accused of sneering. Perhaps there was something in it. Perhaps I really was the embittered, screwed-up ex-husband that my ex-wife liked to depict me as. It did seem a bit mean on my part, just as Pam was beginning to take me into her trust and reveal the intimate secrets of her sisterhood, that I should come back with a cheap jibe.

'I'm sorry. I didn't mean to poke fun. I'm really very sympathetic. In fact, I was wondering whether I could qualify as a donor.'

'You'd never get approved·by the selection board,' said Pam.

'Why not?'

'Because you're not the sort of person we're looking for.'

'And what sort of person are you looking for?'

'Tall, intelligent vegetarians.'

'Sounds suspiciously like eugenics to me.'

'I don't know anyone called Eugene,' said Pam. 'And anyway I don't want to know him. The whole point is to keep everyone anonymous. Once men get involved on a personal level then there would be all kinds of trouble.'

She took another gulp of milk and pulled the sort of contorted face a child pulls when made to take horrid medicine.

'If you got it out of my fridge it's probably off,' I said.

'It's all right,' said Pam. 'I just don't like milk. Never

have liked it. Always used to make me sick when I was little.'

'So why are you drinking it?'

'If you drink up to five pints a day it greatly increases your chances of conceiving a girl.'

'Really. Marvellous, isn't it? Modern science. And for boys I suppose you eat slugs and snails and puppy dogs' tails.'

'There you go again. Taking the piss. You're dead scared really, aren't you? You just can't cope with the idea you're no longer necessary.'

'But would it be such a disaster to have a boy child?'

Pam appeared to give this some thought. In the end she said simply, 'Meryll doesn't want a boy.'

There wasn't much arguing with that. Or I wasn't in the mood for arguing. Particularly not as it sounded like Meryll had just returned. I exited through the French windows and down the alley, re-entering via the kitchen door and then crept up the stairs. As I passed the committee room door I could hear Meryll telling Pam, in firm tones, to drink up and stop being such a namby-pamby.

During the next twenty minutes or so there was a fair amount of coming and going, or mainly coming I quipped to myself. I tried to concentrate my impoverished attention on balancing the petty cash book. I was nearly seventy-five pounds short. I wondered whether I could get away with writing it off against sundries, or whether the sniffer dogs of corruption in high places would find me out. Meryll was one of the auditors. Ted Clarke was another. Neither of them was exactly my staunchest supporter. I was in the middle of once more checking through my collection of receipts, miscellaneous scraps of paper hoarded in an old shoebox, when someone knocked on the door. It wasn't so much a loud knock as a flurried one, suggesting someone seeking refuge rather than demanding entry.

'Come in,' I called.

Alan Sayeed cautiously poked his head round.

'Joseph, what a relief. A sane face at last. Mind if I join you a moment?'

'Of course not,' I said. As a matter of fact I really resented the way Alan felt free to barge in just when he felt like it. Being his agent hardly entitled him to twenty-four hour a day attention.

He came in and sat down gloomily on the edge of the bed, elbows on knees, head cupped in hands. He looked tired and petulant.

'What's up?' I said.

'Oh nothing,' said Alan. 'Absolutely nothing up at all. I guess that's the problem.' He laughed a little bitterly.

'You look a bit shattered.'

'Shattered. That's the understatement of the year. I feel like I've just been steamrollered. I don't think I've had more than four hours sleep all week. What with meetings to be attended, talks given, articles written, lobbies organized. Believe me, it takes it out of you, Joseph. It's draining. There's a limit to what any one person can be expected to do.' He sounded aggrieved, as if I was somehow to blame.

'It's important to know where to draw the line,' I said in an avuncular tone.

'You're so right,' said Alan, with rather more enthusiasm than I felt the remark really deserved. 'You're so right. Drawing lines is what it's all about.' He leant his head back against the wall. It fitted in neatly with a row of dark grease marks on the primrose-flowered wallpaper. 'My God, it's good to enjoy a bit of sane company for a change. You know there are times, Joseph, I really envy you your life style.'

'Me,' I said. I could not quite prevent my voice rising an octave or two. 'You envy me.' I knew Sayeed had a nice line in flattery, essential to any successful politician, but this seemed a trifle over the top, not to say tactless. 'I can't see that there's anything very enviable about my condition.'

'Oh, I don't know,' said Alan. 'You always seem to be leading such a calm, controlled sort of existence. I guess that's one of the perks of celibacy. You only have yourself to think about. It's so much easier to draw the lines.' Alan smiled his ingenuous smile.

152

Celibacy eh? I rotated the word around in my mind. And what gives him the right to assume I'm celibate? On the other hand, he was more or less right wasn't he? One inconclusive roll on the floor with Lorraine over the last six months hardly amounted to a full-blooded sex life.

'Did you know that the state of celibacy actually means the state of being unmarried and has no connection with sexual activity or absence of it? It is in fact one of the most misused words in the English language,' I said.

'Is that so,' said Alan. 'Well, it just goes to underline what I'm getting at, doesn't it? You've got the leisure to acquire all this useless knowledge. During the last few weeks I haven't had a moment to myself. It's not just the politics, though that's bad enough, God knows. There's also Andy to take into account.' Alan frowned, two perfectly parallel little frown lines puckering up his noble brow. 'Don't get me wrong. Andy is a most wonderful woman and I wouldn't have her any other way than the way she is. But she is, how can I put this, a little difficult at times. You've lived with her, Joseph, so you must know what I mean.'

So, he's come round here to complain about Andrea, I thought. He holds me responsible for her being just a little bit of an overbearing self-obsessed tyrant. He obviously feels he's been palmed off with shoddy goods and that I, as the retailer, owe him some sort of compensation.

'Andrea's very much her own woman,' I said.

'Andrea is a very wonderful person,' said Alan, with just a hint of aggressiveness, as if I might have suggested something slightly less than total commitment to this view of things. 'In many ways she is an extraordinary person. And I don't want you for a moment to think that I am in any way getting at her behind her back. Because I'm not.'

'Oh I don't,' I said hastily.

'There's nothing I disapprove of more than slagging others off behind their backs.'

'Too right.'

'All the same, you must know as well as I do that Andrea can be very demanding at times.'

'I take your point.'

'I mean, I'm a committed feminist. I wouldn't be here if I wasn't, would I? I believe men should shoulder their fair share of the domestic burden. But you've got to be pragmatic about these things. There has to be a bit of give and take. And then on top of everything this is my third SIGs meeting this week. Believe me, Joseph, I just can't keep going much longer.'

I had the strong impression that Alan was about to break down into tears, when there came the sound of footfalls on the stairs. Alan went rigid. The steps went towards the bathroom. Then came Meryll's voice cooing strangely.

'Alan, are you in there?'

Alan continued to sit where he was, rigid and silent.

'Alan?' cooed Meryll again.

Alan still didn't move a muscle. The steps came towards us.

'Alan, is something wrong? Only everyone is downstairs, ready and waiting.' Alan couldn't have looked more frightened if it had been the Gestapo.

'Just give me another five minutes,' he croaked.

'But you've already had nearly twenty. And some of the women have got trains to catch.'

'For Christ's sake stop pressurizing me will you. Just another five minutes, OK.'

I had never heard Alan sound so desperate before.

'Please try and hurry,' said Meryll, like an impatient nurse to a constipated child.

'I'm doing my fucking best OK,' shouted Alan.

Meryll's steps retreated. Alan was still sitting on my bed twitching a bit and looking oddly bashful.

'Bitches! You agree to do them a favour and they treat you like you were a tube of toothpaste. One squeeze and out it comes.'

'You're part of this SIG business, I take it?'

'I service about ten different groups in London,' said Alan, not without a touch of hubris.

'Really.'

'Only to tell you the truth, Joseph, this afternoon I just don't feel up to it. Perhaps I'm going down with a bug or something. But I just don't seem to have what it takes.'

'So why don't you tell them that?'

'You're joking. You don't seriously expect me to go down there and say, sorry girls, the pump won't work, the well's run dry, you'll have to come back another day. Some of those women have travelled miles for this.'

'So what's the alternative?'

'Besides, it's not just my reputation I'm thinking of here. There's a lot of votes in this one, Joseph.'

I was beginning to have my doubts about the way this conversation was going. 'That's all very well,' I said. 'But we're not talking about a commodity you can just pick up from your nearest corner shop.'

'That's why I was thinking, you might just do me a little favour this one time.'

'Oh no,' I said.

'Come on, Joseph. Even if you won't do it as a friend, I think you owe it to the Party. For Christ's sake, all you've got to do is nip along to the bathroom and jack off into the old jam jar for me.'

'But I haven't been approved by the group liaison officer.'

'Jissom is jissom,' said Alan. 'Who the hell's going to know the difference? Black man's looks just the same as white man's you know.'

'Yes but . . .'

'For Christ's sake stop making excuses. Just tell me, are you my agent or aren't you?'

'OK,' I said. 'OK. But I take no responsibility for any repercussions.'

'Just get along there and wack your wad in and no-one will ever be the wiser.'

So I took the jar. I have to admit it wasn't entirely an act of selfless generosity. The idea of getting one over the SIG quality control fascists did have an appeal all of its own. I was back in a couple of ticks.

155

'Fast work,' said Alan. He seemed in a much brighter frame of mind than when I'd left. He held the jar up to the light. 'Well, let's hope you make up in quality what you lack in quantity.'

'I wasn't really in the mood for making an orgy of it,' I said. 'You could try thinning it if there's not enough to go round.'

'What, with turps? No, this will do. Beggars can't be choosy. By the way, have you heard the latest? Mullins has resigned. There's going to be a by-election. I just caught it on the radio.'

'Oh my God.'

'So why the suicidal depression? It's great. It means we should get plenty of publicity for our cause.'

'By-elections are funny things,' I said. 'They can produce unpredictable results.'

'So long as we make our appeal directly to the wankers, I mean the workers, we'll romp it,' said Alan.

At which point Meryll's voice came softly cooing up the stairs again. It was like listening to a crow masquerading as a pigeon.

'Better let the old dykes have their pint of blood,' said Alan, 'before they claw us to death.' He gave me a smile of male complicity and went off down the stairs with the jar, Robertson's Silver Shred as chance would have it.

After Alan's departure I returned to my accounts. Only a few minutes had elapsed before I heard the side gate bang, which suggested he had chosen to sneak out the back way. I didn't blame him for making a hasty exit. No point in hanging around for those who might want seconds. I was just pondering the possible advantages of solving my own cash flow problems by organizing a sponsored wank for SIGs and misappropriating some of the funds, when there came a strangulated cry from the front garden, followed by a flurry of female voices squawking alarm signals to each other. I looked out of the window. The aluminium ladder was lying at a curious angle across the crazy paving pathway and Charles was struggling on his back in the privet, his panama hat upturned on the ground as if he was holding a collection for having completed some extraordinary acrobatic feat. The circle of outraged women who surrounded him, however, looked more intent on causing him grievous bodily harm than throwing him their loose change.

I ran down the stairs to offer my assistance. In retrospect, this seemed a rather foolhardy thing to have done, but such is the impetuousness of youth and in my case the boredom brought on by double entry book-keeping.

'What's going on?' I said, sidling up to Pam, who's cheeks had turned the dirty grey colour of over-thumbed pastry and who was shaking like a junket, or a junkie, depending on your cultural prejudices.

'He's ruined everything,' she sniffed, jabbing a finger at Charles.

Charles was still flailing in the privet and shouting, 'Madwomen. Mad. Crazy. Out of their tiny minds. Tried to murder me. Call the police Joseph. Call the police. Tried to assassinate me. Would somebody do something? Do something to help for God's sake.'

The women, for their part, were busy arming themselves with sticks and dustbin lids and such like, and chanting, 'Dirty old man. Cut his fucking balls off. Poke his eyes out. Intruder. Violator. Rapist.' And other well-known rallying cries of the movement.

'Could you try and be a little more specific about the details of what happened?' I suggested to Pam, removing her slightly to one side, away from the central area of fracas and altercation.

'I'd just infused the catalytic converter into my womb,' she sobbed.

'You what?'

'You know. The stuff. I'd just squirted it up.'

'Oh right.'

'And I was lying on the floor doing my deep breathing exercises and relaxing like it says in the book.'

'Very good.'

'I could see the sunlight on the little yellow leaves of the birch tree.'

157

'Laburnum actually, but never mind.'

'Everything was so beautiful. There was such a feeling of peace and calm in the room. All the women lying on their backs with their hands folded on their stomachs like it tells you. I felt I could really feel the tiny seeds germinating inside me.'

'And what happened then?'

Pam burst into tears.

'You'll feel better for getting it off your chest,' I suggested.

Pam frowned through her tears.

'For getting it out of your system,' I hastily corrected.

'It was just so awful,' she gasped.

'Keep going,' I said. 'You're doing fine.'

'This nose. Oh dear. Squashed against the glass. Enormous. Bulging Staring in at us. I was so frightened, I couldn't even scream. Oh dear. Do you think the baby will have been traumatized?'

'Very much doubt it,' I said.

'I bet it will have. I bet it will come out with two heads and no brains and grow up voting Tory.'

'Nonsense,' I said.

'Yes it will, I know it. I know it. It'll be just my luck.' Pam collapsed into a renewed bout of crying.

Meanwhile, Charles had freed himself from the embrace of the privet and was bearing down on me with twigs in his hair and a rent in the thigh of his boiler suit.

'Joseph, explain to these hysterical females will you that I was working on the front of the building prior to their arrival and that I have no interest whatsoever in staring up their fannies.'

'I think what he says is more or less correct,' I said, as non-committally as I could manage.

'So why was he fuckin' peering through the window,' said Meryll, 'Eyes popping out of his fuckin' head. Invading our privacy. Violating our space.'

'That's a fair enough point,' I said, turning back to Charles. 'Why were you?'

Behind Meryll stood the mob with their padded shoulders and bulging thighs and climbing boots with crenellations so deep they resembled an aerial photograph of the Grand Canyon. There was no way I was going to stick my neck out on this one.

'Because I'm an artist,' said Charles. 'As an artist I am naturally curious as to the world around me.' He gestured vaguely at the world around him. Dog turds. Satellite dishes. A fridge lying in the shade of a buddleia bush quietly leaking CFCs. It was your average street scene of urban squalor and moral decay.

'You're a fuckin' pervert,' said Meryll. 'A dirty-minded fuckin' pervert.' Her earrings jangled alarmingly every time she said, 'fuckin' '.

'My dear lady,' said Charles, drawing himself up to his full height. 'I would have to be perverted indeed if I was seeking to obtain sexual satisfaction from a bunch of Sapphic devotees, belly up, waggling their feet in the air. There is more erotic pleasure to be obtained from a walk round Regent's Park Zoo.'

'Huh!' Meryll was momentarily silenced. But only momentarily. 'So why didn't you fuck off out of it when asked to fuck off out of it?'

'I do think you need to address yourself fully to that question,' I suggested to Charles. 'Was there perhaps some degree of unnecessary delay in your departure?'

Charles threw me a contemptuous look as if to say he always knew that I would betray him at the eleventh floor. He stooped down to retrieve his panama and carefully dusted the brim. 'I've already been through all this. I was innocently descending the ladder in order to alter the angle of erection. Really Joseph, there's no need to snigger in that juvenile manner. It's perfectly clear what I mean by erection in this context. All right, I was altering the angle of the ladder to the vertical, if you insist, when I just happened to notice a rather bizarre scene involving a group of young females inserting plastic pea shooters into their vaginas. Naturally I paused for a moment simply to reassure myself that my eyes were not playing deceitful tricks on me. That did not give Meryll and her bully-girl friends the right to open the window and knock me off my balance, endangering life and limb. If it wasn't for that privet hedge I would not be here to tell the tale. It was only a miracle that saved me.'

Obviously there was a certain amount of hyperbole in all this talk of miraculous escapes, seeing as he couldn't have been more than six feet off the ground at the moment he had been pushed. But even so people had been known to die from falling down kerbstones, my great aunt for one. And we were the party of disarmament.

'Seems to me that while Charles was clearly at fault for lingering unduly at window level, his objection to the use of excessive physical violence against his person is perhaps justified,' I ventured in what I thought was an admirably even-handed and judicial manner. 'So why don't we all just forget about it, eh?' But neither of the parties concerned seemed very interested in conciliation procedures at this juncture.

'He wasn't pushed,' said Meryll. 'He threw himself backwards. And if he's so fuckin' innocent why has he been pestering Pam here to do a centrefold for him?' She produced this last piece of damning evidence with something of an oratorical flourish.

'Do we have to go into all that again?' said Pam, who had only just stopped crying and now looked like starting up again.

'Yes, I think we do,' said Meryll.

'Another matter entirely,' said Charles, looking just a tiny bit sheepish.

On my God, I thought. Was there anybody left in this great Party of ours Charles hadn't attempted to take dirty pictures of, and what the hell was he hoping to do with them?

'He tried to take advantage of a naive and innocent girl,' said Meryll, forcing Charles backwards into a japonica, 'a girl young enough to be his daughter. He tried to get her to commit disgustingly obscene acts, against her will, for the gratification of his own foul lust.'

160

'Nonsense,' said Charles.

'They weren't really that disgusting,' said Pam. 'And anyway I didn't do them.'

'I don't think you're in a position to comment,' said Meryll. 'You've been mentally abused.'

'Nothing whatsoever to do with anything,' said Charles. He settled his panama on his head, tamped it into position like it was a plant in a pot, and strode off, muttering about his solicitors.

'I'm on your side,' I said to the women as soon as Charles was out of earshot. 'Pretty poor do, if you ask me. I'm with you all the way on this one.'

21

The morning after the announcement of the election I got a call from Jack White. In the circumstances I thought he might have had the decency to at least sound a bit embarrassed. Instead he came on tough.

'Get your man over here at three this afternoon, no excuses.'

'Right.'

'Our leader wants to have a little heart-to-heart with him.'

'Right.'

'Oh and Joseph?'

'Yes.'

'What's the matter with your voice?'

'I've got a mouthful of cornflakes.'

'I hope you're ready for this, Joseph. We can't afford any more screw ups. Oh and Joseph. The press will be there. So just tell your chappie not to mention building megacentres for homosexuals to go and fornicate in. And a collar and tie wouldn't go amiss either. The working classes like their leaders to be decently dressed. Got that, laddie?'

When I told Alan about the meeting, his first reaction was that he wasn't going cap in hand to the Party bosses. If the leader wanted to speak to him he could come to Docklands East. In fact, it would do him good to see the conditions with his own eyes. But on further reflection Alan decided he would go along after all. An opportunity like this for speaking his mind on the great issues of the day was not to be lightly passed over.

*

After nearly an hour of being closeted together, the two men emerged to meet the media. They stood on the steps of the Labour Party headquarters while various reporters jostled to poke microphones up their nostrils. Throughout these ignominious proceedings Alan smiled stoically, hands in pockets, broad-shouldered, handsome. When his time came he explained that, while he was in favour of extra-parliamentary activity, he was totally opposed to any form of violence. The leader for his part said that of course extra-parliamentary activity was an important part of the Labour movement. What else were the Trade Unions about. But it had to be seen in context. Mother of Parliaments, home of democracy and all that. Unfortunately, just at that point the leader got a speck of dust in his eye, which prompted him to start knuckling. This rather ruined the final shot of them shaking hands. It looked as if Alan had just punched the leader in the face.

Later, privately, Alan declared what a great guy the leader was and how they had spent most of their time together discussing the recent MCC tour of the Indian subcontinent. But while on a national level a sort of rapprochement had been achieved, locally things just went from bad to worse. Matters culminated about two weeks into the campaign at a meeting of the LGC at the town hall.

I had a premonition there was going to be a blood-letting when, approaching from an easterly direction, I got a good view of a particularly gory sunset leeching ominously across the skyline. I dumped the van in the multi-storey and made my way down the stairwell that stank of oil and urine, in none too pleasant proportions. On the third level, a tubercular-looking youth was slumped across the stairway with a piece of paper pinned to his shirt stating that he was homeless. He was wearing plimsolls, no socks, badly ripped trousers and an old duffel coat. In order to get past I had to step over his legs, which gave me an uneasy feeling. I threw a few coins in his tin. He raised his eyes but beyond that there was no flicker of expression.

The town hall was built like the headquarters of a bank. Once through the revolving glass portico there was a large open space with marble floor-tiles, the odd pillar and a fountain trickling down through a tastefully flood-lit jungle of pampas grass and cheese plants. Continuing the watery theme, aquariums shaped like coffins were set into the walls. Having some time to kill before the meeting was due to start, I observed a dead goldfish floating on the surface of the water of the left-hand tank and wondered how long it had been there. It didn't look in too good a shape. The eye had filmed over and part of the underbelly had been eroded away. I was wondering whether there was a security guard I should report the fatality to when Andrea hove into view.

'I don't know what you've got to look so smug about?' she said.

'I wasn't intending to look smug,' I said. 'I was trying to smile pleasantly.'

'It comes across as smug,' said Andrea. 'With the world in the state it is, millions starving, the obscenity of the arms race, I don't think anyone has the right to be self-satisfied, do you?'

'When you put it like that,' I said.

'And I want to make it quite clear, it wasn't me who junked the rent amnesty vote. I had made up my mind to go ahead despite the personal sacrifice involved. But I might have known you'd find some way of sabotaging the whole initiative. And one other thing. You really shouldn't wear pink ties. I'm sure I've told you before. Pink clashes with your eyelids. You look like a poster for a horror movie.'

'It was red,' I said. 'Only the colour ran in the wash. I got some cod grease down it. Incidentally, one of these fish is dead. Do you think we should take any action?'

'What do you want me to do? Cook it for you.'

'I was wondering whether there was a security guard we could report it to.'

'Dead fish are no concern of mine,' said Andrea, 'and frankly, I think it's a great shame you don't spend a little more time bothering about your paternal responsibilities and a little less about matters which are none of your business. I can't recall the last occasion you had Livingstone for a weekend. But it is really quite unreasonable that I should be left with the whole burden of child-rearing while you prance round the countryside like a rep from the RSPCA.' with which resounding words she flounced off into the central debating chamber, briefcase tucked under her arm, head flung back, blue eyes, blonde hair, ponytail. There was something quite quintessentially point-to-point about her. How I adored that breezy no-nonsense style.

The evening started with a report from Alan on the progress of the campaign so far. It wasn't one of his best. He seemed lacklustre and even at times faltering. I wondered whether he'd been overdoing the SIGs meetings again.

There was polite applause. Alan sat down and squeezed the bridge of his nose between thumb and forefinger like a man starting a migraine. Ted Clarke took the floor.

'I'd like to thank comrade Sayeed for his contribution to this evening's debate and say that I warmly endorse everything he has just said. There can be no let up in our onslaught on the Tories, both those inside and outside the Party. And now, if you'll turn to your agendas, you'll notice the next item is printers for election material. In the past we have always used the Bluebell Press. I would like to propose that in future we use the Cambridge Heath Press. The Bluebell Press is totally un-unionized and I don't think it is fitting that this Labour Party should patronize a capitalist and exploitative set up.'

This seemed on the face of it like a fairly uncontroversial proposal. There was a general nod of agreement. It was some moments in fact before I managed to catch the chair's eye.

'I realize it is not really my place as agent to voice an opinion in this forum, but I feel that there are a couple of relevant factors here that the meeting might be overlooking, indeed might not even be aware of.'

At this point I was interrupted by shouts of 'Get on with it' and 'Pull it out Pink'. I paused while the shouting subsided.

'Firstly, I think this meeting should know that the Bluebell Press is un-unionized because it does not have any employees. It is run by one person, a Mr Arthur, who is largely dependant for his livelihood on the business we are able to put before him, and who has served us well these last seven years, frequently working late into the night to help us meet a deadline. I would also add that he is a West Indian and that our withdrawal of support will not be viewed kindly by the West Indian community in this borough.'

More shouts this time accusing me of condescending racist attitudes. I was, however, determined, for once, to have my say. I raised my voice above the mounting protests.

'I think it is also important that it be clearly understood that the Cambridge Heath Press is owned by the Militant, which as we all know is a proscribed organization. While one or two members of this Party are well known sympathizers of Militant, the Party as a whole has never been under Militant's control, and it seems to me to be a mistake that at this stage we should want to take any action that aligns us with an unrepresentative and sectarian group, reopening the wounds that Alan has done so much these last few weeks to skilfully heal.'

By the time I'd finished, the whole place was in uproar. Ted Clarke was on his feet and pounding his table.

'Comrades, comrades. I take very serious objection to the snide insinuation that I was trying to promote the Cambridge Heath Press without revealing their Militant connections. Of course they have Militant connections. Every true socialist in this room must be well aware of that. And I think Comrade Pink is missing the point. The time has come for us to demonstrate quite clearly to the leadership of this party that we are not in favour of witchhunts. For let's make no bones about it, that is what has been going on. And if we don't stand by our comrades in the Militant this time round then next time it will be you who the searchlight is turned on to and who find yourself hauled up before some sham of an inquiry. The Right in this party want nothing less than the total obliteration of the Left. It is their final solution. And we must ask ourselves, are we prepared to just sit idly by and watch the holocaust take place and not lift a finger?'

It was stirring stuff. And Clarke got his way by an impressive show of hands. After that I kept my mouth shut and the rest of the evening's agenda passed off in a subdued and predictable manner.

On the way out I caught sight of Andrea lying in wait for me behind a palm tree. I could tell from the set of her mouth and the way she kept examining her fingernails that it was me she was waiting for. Right then I just didn't feel up to another mauling. I'd had enough for one evening. There are limits even to the masochism of a Labour Party Agent. So I diverted to the one place I knew she wouldn't follow. The Gents.

Once inside, I leant on a cool white porcelain sink and stared at myself in the mirror. I looked dreadful. My hair needed washing. I had pouches under my eyes the size of duck eggs. And my skin colour suggested the final stages of jaundice. I ran a basin of water and washed my face. It was a healing experience. But it still didn't get around the fact that I was running a campaign that fast looked like making the Crimean War seem like a well-organized Sunday school outing. And why? Why? Because there was a majority in the Party that seemed hell-bent on self-destruction. But there was no backing out now. Not halfway through. When it was over I'd be off like a shot. I'd find that bar job in a country hotel somewhere. Or perhaps I'd take holy orders. Anything but this. But in the short term, there were no choices.

I looked up from the sink into the mirror again, only to see Alan Sayeed standing behind me. He was standing there quite motionless, as if he had been observing me for some time. There was something slightly unnerving about that. In fact he was so still I wasn't too sure he was real.

I went and dried my face on the roller towel. My movement seemed to snap Alan out of his trance.

'Joseph. I'm so glad I've bumped into you. We must have a word. Man to man.'

'Well, if it's to be man to man this seems like as appropriate a place as any,' I said. I went and stood in one of the stalls. Alan came and stood next to me.

'It's about Andrea,' he said.

My God, I thought. Even in here there's to be no getting away from her. She sends her envoys in after me.

'What about her?' I said.

'I think you should know that we've decided to separate.'

'Well, that's fine and dandy,' I said. 'I'll make a note for my Christmas card list. It can be so embarrassing to get these things wrong.'

'I realize this isn't easy for you,' said Alan. 'It's not easy for any of us. But I'm telling you now because I think Andrea will be needing your support over the coming few months.'

'My support. You must be joking. Andrea would welcome support from me about as much as a present of an uplift bra.'

But Alan was not to be put off.

'I know you and Andy have not always seen eye to eye on one or two matters. But I also know that deep down she has a tremendous affection for you. And she needs your approval.'

'I think we must be talking about two different women here,' I said. I'd finished shaking myself about thirty seconds back and was beginning to wonder just how much longer Alan intended to go on for. For some considerable time as it turned out.

'Of course, you will make a joke of it. That is the English way. The Anglo-Saxon male fears nothing so

168

much as a public admission that he possesses feelings. But I know you better than that Joseph. I know that deep down you are a caring and loving person who does not turn his back on those in need. But let us not pursue it. I can see that I am embarrassing you. I have made my own position clear, as I think honesty and decency require. And there is something I want to ask you to do for me, as a very special favour.'

Christ, what the hell does he want from me now? I began to panic. This man was omnivorous. Not content with my wife and my sperm and my dignity, and my twenty-four hour a day devotion to duty, he was after something more. Probably one of my kidneys. He was obviously suffering from some sort of urinary tract problem. Why else was he still standing there hand on the trigger when any healthy man would have been zipped up and out of the place aeons ago. This put me in a difficult situation. I either left him in mid-stream, so to speak, or I hung around like one of those lavatory fetishists one was always reading about in the more sordid Sunday newspapers.

I've always envied people who can just walk out on a situation. The get up and go sort. I am by nature one of life's great hoverers. I always end up being thrown out of dinner parties, not because I am especially enjoying the company of my hosts, quite often the reverse, but because I just can't bring myself to say goodbye. It seems so terribly final. Even when they've managed to manoeuvre me to the doorstep I still keep them standing there shivering and yawning while I desperately rehearse a truly staggering range of banalities on such subjects as foreign holidays or soft furnishings, subjects I know nothing about, and care about even less. It was like that with Alan in the town hall lavatories. I should have left but I wavered.

'What sort of favour did you have in mind?' I said.

'It concerns this business of Militant publishing our election literature.'

'Yes, I realize I shouldn't have said anything. I was

169

speaking out of turn. But I was not sure the situation was fully understood by all those who were present.'

'There you go again, Joseph. Always on the defensive. Always presuming there is a world conspiracy against you. What I was about to say is that I agree with you, one hundred per cent.'

This rather took the wind out of my sails. It also co-incided with a loud fart erupting from behind one of the row of closed doors.

'I thought we were alone in here,' said Alan.

'So did I,' I said.

We left the town hall pretty smartly and took a turn or two around the block. It was a warm heavy night. There were a lot of kids on the street, running down the centre of the roads, darting in front of cars.

'If you agree with me it's a bad idea, why didn't you say something at the meeting?' I tried hard to keep up with Alan. He walked like a man exorcising a demon.

'Because it wouldn't have helped,' said Alan. 'A lot of the delegates are already criticizing me for opening up lines of communication with the leadership. They would just have seen it as further evidence that I was selling out.'

'And are you selling out?' I asked.

'I'm serious about winning this election,' said Alan. He paused outside a shop selling pornographic videos. 'Look at this city. Look at the state it's in. Look at the condition of its people. It's getting too late in the day for playing the ideological purity game.'

This man's changed a lot in the last few weeks, I thought. The Left would say it was opportunism. Perhaps it was. But then again perhaps a bit of opportunism was no bad thing.

'I still don't see how I can help,' I said.

'You're the guy who does the donkey work,' said Alan. 'It's all very well for Clarke to mouth off about how Cambridge Heath should do the printing, but you're the poor sucker who's expected to deliver the copy, right?'

'So.'

'So, it's obvious isn't it. You accidentally deliver it to the wrong place. Once the stuff is printed it will be too late for Clarke to do anything about it.'

We were now heading away from the river towards an area of vacant parking lots and scrap-metal yards and light engineering works, most of which had been closed down during the recession of the early Eighties. Alan was kicking a McDonald's fast food carton. He was pretty neat with the footwork.

'It doesn't sound like a very democratic procedure to me,' I said.

'Perhaps not,' said Alan. 'But when everyone else around you is playing dirty, sometimes it's necessary to play a little dirty, too.'

'How do you mean?' I said.

But before Alan had time to answer there was a crash from across the road. A gang of kids, aged from about eight to ten, Livingstone's sort of age, had just put a brick through a sweet-shop window, one of the few shops left that wasn't boarded up at night. Alan and I both just stood there watching in paralysed fascination. An old man stuck his head out of an upstairs window and shook a fist, like a cartoon figure. It was a ludicrously stylized gesture.

'See what I mean? This city's falling apart,' said Alan. 'There's a whole generation of kids out there who don't know the difference between right and wrong. And can you blame them. We live in a grab culture. And I'll tell you something else, Joseph. There's some damn funny business going on in this by-election.'

'What are you getting at exactly?' I said.

Alan glanced at his watch. 'Can't talk now. I promised Andy I'd call her. Let's meet for lunch tomorrow. How about the NFT cafeteria? I'll be up in town. It's kind of handy for me.'

'Okay,' I said. I didn't really want to drag all that way for a nasty salad in London's answer to H-Block. But I was only the agent. It wasn't my job to be sniffy.

'And you'll switch printers for me,' said Alan.

171

'I'll take the copy along to the Bluebell, tomorrow first thing. Just so long as you're sure that's what you really want. There'll be repurcussions you realize. It's not the kind of action Clarke's going to take lying down.'

'Sod Clarke,' said Alan, giving me a hug. 'I knew you wouldn't let me down, Joseph.'

22

When the phone goes at about 3 a.m. it's like the rattle of
death. I turned over to face the wall, pulled the blanket
over my head and tried pretending that none of this was
really happening, or even better none of my life had
really happened yet. I was back at the age of one, with a
clean slate and a different set of parents. Why not? It
makes just as much sense as black holes and cosmic
strings and all the latest discoveries of so-called science.
But the damn thing just wouldn't give up. I began to
wonder whether it was really the phone or whether it
was a bad attack of tinnitus. I staggered out of bed,
knocking over the glass of water I like to keep beside me.
I never touch the stuff but I like it to be there in case of
need.

'Hello,' I croaked.

'Is that Joseph Pink?' came this sugary voice I had
never heard before.

'Speaking.'

'Good morning, Joseph. Forgive me contacting you at
this early hour, but I thought it important to let you
know at the first opportunity. There are certain persons
abroad desirous of causing you unpleasant personal
injury if you don't comply with their wishes. You take my
meaning?'

'Who is this?'

'Someone who has your best interests at heart, Joseph.'

'What the hell are you on about? What persons? I
don't understand.'

'I think you understand perfectly well. Let's not be coy about this. If you want to keep your face in working order you'd be well advised to do as you're told.'

I put the phone down. Almost immediately it started ringing again.

'Joseph, you're not being very co-operative. I've gone out of my way to help you. And me and my friends, we don't appreciate ingratitude.'

'Piss off.' I slammed the phone down again. This time it stayed silent. I went back to bed, creeping on tiptoe in case any sudden movement on my part triggered it off again. It seemed docile enough now. But there was no more sleep for me that night.

23

I was the first to arrive at the NFT cafeteria. The queue
was already a couple of miles long and getting longer by
the minute. It seems the desire for culture stimulates an
even greater desire to eat, which is understandable considering the stomach gnawing tedium of the films that
get shown. Black and white documentaries about food
queues in the Eastern Bloc for the most part, with
subtitles. I snuck in at the front end. I only wanted a
coffee and one of their preshrunk vinyl-wrapped bap
things. That didn't make it the morally correct thing to
do, of course, but there are times in this life you have to
manipulate the system a little and this was one of them.
And who were all these people anyway that they had the
time to go dinking about in Britain's premier nuclear
bunker complex in the middle of the sodding day. Why
weren't they at their desks, head down, earning an
honest penny? Jesus Christ, if this general drift towards
greater leisure went much further there would be no
advantages left in being a lousy party agent. I wasn't in
the best of moods.

The main drawback with jumping cafeteria queues,
apart from the mass hatred it engenders, is you don't get
an opportunity to pick up a tray. So I balanced my bap on
top of my coffee in one hand and clutched my Tesco
carrier in the other and teetered my way towards a seat
near a window which afforded a good view of a couple of
scrofulous pigeons copulating away like there was no
tomorrow. Beyond the pigeons, a police launch was

turning slow circles as if someone had pulled the plug on the river and it had got caught up in the vortex.

'Sorry I'm late,' said Alan, straddling the back of a chair like he'd just stepped out of a Western. He was wearing this really slick suit and his hair was all shiny with some coconut-oil gunk he put on it. In fact he was so bright and healthy looking it hurt my eyes just focusing in his direction. 'I had to pop into the bank on my way over,' he continued. 'And as it turned out I'm really glad I did.'

'Don't tell me,' I said. 'These guys with stockings over their heads came in, flung you over the counter and in your ensuing conversation you persuaded them a vote for Labour would immensely improve their pension rights.'

'No,' said Alan. 'I'm overdrawn. But what's eating you?'

'My stomach ulcers. But if you want something of your own you'd better join the queue fast.'

Alan shrugged nonchalantly. 'That's OK. I'll make do with some of yours. I told you I've got liquidity problems.' He unwrapped the bap and tore off two thirds of it.

'Help yourself,' I said. I wasn't feeling much like solids after all.

'Joseph, what's wrong? You're looking terrible.'

'I had an alarm call at two-thirty this morning. Someone threatening to ruin my charisma. Spoilt my beauty sleep.'

'You're joking. Who was it? The NF.'

'Not exactly, though I dare say they have friends in common.'

'You should go ex-directory.'

'Look, I appreciate your concern, but it's really a private problem. What was it you wanted to see me about? Other than your cash flow.'

Alan masticated on a lettuce leaf, helped himself to some of my coffee, masticated some more. 'Tell you the truth, it all sounds a bit ridiculous in the cold light of day.'

'Most things in life are ridiculous. Look at those pigeons, for instance. It all depends on your point of view.'

'I guess you're right. OK. See what you make of this. A few weeks back I was parked in a side street near to your place. It was after one of those awful Campaign Meetings. I got in, started the engine, when all of a sudden this woman lurches up and starts banging on the windscreen. Could I give her a lift. Well, I'm pretty used to having women throw themselves at me. You know how it is? OK, perhaps you don't. But I do.' Alan batted his eyelashes.

'Get on with it,' I said.

'Well, this one was a bit different. For a start she was very young, no more than eighteen, I'd guess. But also there was a sort of desperate look about her, which, out of simple humanity, I couldn't ignore. So I told her to get in.'

'You're such a humane bastard.'

'There's no need to pull that face. I didn't lay a finger on her. In fact, I gave her a heavy lecture about how she was playing a dangerous game hitching lifts off strangers at that time of night. I was pretty certain she was expecting me to ask her back to my place. But I don't need that kind of scene. I just took her to where she wanted to go, which was some street off the Mile End Road. Problem was she wouldn't get out the car. She just curled up on the front seat and gave me this pussy cat look and said couldn't she spend the night there. She had nowhere to sleep and so on. Well. I couldn't very well just leave her there. On the other hand I didn't want to start getting heavy. Then I hit on the bright idea of offering to buy her a meal. She jumped at that. So I took her to this late night Chinese place and we got chatting about my work, the Labour Party, homelessness all that stuff. She was very interesting. Very well informed.'

'Perhaps we could get her a postal vote.'

Alan laughed and drank off the rest of my coffee. 'You don't get much in these cups do you?'

'They're a very cunning optical illusion,' I said. 'They appear to hold a third of a pint or so but actually contain only five millilitres. And you're just had four of them. But before you go for a refill, would you mind telling me the rest of the story. I was just getting interested.'

Alan arranged his fingers symmetrically on the table top and stared at them. 'She claims to have top secret information concerning the penetration of the Labour Party by M15 agents. According to her they have infiltrated a number of key positions in the organization. Not just to monitor our activities but as part of a large scale plot to undermine our credibility with the electorate. Ok, she didn't use those exact words but that was the general drift.'

Alan looked up and fixed me with one of his intensely sincere stares. I made a sceptical adjustment to my eyebrows.

'Bit of a coincidence wasn't it? She had this sensational story up her sleeve and she just happened to hitch a lift from a Labour Party candidate.'

'You're suggesting, once she found out who I was, she made it all up to please me?'

'Sounds like a serious possibility.'

'Sure. It's possible. But she sort of anticipated your objection by telling me that it wasn't just chance she picked on my car. She'd known all along I was the Docklands East candidate. And she'd been lying in wait in order to warn me. Only before giving me the warning she wanted to make certain for herself that I was worthwhile her taking the trouble.'

'And you passed the test.'

'Seems like it.'

'Still doesn't mean she wasn't lying. Could just be she has a good line in flattery. What happened next?'

Alan looked embarrassed. 'I took her back to my flat. I made up a separate bed for her on the sitting room floor. The next morning she was gone. So were half my valuables.'

'I see. Did you inform the police?'

'You've got to be joking. I felt a big enough fool without having that crowd down on my neck. The press would have got on to it. I'd have been a national laughing stock. As a matter of fact you're the first person I've mentioned it to. I haven't even told Andrea.'

'And I take it after the theft you lost faith in your little hitchhiker's story?'

'Yes, I did. For a while. Only lately certain things have been happening that have started me thinking again. So what if she went through my wallet. She was probably on smack. She was probably desperate for a fix. It doesn't necessarily mean everything she said was a pack of lies. And you know, Joseph, there really is something self-destructive about this party of ours. I don't want to sound paranoid about this. But there are certain comrades who just recently seem to be following a course of action calculated to bring us maximum bad publicity.'

'You're referring to Clarke, I take it?'

Alan was silent a moment. He puckered up his brows and looked pretty much like a big school kid who had been asked to split on his mates. 'I didn't really want to get into personalities. Ted was very good to me in the early days of my joining the Party. Let's face it, I would never have got anywhere without his backing. He was an astute manoeuvrer when it came to manipulating delegates in my favour. And he was very against extreme ideas like the rent amnesty because of the risk it involved to my career. I always presumed when the by-election was called, and I became the official candidate, Ted would be the first to recognize the need for me to broaden my appeal. I mean activists and voters are different kinds of animal. They need handling in different ways. You and I know that. Clarke knows that. Anyone who's serious about the political game knows it. But since this election was called Clarke has moved in the opposite direction. He's done everything in his power to wreck my campaign. The other day he even released to the press that article I wrote for the homosexual forum

179

magazine. OK, I still stand by everything I said there, but there's a time and a place. And now to cap it all there's this crazy business of going out of our way to associate ourselves with the Militant. I mean no-one in their right minds would do that in Docklands East if they were serious about winning this election. But all of a sudden it's like tactics is a dirty word.'

'Slow down, Alan. Slow down. If I get you right what you're suggesting is that Clarke is in the pay of M15 with a brief to destroy the Labour Party.'

'I don't know what I'm saying. It sounds preposterous when you put it like that. But on my bad days that's what it feels like is happening.'

'This hitchhiker of yours. Where did she say she got her information from?'

'She didn't. I asked her but she kept saying I'd have to take it on trust. OK, I realize that's not very satisfactory. I just wish I could get hold of her again somehow.'

'Did she give you her name?'

'Janine. Nothing else. Not a lot to go on, is it? I don't even suppose it's her real name. There must be hundreds of young, blonde, blue-eyed dope addicts in this city of no fixed address. What's the matter, Joseph? You look like you've seen a ghost.'

'You said Janine?'

'That's right. Do you know her?'

'Not exactly. But if she's who I think she is, she's dead.'

'Dead.' Alan stared first at me and then into the dregs of the coffee cup. 'What happened?'

'An overdose.'

'Deliberate?'

'Who's to say.'

'Poor kid. Christ, is that the time? I've got to split. I've got a meeting with the Walworth Road top brass in ten minutes. Let's talk later, Joseph.'

So Alan hurried off and I sauntered back alone across Hungerford Footbridge. Halfway over I paused to stare down into the dull murky waters. The weather was overcast and there was no reflection of light. I wondered what the police launch had been searching for, a suicide, a canister of poison, an attaché case of confidential documents. The river was just a vast drain for all the city's evil secrets. And like most of London's drains the stench was beginning to rise. I observed a couple of yapping gulls feeding off the refuse and then moved on.

I dropped down into Charing Cross tube and caught the District Line going East. A twitchy pustular youth sat down opposite me wearing a black tracksuit and hugging an Arsenal kitbag like it was a baby. Once we got to Tower Hill the carriage emptied out. The doors reclosed with a thud and we were back in the tunnel – just the youth and myself. He didn't waste any time. He unzipped his kitbag and took out a knife with a six-inch blade and began testing the sharpness of it with his thumb and glancing across at me and smiling in a nervous, rather shy sort of way. I began to feel pretty twitchy myself. I still hadn't quite shaken off the threatening phone call. I didn't know whether to make a grab for the emergency handle or to sit it out. In the end I chose to sit it out. It was the right decision. A sudden movement might have panicked him. Instead he took to cleaning his fingernails out with the point. When we drew into Whitechapel he put the knife back in the bag and made a run for it like the hounds of hell were after him.

24

The crematorium was a neat little red-brick building with a tall thin chimney at the rear, from which the occasional plume of smoke issued into the vacuity of the sky. I sat near the back. There was a long and rather tedious reading from William Morris's *News From Nowhere*. I fell to musing on what sort of funeral I would like for myself. I rather fancied a solemn procession of long grey overcoats, coffin slung on a gun carriage, driving snow. But perhaps that was rather too Stalinist in tone. The quiet country churchyard, the spongy hummock, the smell of rotting apples and the ritual turning of the wet sod was more in keeping with English values. Of course, Andrea would never approve of that. Bourgeois sentimentality about worms and nature. And remember what Marx had to say on the subject of rural idiocy. Andrea would want a street party with a reggae steel band, having previously donated all my organs for medical research. But why was I worrying about any of this? I had received another threatening phone call that morning. Chances were one of Stentor's contractor friends would shortly be setting me in concrete beneath a secluded little stretch of the M25's fourth carriageway.

Suddenly I realized the congregation had doubled up on their chairs, foreheads clasped in hands, a posture that I normally associated with the imminent onset of diarrhoea, but in the present circumstances I presumed meant the moment had come for a little silent meditation on the late departed. I had obviously missed out on a crucial signal. I hastily adopted a similar position. After prayer we stood up to sing Jerusalem. The coffin trundled towards a hatchway draped in electric-blue fibre-glass curtains. And it was all over. One or two mourners began shuffling uncertainly towards the aisles. Then the momentum gathered pace and there was an almost unseemly rush for the doors.

Outside it came as something of a pleasant surprise to discover it was still daylight and the world was still much the same as when I saw it last. It was a bit like coming out of a matinee performance at the cinema. But these optimistic feelings didn't last long. I had just caught sight of Meryll bearing down on me Gorgon-style, her crash helmet tucked under her arm like an auxiliary head.

'I suppose all that Zionist crap was your idea.'

'Zionist crap?' I queried.

'Well, what else would you call it. All that Jerusalem bollocks. Why can't we sing The Internationale for a change. Are we afraid of being socialists or something?'

'Ah, I see, you're objecting to the choice of hymn. The words are by Blake,' I said. 'As far as I am aware he was an uncircumcised Englishman.'

Meryll pulled her I'm-about-to-throw-up face.

'I know who fuckin' Blake was and I don't want to know about the state of his prick thanks.'

'I'm sorry. How insensitive of me.'

'The guy was obviously some kind of rapist freak, obsessed with images of penetration. Arrows of desire. Yuck. That kind of filth should be burnt.'

'As a point of information he was also a socialist prophet. If you read the words carefully it's really a critique of industrialization. Dark satanic mills et cetera. Get it?'

'Oh for fuck's sake. I can read, you know. How typically male. Always thinks he must interpret for the little woman. As if he's got some god-given monopoly on truth. Well balls to that. What I'm saying is why can't we sing The Red Flag once in a while?'

'Fair point.'

'Right. Well, perhaps you'd like to take it on board instead of being patronizing.'

'Fine. Fine. Only Melrose did specifically request in his will that we sing *Jerusalem*.'

But it was too late. Another muffed punch line. Meryll had already rammed her helmet down on to her head and all communication was terminated. I could only observe her mouth continuing to work inside its upturned gold fish bowl until the visor became obscured behind a film of condensation.

'You don't believe Melrose's death was really an accident do you?' said Julian, strolling across the green sward, pocked with dog shit, hands in pockets, wearing cricketing flannels and a baggy pullover, and chewing gum.

'Well, accidental death was the verdict of the inquest,' I said.

'Rigged,' said Jonathan, wearing floral shorts and dark glasses.

'So how do you explain it?' I said.

Melrose had died parachuting from six-thousand feet while listening to Wagner on his Sony Walkman. He had been in mid-descent when there had been a sudden change of wind causing him to drift on to a forty-thousand-volt electrical pylon. He had been virtually incinerated on the spot.

'Melrose was one of the most experienced descenders in the business,' said Jonathan. 'He wasn't the kind of man to be thrown by a puff of wind from the wrong direction.'

'So what was it then, suicide?' Melrose had always said to me that he would take his own life when the time came that he felt he was no longer making a positive contribution to society. But he had been as fit as a flea right up until the last minute, and the manner of death seemed a trifle bizarre even for someone of his eccentric tastes.

'The CIA had him rubbed out, of course,' said Julian, shifting the gum from one corner of his mouth to the other and showing me his back molars.

'And why should they want to do a thing like that?'

'Obvious isn't it?'

'Not to me, I'm afraid.'

'The Hilda Morrell connection.' And with this enigmatic remark they moved off in unison towards a newspaper kiosk.

I was about to approach Jack White, whom I badly wanted a private word with, when I felt someone tugging at my sleeve. It was Pam.

'Oh dear. Terrible isn't it,' she sniffed.

'Yes, it is,' I said.

'I was terribly fond of him.'

'I think we all were.'

'He was such a gentle man. I shall miss him. Terribly.'

'Yes.'

'I know it's stupid of me to get upset like this. He had a good life. And what is death if it isn't part of the cycle of creation.' She patted her stomach.

Is Pam trying to tell me something here, I thought. I felt a wave of panic rise from the pit of my own stomach.

'Are you coming with us to scatter his ashes on the allotment?'

'I'd like to,' I said. 'But unfortunately I've got a pressing engagement.'

I felt a bit of a creep ducking out of it like that. And I'd never even got round to printing Melrose's pamphlet on leaf mulch. I made a mental vow to finish it off and publish it as a sort of obituary notice. I just got to Jack's car before he had time to take off. He stuck his head angrily out the window.

'Joseph, what the hell are you playing at? You trying to kill yourself or something. Because you needn't think I shall be attending your frigging funeral as well. One wake a week is quite sufficient thanks.'

'Are you going towards the centre?' I said.

Jack looked at me with suspicion. 'Why?'

'I thought you could give me a lift.'

He began humming and hahing about the complexity of his movements.

185

'Oh come on Jack. I've got an election to organize. My shoe leather's nearly through. Have a little charity. I'll pay you for half the petrol.'

'Oh get in then.' He flung the door open.

Jack drove an early 1970s Ford Cortina with a stripe down the side. 'At least it's not one of these frigging foreign jobs that all your Trots drive around in,' was one of his standard remarks. Getting into it was like getting into a giant garbage can. It was full of old cigar boxes, newspapers, raffle tickets, unopened membership applications, empty milk bottles, straw, sawdust and a suffocating smell of smoke.

'The seat belt doesn't work too well,' said Jack. 'Just drape it over you. I don't want to get fined for doing some bugger a good turn.'

I waited until Jack had managed to struggle into third gear before broaching the subject that was uppermost in my mind.

'Remember that girl called Janine?'

'Ah Janine.' Jack came on all lugubrious. 'Another dear friend who alas is no longer with us. But then none of us are long for this mortal world, Joseph. My own days I fear are numbered. I cannot seem to shake off this wretched cough.' He coughed pathetically.

'How well did you know her?'

'Oh, not well at all. She was but a brief glimmer of light in the rheumy corner of an old man's eye. But if it's a little visual delectation you're interested in, Joseph, there's a very nice bit of tit and bum down at the Unicorn these days. We could have a bite to eat there one lunchtime say.'

'Did she ever talk to you about how the Labour Party had been infiltrated by M15?'

Jack chuckled. 'Oh rum. Very rum.'

'Did she discuss it with you, Jack?'

Jack swerved to avoid a milk float. It was about the only thing on the road that was moving slower than we were.

'I've told you, Joseph, I knew the poor child no better than yourself.'

'Stop bullshitting, Jack. You knew her quite well enough to screw her whenever you got the chance.'

Jack crashed the gearbox, slammed on the brakes and slowly drifted to a halt on a double yellow line.

'Has anyone ever told you, Joseph, that you have a mind like a sewer?'

'Jack, I saw you and her with my own eyes on a Ronayne bedroom floor.'

Jack took a couple of deep breaths and assumed his world-weary long-suffering expression. 'I think you'd better walk from here, Joseph. You can send me your share of the petrol money by postal order. I don't want one of your dud cheques.' And with that he got out of the car and flounced off.

I went to chase after him but the passenger door had jammed. By the time I got myself out he'd already disappeared from view. I found him easily enough inside a Joe Coral betting shop, watching the three-thirty at Newmarket. I decided on the apologetic approach.

'Look Jack, I'm sorry. It doesn't really matter what your relationship with her was. All I want to know is did she ever mention M15 to you in connection with the Labour Party?'

Jack covered his ears with his hands. 'Is there to be no sanctuary from the hound-dogs of socialism? This is consecrated ground you are defiling, Joseph. We are gathered in this place to worship the great god of chance. And we do not welcome the intrusion of profane subjects.'

'Jack, this is ridiculous.'

Jack made an impatient gesture with his hand. 'Lower your voice can you. Have some respect. This is not one of your dives for all the scum and riff-raff of the earth.'

I looked around me. Scum and riff-raff seemed like a pretty fair description of the clientele. The three-thirty had just finished. There was a hardly perceptible movement, a slight fluttering of newspapers. The winners showed no more emotion than the losers. Jack swore under his breath and turned towards me.

'Look laddie, OK, perhaps Janine and I did enjoy a

little carnal knowledge together. But what the hell has it got to do with you or anyone else except me and her? And she's dead so that just leaves me. Dear God, perhaps I loved her. Has that possibility occurred to you? Perhaps she was my little chink of heaven. My last chance to grasp the beauty of this world. How does that appeal to you?' Jack seemed near to tears. But then his rheumy eyes, to employ his own phrase, watered easily.

'All I want to know is whether she ever talked to you about a plot to destroy the Party from the inside?' I pleaded, wondering what I had to do or say to get Jack to concentrate on the real issue.

'I've been telling you about the existence of such a plot for years, Joseph.'

'Sure you have. Trotskyist infiltrators. Plants from the SWP and the IMG and the WRP and all the rest of them. But this is different. Because this time the plants are from the Right and they are being funded by our so called security forces. Janine must have talked to you about this?'

'Look laddie, I was interested in Janine's body not her mind. Her mind was a cess pit. Like most cess pits it was full of all sorts of crap. I didn't care to wallow around in it too much.'

'Well, thanks for your help,' I said.

I made to move off but Jack caught hold of my arm.

'If I was you Joseph, I'd forget all about Janine.'

'Thanks for the advice.'

'On the other hand . . .' He began to cough.

'Get it off your chest, Jack. You're going to miss the next race at this rate.'

'If you really insist on sniffing round places you have no business sniffing, then there is someone I could put you in touch with, laddie, who might be able to help you further.' Jack drooped his eyelid, always a bad sign. But having come this far I could hardly back off now.

'OK,' I said. 'What's the deal?'

'Meet me at nine-thirty tomorrow evening in the Prince of Wales. It's right by King's Cross. Anyone will give you directions.'

25

The route from my flat to the tube station took me along
the back of Docklands General Hospital. It was a grim
Victorian edifice with black fire escapes and high black-
spiked railings. Nurses scuttled between the buildings
with dark cloaks pulled around their bent shoulders like
the carapaces of giant cockroaches. Every other week
you read in the papers about another ward being closed
down. I only ever knew three people who had been
admitted to Docklands General and none of them had
come out alive.

I was approaching the crossroads a little way past the
main entrance when I noticed a young woman standing
on the corner. This, in itself, was not a particularly note-
worthy occurrence. But this woman was different. For a
start I knew her. And for seconds she was chained up.

'Pam, what the hell's going on? I mean who did this to
you?'

'Meryll,' said Pam, matter of factly, as if it was just the
most natural thing in the world to go round chaining your
best friend up to a set of railings covered in dog piss.

'Meryll! Christ! What's got into her? She gone nuts or
something?'

'It's a symbolic action,' said Pam with her usual nasal
whine.

'A what?'

'A symbolic action.'

'Symbolic of what? Woman's inhumanity to woman.
How are we going to get you out of this? I think perhaps I
should call the fire brigade.'

'Don't be silly, Joseph. It's part of a national day of protest. Women are doing it all over the country.'

'You mean to say you're chained up like this voluntarily.' I had a sort of sinking feeling. I had just noticed a small and rather soggy cardboard placard on which someone had daubed the rallying cry: Support the Walthamstow Women.

'Well you don't think Meryll would do this to me if I hadn't agreed to it, do you,' said Pam, clearly shocked by the implications of such an idea.

'No, I guess not.'

'Sometimes, Joseph, I wonder whether you're all right in the head.'

'I'm sorry.'

'It's part of a twenty-four-hour vigil. I shall be fasting and meditating.'

'Good. Great. Best of luck and all that. But Pam?'

'Yes.'

'Isn't it rather dangerous? Particularly if you're planning to be here all through the night. This is a pretty rough area.'

Pam looked at me with great condescension. 'As long as I have confidence in myself, in my own power to control my own life, nothing untoward can happen to me. It's all a matter of having that confidence Joseph. Meryll describes it as an aura radiating out from certain special people like a protective electrical field. I think that's rather a good description, don't you?'

'Smashing. Look, it's all very well for Meryll to talk in these terms of scientific voodoo, but I don't see Meryll here, chained up, risking her neck.'

'Meryll's in charge of refreshments.'

'Is she so. Well, isn't that just fine and dandy for Meryll.'

'I sometimes get the impression, Joseph, that you don't like Meryll.'

'Let's just say I have certain reservations about who was the biggest monster, her, Joseph Stalin or Adolf Hitler.'

'Joseph!'

'OK, OK. I know. I'm not being entirely fair to Stalin. He was in a difficult situation. But really Pam, are you sure this is such a good idea? I should hate to come along this way tomorrow morning and find you'd been cannibalized.'

'I shall be all right, Joseph.'

'You're a brave woman.'

'We must be prepared to fight for what we believe in.'

'I suppose you're right.'

'It's not just for me. I also have my daughter to think of. I want her to grow up in a beautiful clean world.'

'Your daughter.'

'I'm pregnant, Joseph.' Pam beamed at me. I don't think I'd ever seen her look quite so radiantly happy before. It was like she was all lit up from within. I felt like I'd just been slugged on the back of the neck. If Pam was pregnant I was more than likely the father. 'Well, aren't you going to congratulate me?' she said.

'But that's wonderful Pam. Truly wonderful. I hope both you and the child will be very happy.'

'I'm so excited. Meryll and me are buying this caravan. We've already seen it. It's in an orchard in Kent. It's got a stove and these sweet check curtains. And Daphne is going to grow up with apple blossom falling on her blonde curls as she picks the wild flowers. Imagine it, Joseph. I can hardly wait.'

Pam clasped her hands together and closed her eyes like a woman in rapture.

'But Pam,' I said. 'What if it's a boy?'

Pam opened her eyes and stared at me pityingly. 'It's not a boy, Joseph. I can feel it inside me. I know it's not a boy.'

26

The Prince of Wales was at the end of a dismal street with a high brick wall along one side and shabby tenement dwellings along the other. The whole lot was due to come down, and hanging in the background, silhouetted against the evening sky, was the black shaft of a crane. The Sword of Damocles, I thought to myself. I guess Damocles was into the demolition business before Costain, McAlpine and all the other Johnny-come-Latelies had even cut their teeth on their first slum clearance project. But there had been delays with planning procedures and financial packages, and in the interim, as if in defiance of the new clean world of steel and glass office blocks, with their courtyards and conference centres and secure underground car parks, a kind of twilight existence had sprung up. The area around the Prince of Wales had become a centre for dope dealers, alcoholics, prostitutes, runaways, bankrupts, illegal immigrants, refugees from war and famine, petty criminals, vagrants and miscellaneous socially misplaced persons, among whom, I should also now include party agents and their bosses.

I found Jack seated by himself with his watch placed ostentatiously on the wooden table top next to his G & T.

'Not late am I,' I said.

Jack said nothing. Just continued to stare at his watch.

'Bumped into an old friend on the way over.'

Jack still said nothing. I felt he was rather overdoing the remonstration bit and was just about to tell him

192

where he could stick his digital timepiece when I noticed he was holding two fingers of his left hand on the pulse of his right and counting.

'Just checking the old ticker. Had a spot of indigestion last couple of days. Can't seem to throw it off. So, what's your poison, laddie?'

'Pint of Guinness would make a nice change,' I said.

Jack ordered a pint of what he referred to as Irish bile and also took the opportunity to get a refill for himself. Despite his digestion problems he seemed in remarkably good spirits. I couldn't recall him ever voluntarily buying the first round before. It was suspicious.

'So who is this person who can tell me about Janine?' I said, when we had settled in with our drinks.

Jack looked cautiously over one shoulder, then the other, then hunched himself inside his old tweed coat, before announcing in a stage whisper, 'One of the fallen sisterhood, Joseph. One of the fallen sisterhood.' He jerked his head towards a group of women at a nearby table.

'You mean . . .'

'Yes, Joseph, our contact is a painted lady, a butterfly of the night, a denizen of the underworld. But I'm afraid that is the sort of company our little friend used to keep. Are you still sure you want to go through with this, Joseph? I don't want it said that I have led you astray. I know how sensitive you are about such things.'

'Just cut the sarcasm, Jack. Is she here now?'

Jack held up a hand. 'Not so fast, laddie. Not so fast. This is not something that should be lightly rushed into. You know the greatest single problem facing Western civilized man today?'

'No,' I sighed.

'Premature ejaculation. It is one of the compensations of getting old, Joseph, that you discover the joys of taking your time. You learn to savour every little moment. Instead of going off half-cock. It is the difference between a Wimpy and a five course meal at the Savoy.'

'Sure,' I said. I forbore to ask him how this philosophy

of life fitted in with a quick scrap on the Ronayne coat-room floor.

'How are things with Andrea?' asked Jack, lighting up one of his nasty thin cigars and blowing smoke in my face.

'Oh fine,' I said.

'I sometimes worry about you, Joseph.'

'No need to concern yourself on my behalf.'

'But I do. I do. I worry that you have not entirely rid yourself of the influence of that woman.'

'There's a bit of tension now and again. But generally we rub along OK.'

'I was married once,' said Jack, blowing a plume of blue smoke reflectively towards the nicotine stained ceiling.

'Oh really,' I said. I had heard rumours to this effect but I had never bothered about getting them authenticated.

'Yes, we enjoyed two years of conjugal bliss and then one day she just up and left. No other man involved. She said she just wanted a change. Fortunately there were no children. I was very young at the time and to tell you the truth, Joseph, I was rather upset. Now, of course, I realize it was the best thing that could ever have happened to me.'

'In what way?' I said. I didn't really want to listen to Jack's emotional life history. It wasn't what I had come for. But I got the impression he regarded this revelation about his marriage as doing me a great honour. I was being entrusted with a rare secret. And if I wanted him to co-operate on the Janine front then I, at least, had to show an interest in his tales of female perfidy. There was a sort of bargain being made here. I had no alternative but to play along.

'It taught me a fundamental truth about handling women, Joseph.'

'And what's that?' I said.

'You must never make yourself vulnerable. You must never put yourself in a position where they can kick you in the teeth. Because if you do, they damn well will, laddie. Sooner or later, they damn well will.'

I stared across at Jack. He looked a bit feverish. Perhaps he was going down with a bug or something. But there was more to it than that. It occurred to me that evening, for the first time really, that Jack's appearance was beginning to teeter over the edge of seediness into a condition altogether rather more squalid. His hair was too long and in bad need of a wash. His coat had burn holes in it. His hand shook as he lifted his glass to his lips. I was about to ask him whether he wanted another, when I caught a glint in his eyes.

'Don't turn round Joseph. Whatever you do don't turn round. Your contact has just walked in through the door. Keep your head down, laddie. She's staring in our direction. It's OK, she hasn't seen us. She's ordering a drink. So take it very slowly. We don't want to startle our little love bird from its roost before you have had a chance to stroke her wings, now do we? Slowly. See who I mean? Standing by the bar. What about that plumage, eh?'

I saw who he meant all right. And when I did I almost fell off my stool. The red stilettos, the black fish-net stockings, the short black leather miniskirt, the wide red plastic belt drawn in tight, the silky blouse, the red mouth, the pale cheeks, the blacked out eyes. Celia. Celia in the fancy costume that I had once glimpsed in her wardrobe. Celia without her glasses and with her hair loose down her back. She was with another younger woman who was wearing little leather ankle boots and a short white fur coat.

Jack was doubled up with laughter. 'You'd never think she'd suck cock with a prissy mouth like that would you,' he snorted. His laughter turned into an apoplexy of coughing. I wished him dead on the spot.

I pushed my way impulsively through the crowd without thinking out any clear strategy for handling this situation. That was a mistake. Though even if I had stopped to think I don't know that I would have ended up doing any different. I was standing right next to Celia before she noticed me. In fact it was her friend who drew my presence to her attention.

'I think you've got an admirer,' said the friend, nudging.

When Celia saw me she closed her eyes and breathed in very deeply.

'Hello,' I said.

'Oh my God,' said Celia, with heavy emphasis on every syllable. 'I always knew sooner or later something like this would happen. Oh my God.'

'Celia, can we talk?'

'Not here, Joseph. Not here.'

'Well, somewhere else then.'

'Can't you see I'm with someone.'

'Yes, I'm sorry to just barge in like this. But it's about Janine. Jack seems to think you might be able to tell me something about her.'

'Not now, Joseph. Now now.'

'Janine, wasn't she the flaky kid who done herself in?' said the friend.

'Celia it's really rather important.'

'Get lost, Joseph.'

'Why's he keep calling you Celia?' said the friend, who was obviously enjoying the way this situation was developing.

'It's just a name he likes to use,' said Celia. 'Come on, let's get out of here. The guy's a creep.' She grabbed her friend's arm and made towards the exit. I followed.

'Look, Celia, if you're feeling embarrassed about whatever it is that's going on here there's really no need to be,' I said.

'What's the matter with him, acid or something?' said the friend, turning to stare at me as Celia dragged her away.

'He's just one of these fucked up guys that like to talk all night,' said Celia, breaking into a run, which wasn't easy in her tight skirt.

I chased after them down the dark narrow street, under scaffolding, through puddles, past lamp posts, between parked cars.

'Celia. Celia. You're over-reacting. Look, I realize it's a bit awkward for you having me drop into your secret life like this. But I absolutely accept without any reservation whatsoever your inalienable right to be a prostitute in your spare time if that's what you want. I mean I'm not even shocked. I might have looked shocked but it wasn't really shock it was just surprise. And Celia. Celia, I promise you I won't say a word about this to Charles or anyone. Celia.'

But it was no good. They just kept on running. And I was beginning to attract rather a lot of attention.

27

I usually eat my cornflakes in a semi-somnambulistic state. That's why I was more than halfway through before the taste of turps penetrated that bit of my brain which deals with messages from my taste buds. Perhaps I was getting paranoid, but my first thought was the milk had been poisoned. There had been more strange phone calls over the last two days. I sniffed the bottle but it smelt OK. The cornflakes smelt like they always smelt, man-made fibre dust. So there had to be an alternative source of contamination.

I went to the sink to tip away the soggy mess that remained in the bottom of the bowl. And there was my answer. The sink of grimy water that I soak my dishes in was floating with a rainbow of oil. That bastard Charles Ronayne had been rinsing his paintbrushes in with my washing up.

I went out the front to have words with him about it. It was raining, not hard but a steady penetrating drizzle. The front of the building had taken on the appearance of a demolition site. Charles had rigged up a sort of canopy of plastic that went from the guttering horizontally out-wards for about four feet and then down to the ground. He was working inside this tent-like structure, lit by arc lamps and accompanied by a tape of Handel's *Messiah*.

I poked my head in. It was some minutes before I could attract his attention. When he saw me he flapped his great paws at me and ushered me out as if I'd just blundered into some sacred chamber where he was the officiating priest.

'I don't want sightseers,' he said in his lordly style. 'Not at this stage. A work of art can only be properly understood in its final state. I don't go along with the school of thinking that spends more time on the preliminary drawings than the end product.'

'Charles, I'm not after any sneak previews. I'd just appreciate it if you didn't rinse your brushes in with my washing up in future, OK? I like to take my turps as an after dinner liqueur.'

'If you washed up on a more regular basis it wouldn't be a problem,' said Charles, quite unapologetic. 'It's not my fault that you have slovenly habits.'

'That's all very well, Charles. But I do happen to live here. And this renovation work of yours is beginning to interfere with my life style. I mean not only are you trying to ruin my digestive system, but my windows are now permanently shrouded in plastic. I inhabit a sort of gloom world. Except when you turn the searchlights on. Then it's more like being inside an operating theatre.'

'We all have to make sacrifices in life,' said Charles. 'And I think the final result will more than justify any small personal discomforts you might suffer during the creative process. The end justifies the means. That is part of your creed, is it not?'

I hadn't got the time to argue with Charles any longer. I was due to start canvassing on the Albany Estate in fifteen minutes. Besides there was no real point. Trying to communicate with Charles was like trampolining in a quagmire.

The arrangement was we'd all meet outside the Regal. I studied the posters for *Sinning With Sexy Susan* in some detail. It was ten-thirty before Alan showed. He arrived looking somewhat jaded. Even his rosette was wilting.

'Sorry I'm late. Someone posted a pile of shit through my letter box again. Third time this week.'

'You call the police?'

'What's the point? They'd either think I'm defecating

199

on my own doormat or else I deserve everything I get and worse.'

'Take your point.'

'I'll tell you something.'

'What's that?'

'This country is full of racists. And I'll tell you something else. If I knew what I know now about this business, I'd never have got involved at this kind of level.'

'Don't get dispirited,' I said. 'We've reached that point in the Campaign when everyone always feels a bit low. Things will improve, you'll see.'

Alan looked unconvinced.

'The rest gone on ahead, have they?'

'There is no rest, Alan.'

'What do you mean? I thought this was supposed to be a mass canvass. Hit the Albany in force. Impress them with the numbers of our supporters.'

'It's a bad day of the week. A lot of people are working.'

'Like hell they are,' said Alan. 'Are we the Party of the unemployed or are we not. And where's Clarke. I thought he was supposed to be here.'

I shrugged.

'Typical,' said Alan. 'He's too damn busy trying to put the shit up the bourgeoisie to be bothered with building real support in the local community. Which reminds me, have you made any progress with your Janine enquiries?'

'Nothing very tangible as yet,' I said. I didn't think this was an appropriate moment to go into the Celia fiasco. I wasn't sure there would ever be an appropriate moment.

'Pity,' said Alan. 'A juicy scandal about how this country's security forces are out of control is just what we need to turn this campaign around. Somebody must have known her. She must have had friends, family, a history for God's sake. She didn't just arrive out of nowhere.'

'I think we'd better make a start on the leg work,' I said. 'Before we get moved on for loitering.'

The Albany was one of the older estates. Four racks of flats built around courtyards with long walkways and stairwells that stank of cats and worse. The basic architectural concept seemed to derive from the prison quadrangle. Most of those who came to the door were women with long straggly hair, bruised-looking faces and kids tugging at their skirts. All they wanted to talk about was the damp running down the walls and the broken windows. Alan made the usual bland promises and the woman said they'd vote for him, though it was obvious they'd never make the effort. It made the canvass returns look good though.

We suffered the usual quantities of personal abuse, doors slammed in faces, remarks about nigger lovers, that sort of thing. It was all in a morning's work. It wasn't until we were halfway across an open space designated as a children's play area, but possessing more of the qualities of a bomb crater, that the real trouble started. The first thing I was aware of was the implosion of a whooping noise in my eardrums. Then I saw what looked like a group of football supporters, big boots, shaved heads, Union Jack T-shirts, limbs like raw sides of beef, charging towards us.

'I think we'd better get out of here,' I said.

'Don't you think we should find out what they want first,' said Alan. I had always been impressed by his physical courage.

'No, not this time.'

I had already begun to run. I went like hell. I am not exactly fit, but naked fear got my heart pumping just that extra few fluid ounces of blood. I think I had probably managed to increase the distance between myself and the pack by a few yards, when I came to a brick wall. It wasn't very high, but in my haste I caught my foot on the top of it and fell awkwardly. Picking myself up on the other side, I discovered I could hardly move my right leg. I distinctly recall seeing a butterfly settling on a stone, a red admiral I think it was, or possibly a peacock. Then there came a stunning blow to my right ear. I was not so much aware of any pain as of a dark vortex, like a spiralling fire escape down which I was hurtling at great speed.

28

'How are you feeling now, Mr Punk?' A black nurse with fuzzy hair was holding my wrist and counting. The fuzziness probably had more to do with the trouble I was experiencing focusing than any indigenous racial characteristics on her part. I tried to say that I was feeling fine and that my name was Pink, but the effort involved in formulating the right sounds was beyond me. Anyway the nurse didn't seem too interested in my answer. She seemed to be having difficulties enough of her own with the counting. I remember thinking she was either innumerate or my pulse was fading fast. Oddly, I wasn't alarmed by these thoughts. On the contrary I felt rather light-headed. Through the large window at the end of the ward was a view of tree and cloud. I felt slightly delirious with the innocent beauty of the world. I wanted to hug it to me. I wanted to cry. The nurse dropped my hand on to the counterpane, muttered something and scribbled some notes on to a board.

It seemed like several light years had elapsed since my dash across the play space. I later learnt it was, in fact, only a few hours, and that I had been taken by ambulance to Docklands General. It was evening before the doctors came round. Their arrival was preceded by a flurry of activity. A young dark-haired man, labelled Dr Tarrant, came and peered at me. Despite his white coat and the stethoscope draped around his neck he didn't entirely dispell the impression of being a prep school boy dressed up as a doctor. He did a few pull-ups on the bar at the end of my bed. 'Mr Prink?'

'Pink'

'Mind if I take a quick look?'

'Sure. Go ahead.'

I lay passively while the doctor stared, probed, prodded and pummelled. Once or twice I let out a yell of pain, which seemed to satisfy him for he would then move on to another part of my anatomy.

Suddenly Dr Tarrant became bored. 'Cover yourself up,' he said, as if I had been indecently exposing myself for the last ten minutes. He had moved on to the next bed before I had finished grappling with my pyjamas.

'But doctor, what's the matter with me?' I called.

Dr Tarrant thrust his head back through the curtains that were still drawn around me. In this disembodied state he looked like an impish gargoyle.

'Nothing to worry about, spot of concussion, few cuts and bruises, twisted ankle. We'll keep you in a couple of days for observation. You'll be as right as rain in no time. In the pink, you might say.' He beamed at me.

I felt like a charlatan.

The supper trolley was wheeled in by a sullen-looking girl. She slouched at the end of my bed trying to match my name with the names she had on her plates. She wasn't having much success. 'Anything by mouth?' she eventually asked in her surly manner.

'I think so,' I said.

'Well, there's nothing for a Prick down here.'

'It's Pink,' I said.

'Nothing for a Pink either. Did you fill in one of these menu cards?'

'No.'

'You can only have a meal if you filled in one of these menu cards.'

'But I wasn't given one.'

I was beginning to feel like I was back in my first year at school. Indeed, we seemed to have reached an impasse of quite insurmountable proportions when the girl said, 'I suppose you could have Mr Sooter's. Fricassee of chicken suit you?'

'Sounds fine,' I said. 'But what about . . .?'

'Oh, I don't think he'll be wanting any fricassee where he's gone,' she laughed and plonked the polystyrene container down in front of me.

'You mean . . .'

'This afternoon. Best thing really.' She clattered on down to the far end of the ward. I peeled the cellophane back. The chicken was decidedly on the emaciated side. I wondered which one Mr Sooter had been and what he'd died of and whether he'd been looking forward to the meal I was now eating on his behalf. There was something just a bit predatory about it. But I was ravenously hungry. And this was the NHS. You had to stick up for yourself in a place like this. It was no good being squeamish about dead men's dinners.

'There's two visitors for you,' said the nurse.

Two men approached. They were policemen. They were in plain clothes but I guessed they were either policemen, or members of the Militant, from the spivvy suits they wore and the sharp line of their haircuts around the ears and the back of the neck.

They sat down one on either side of my bed. 'My name is Chief Inspector Detmold,' said the older, unfamiliar, one. He had a taut muscular face, neatly tonsured sideburns turning a steely grey. 'Just in case you should require it on some future occasion.' He smiled. His voice was soft, mellifluous almost, but when he smiled you could see he had teeth like a ferret's. 'And this is Detective Sergeant Johnson from Special Branch.'

I looked at the henchman. He was a good ten years younger with a smooth fleshy face pitted with a surprisingly large number of shaving nicks. I briefly wondered whether this was evidence of a carelessness towards his own physical well-being, perhaps to be expected in a man of action, or whether there was some other explanation, such as inadequate bathroom lighting. He didn't look as if he'd welcome conversation on the subject so I didn't start one. Indeed, he was decidedly on the morose side, seemingly preoccupied with examining the dirt in his fingernails of which there was a considerable quantity. I had the odd feeling I might have seen him somewhere before, but I couldn't quite place him.

'So tell me in your own words, Sir,' said the Chief Inspector, 'exactly what happened. Take as long as you want over it. And be particularly careful not to leave anything out, no matter how trivial or silly it might seem to you.'

So I told them. The Chief Inspector leant back on his chair, fingered his stubble and stared at me through half-closed eyes in a shrewd manner, while Detective Sergeant Johnson took notes. At least I presume that was what he was doing. It is possible he might have been composing a shopping list, in which case I hope he included a new razor and a nail brush.

'Explain to me again will you just what it was you were doing down on the Albany Estate?' said the Inspector when I had finished my piece.

'Canvassing. I'm the party agent.'

'Canvassing eh? And what your particular line, Mr Pink? Tupperware. Naughtienighties.' He smirked across at Detective Sergeant Johnson of Special Branch who smirked back.

'I'm the Labour Party Agent for Docklands East,' I said. I was quite certain they knew very well what I did. This was just some elaborate charade to humiliate me.

'Labour Party Agent, eh,' said Detmold with exaggerated surprise, 'Well, not so very different really. All trying to sell something, aren't you? It's just the other chaps have had a bit more success of late. Not exactly flavour of the month is it, Labour. Seems the great British public don't want to be told what to do by a bunch of smart-arsed commies, just out of university. But we mustn't get bogged down in politics, fascinating subject though it is. Back to business. When you first set eyes on these young punks...'

'Skinheads,' I said.

'I thought you said punks?'

206

'No, I called them skinheads.'

'Just as you like, Sir. Punks, skinheads, makes little difference. When you first saw them, what were they doing?'

'They were jeering and sticking their fingers up and then they started a charge.'

'And it was at that point you began to run across the park.'

'Yes.'

'You're quite positive that was the sequence of events?' interrupted Detective Sergeant Johnson with sudden and unexpected hostility. It was the first time he had as much as opened his mouth.

'Yes.'

'You didn't start running first and then they gave chase?'

'Not as I recall it, no.'

'But it is possible that it was you who started the running?' The Sergeant seemed to be getting very het up. A nerve had started twitching in his left cheek.

'Yes, I suppose it is possible,' I said.

The Sergeant turned to his Inspector with a look of triumph on his face.

'I don't really see that it makes much difference,' I added.

'I think that's up to us to decide,' snapped the Sergeant.

'The point Detective Sergeant Johnson is making,' said Detmold, in his slower, gentler, man of the world manner, 'is that there will be those who will argue that by starting to run you were provoking the others to chase after you.'

'But that's ridiculous,' I said.

'Of course it is, of course. To you and me it is ridiculous. But you must remember that we are rational civilized people with wives and children at home in need of our protection and care. I'm afraid your average liberal-minded, do-gooding juror doesn't always see it in the same way as you and I. That's why, before we bring a case, we have to be quite certain it will stick. Now, you said you tripped over a low wall, twisted your ankle, paused to observe a butterfly on a stone and then experienced a heavy dull blow behind the right ear?'

'Correct. Except I didn't exactly pause to observe the butterfly. I just happened to notice it was there.'

'And you didn't see who inflicted this blow?'

'No, it came from behind.'

'May I put it to you, Sir, that what you actually experienced was the delayed sensation of a bang on the head caused by falling.'

'That's absurd.'

'Just answer the question yes or no,' snapped Detective Sergeant Johnson, the twitch starting up again.

'Why don't you ask the doctor who first saw me whether the blow looked like an injury from a fist or from hitting my head against a rock on the ground.'

'Who said anything about a rock,' screeched the Sergeant with manic glee.

'Rock, brick, stone. It's all much of a muchness, I would have thought.' I was becoming exasperated.

'There's really no need for you to get excited, Sir,' said the Chief Inspector, in his calm voice that was beginning to irritate me even more than the Sergeant's hysterical interruptions. 'Our only concern here is with establishing the truth. Now, if you would kindly cast your mind back to the events of this morning. How many youths did you say there were?'

'I didn't.'

'Don't let's beat around the bush, Sir. We are all busy people. I realize in the Labour Party work is something of a four-letter word, but there are some of us who can't afford to sit around on our bums all day waiting for the bananas to fall off the coconut trees, if you take my meaning. Now, approximately how many youths were present?'

'At a guess between three and five.'

'But not as many as ten?'

'No.'

'You're quite certain about that?'

'Yes.'

'And would you recognize any of them again?'

'Probably not.'

The Inspector looked sagacious. There was a faintly unpleasant rasping sound as he moved his roughened fingers across his early evening stubble. Then the sound stopped abruptly.

'And what impression did you get of their skin colour?'

'They were white.'

'Pale white? Or did one or two of them perhaps have slightly swarthy skins? The sort that some Greeks or Cypriots have for instance.'

'Possibly. It would be difficult to say at the distance I first saw them. My general impression was of whitish skins.'

'And could you, Sir, at the distance of one hundred yards, tell the skin colour of a Turk from the skin colour of an Arab?'

'Probably not.'

'And would you agree with me in saying that your friend, Mr Sayeed, has a skin colour no darker than that of the average Arab?'

'He is fairly light-skinned for an Asian, yes.'

'So some of the youths might have had skins as dark or possibly darker than Mr Sayeed's?'

'Look, where the hell is all this leading to. You are putting words into my mouth. You are twisting everything I say.'

'Steady on, Sir. Steady on. That is a serious accusation you are making there. A most serious accusation.'

'I'm sorry but . . .'

'You are in effect suggesting that we are not conducting this interview in a proper and professional manner.'

'I'm just feeling a bit upset and tired, that's all. I do have feelings you know.'

'Policemen too, Sir. Policemen too. We also are human. We have mortgages and hobbies and wives at home in need of our care and protection. And may I remind you that it was your friend Mr Sayeed who called us in. We don't object to that. Of course we don't. It's our job. People always call us when things turn nasty. When there's blood on the road or a body in the cellar. But don't try and make fools of us by selling us the party political line, when you know only too well it doesn't fit the facts.'

'I'm sorry? I'm not quite following you.'

'Your friend, Mr Sayeed, told us that it was definitely a racialist attack. I think it would be true to say that it suits certain political parties on the Left to stir up racial tension by this sort of talk. But your own evidence, Sir, your own evidence clearly indicates that a number of the attackers could well have had skins of a darker shade than Mr Sayeed's. Also Mr Sayeed himself was left quite unhurt, which does not exactly fit in with his racial persecution theories. Furthermore, we have to accept the possibility that this attack was at least in part provoked by your own behaviour. By your own admission, you had already stirred up considerable local antagonism by harassing innocent people on their doorsteps. And finally there is some doubt as to whether your injuries were inflicted by a third party or were the result of an accidental fall. All in all, Sir, even assuming we can track down your suspected assailants, it does not add up to a very convincing case. Good night to you, Sir. We both hope you will be feeling much better shortly.'

29

On being discharged from the hospital I caught the bus home. My limbs felt lighter than I remembered them and unusually well-co-ordinated. The sensation was a little like floating and not at all unpleasant.

I swung my way on to the upper deck, thinking of all the delightful views into other people's bedrooms I might enjoy during the journey. I don't wish to give the impression that I am a rabid voyeur, far from it, but I have always enjoyed the odd glimpse into the domestic settings of others. Girl reading book, woman brushing hair, gentleman with oiled moustachios playing an upright piano, that sort of thing. I was quickly disabused. The bus windows were opaque with years of cigarette smoke. You couldn't see a thing through them. In addition, most of the seats had been ripped up and the air was so stale it was like putting your head inside a used Hoover bag. Hardly surprisingly the upper deck was empty of fellow travellers, apart from a couple of twelve-year-olds who seemed to be indulging in an act of fellatio down the front. I sat near the back and amused myself with reading the graffiti: 'Kill nigger lovers', 'Sayeed is a commie pooftah', 'Use a spade to dig a grave'. It was all rather dispiriting. The only one I felt any sympathy with was the desperately scrawled message. Louise, forgive me. I thought of adding, and Celia ditto, but hadn't got an appropriate felt tip.

By the time I got off the lightness in my limbs had gone. It had been replaced by a spongy sensation which was far less agreeable. I went straight to bed and must have fallen asleep because some hours later I woke to discover Celia standing beside me looking down as if from a great height. I wasn't at all surprised to see her there. Rather the opposite. It was as if I had all along been expecting her to call. Or, more than that, as if I had myself conjured her up out of thin air. She was wearing the long grey raincoat with the belt tied tightly around her waist, which was surprisingly waspish, and the collar turned up against the weather, even though I recalled the weather as having been fine when I got off the bus. She looked rather forbidding. Perhaps it was the width of the padded shoulders and the serious greyness of her eyes. She was bearing a bunch of black grapes covered in a misty purple bloom.

'I should warn you, they're Cape,' she was saying. 'They're all I could get hold of. I came over in a hurry. I won't be offended if you don't eat them.'

I propped myself up on an elbow to receive the proferred grapes and placed them on a stack of old *Guardians* that served as a bedside table.

'Have a seat,' I said, hastily brushing aside the stale toast crumbs and dead skin cells that littered the sheets, not so much jaundiced now as terminally grey.

Celia sat down a little further away than I had indicated on the edge of the counterpane, smoothing her coat beneath her as she did so.

'I can't stop long,' she said, and then added, frowning at me, as if she disapproved of what she saw, 'I heard about what happened from Alan. Is it very painful?'

'Only if I smile,' I said. I affected a machismo nonchalance that Andrea would thoroughly have disapproved of. But then she also disapproved if I whinged and whined and made a terrible fuss. With some women you couldn't win.

Celia almost smiled and then thought better of it and shrugged instead and looked down at her small hands, placed demurely in her lap, as if she were posing for a photograph.

'Look,' I said. 'I really must apologize for what happened the other evening.'

212

'There's no need. In fact the truth is rather worse than you imagine.' Celia picked at a thread of cotton on her skirt.

'The truth. What is the truth?'

Celia stared at the floor. There followed an awkward silence. I crushed a grape in my mouth which promptly sent my taste capillaries into a spasm of over excitement. I ate four more in quick succession and offered the same to Celia. She shook her head vigorously. I spat the pips neatly into a cupped hand and then stockpiled them in a crevice of sheet.

'Look it really doesn't matter,' I said. 'Forget I asked. What you do in your private life is entirely your own business.'

Celia laughed a short laugh and then smothered it, passing a hand across her mouth.

'So you really think I'm a rich, aging floozy who gets her kicks by freelancing as a tart on a Saturday night, do you?'

'No, of course I don't.'

'Why not?' Celia turned on me, combative.

'It just doesn't seem in your character, somehow.'

'You think I haven't got the guts, is that it?'

'That wasn't what I meant.'

'Well, you'd be right, I haven't. I'm one of those who likes to get their thrills a little more vicariously than that.'

'I'm sorry. I'm not really following you too precisely.'

'You've never heard of social work, Joseph, charitable endeavours, do-gooding?'

'Yes, of course, but . . .'

'That's my game. That's what I get off on. I'm a secret voyeur of the low life. Only I pretend I'm doing it for their benefit. That way you can't lose. There's no risk.'

'You mean . . .'

'That's right. I work with prostitutes. About two years ago I joined a voluntary organization set up to help young girls in danger. The idea is you don't approach them as middle-class respectable professionals based in clinics and welfare centres, but as one of themselves, only a little further down the slippery road, aging whores, who know their way around the pub and street scene, who know the pitfalls and the pratfalls. I guess it was the play-acting bit that appealed to me most. I've always enjoyed dressing up. I even went to workshops on tarty behaviour. There was one time I had to go to a garden party in a see-through blouse and no bra. That was one of our assignments. The ridiculous thing was no one seemed to notice.'

'I noticed,' I said brightly, struggling to sit upright.

Celia looked disapproving, as if it was really rather indecent of me to have mentioned that I'd noticed, and promptly changed the subject.

'I believe you wanted to know about Janine?'

'Yes,' I said.

'What did you want to know?'

'Anything you can tell me.'

'She was one of my clients. One of my more spectacular failures.'

'Did you introduce her to Jack White?'

'Joseph, give me some credit for having a little common sense and human decency. What are you suggesting? That I was running an escort service for the more tawdry members of the Labour Party.'

'I'm sorry.'

'Oh, don't apologize. In some respects it's not so very far from the truth. I got Janine a cleaning job at the Gransbury in an attempt to wean her off some of her less desirable activities. I didn't realize that the Gransbury also happened to be Jack's local. The pub manager was quick to see that Janine was a wasted asset behind the scenes and soon had her up front taking her clothes off for the lunch-time punters. Jack spotted her and Bob's your uncle. He even brought her to the potluck supper. Apparently, he was quite smitten with her. Asked her to marry him according to Janine. Of course, as far as I was concerned it was a disastrous liaison.'

'Because it blew your cover.'

214

'Exactly. I didn't really want my secret life broadcast round the Party, any more than I wanted Janine to find out I was an undercover social worker. So I told her this sob story about how I had been forced into prostitution in order to raise money for a new experimental treatment for my desperately sick brother in America. How it was Charles who owned the house and everything in it and he was too mean to spend a penny of his own. And, of course, I told her how it was vital that not a word about my street life got out.'

'And she believed you?'

'I think so. I'm a very good liar, Joseph. My whole life has been built upon lies. I should be good at it by now.'

'And then Janine went and overdosed.'

'Yes. And you know what I felt when I first heard she was dead? Relief. Intense bloody relief. At last she was off my hands. And my secret was safe. So, now you know everything.'

'Not quite everything,' I said.

Celia looked slightly irritated, like a woman who did not welcome contradiction. I continued regardless.

'A week or so before she died she hijacked Alan Sayeed in his car in order to tell him that M15 had infiltrated the Labour Party.'

'The silly child. I warned her against doing that.'

'So you know something about this story?'

'She told me about it, yes.'

'But you didn't believe her, is that it?'

'She was full of wild stories, Joseph. You have to be careful how much credit you give to them. At different times during my knowledge of her she also claimed an affair with a royal prince and sex on a yacht with all four members of a famous rock band.'

'You think she was lying.'

'Let's just say you'd be well advised to treat her remarks with circumspection. As a matter of fact I think she might well have made the whole M15 thing up in order to please me. She knew I had Left-wing sympathies.'

'But in that case why should she also go to all the trouble of telling Alan the same thing?'

'Sometimes, Joseph, people make things up and then they come to believe them.'

'Perhaps. I'd still like to know more about how she came by her information.'

Celia looked coldly at me. Her mouth was just a little tight, a little prim.

'Those grapes haven't been washed, you know.'

'Neither have I. We should get on well together.'

'Just don't blame me if they give you the runs.'

'Janine's story. Where did she get it from?'

'OK. If you insist. She was working the West End in the early hours when this punter staggered out of some expensive restaurant. He stood on the pavement for a few minutes saying goodbye to his cronies, and then he began looking around for a taxi. It was only then he spotted Janine. He prowled up and down a few times in the customary manner but he didn't approach her. Janine thought she recognized him from photos in the papers but then again Janine was always recognizing famous people. After about five minutes some one else came along and picked her up. She was a very attractive girl. She never had to wait very long for a client. In fact, if she'd been a bit more together she could have been in a whole different league of call-girl. Anyway, about thirty minutes later she had finished with her client and discovered the first man was still hanging around. This time he did approach her and they went to a different hotel of the man's own choice. Quite a smart place, but afterwards she was confused about where it was and what it was called.'

'That doesn't exactly help the credibility of her story.'

'It was a very upsetting experience. She claimed it damaged her mind.'

'What did he do to her for God's sake?'

'You really want me to go into all the detail?'

'Yes.'

'OK. Firstly, he made her undress in this very ritualistic.

216

manner. Pretty much par for the course that. Then he tied a pillowcase over her head and made her kneel on the bed and tied her wrists to the bars. He had obviously selected the room with care in advance or used it before. It had all the necessary accoutrements. At this point she apparently said she would want extra for being tied up and having her head bagged and he agreed to pay her a fairly large sum. He then asked her lots of questions about her previous customer, along the lines of how many times had he done it, in what positions, had she enjoyed it, and so on. She made up lurid answers because it was obviously what he wanted to hear. She wasn't too clear about what followed because of course she couldn't see what was happening. But she felt this cold jelly-like substance being attached to her buttocks and breasts and then what must have been wires were taped to these areas. She began to get scared at this point and tried to free herself but without success. Then the shocks started. Quite slight ones to begin with, but gradually stronger and more violent until she was screaming and convulsing. She blacked out. She had no idea how long for. When she came round, he was gone. So, too, were all the wires and whatever else he had used. But she could still smell a petroleum type of smell on her skin where they had been attached. And he must have left in a hurry because he had forgotten his briefcase. Janine thought he might have panicked, perhaps fearing he had gone too far and caused her heart to stop.

'Anyway, she began going through the case hoping to find the money he owed her. It was full of papers but no cash. So she stuffed the papers in her own bag and cleared out. Later that night she read through some of them. Apparently they gave details concerning the organized disruption of the Labour Party. Docklands East was a targeted constituency.'

'And where are these papers now?'

'Exactly. That's the problem. She was never able to show them to me. She was living in a squat at the time. They disappeared, got stolen, or thrown away by

217

mistake, or perhaps they never existed. Who's to say.'

'What about the guy with the do-it-yourself torture kit?'

'Oh, later we went through some old newspapers together and she identified him as a senior Conservative MP. But what does that prove? Her word against his. And anyway she's dead. So there you are, the classic story of the minister and the whore. I hope it's of use to you, Joseph.'

'All the same, it's an odd sort of story to make up, isn't it? Not really of a piece with princes and rock bands.'

'I dare say something very similar really happened to her. Perhaps even the famous politician bit is true. When all is said and done it wouldn't be the first time a senior Conservative was mixed up with prostitutes. The only real question is, is it all true? And even if it is, what can we possibly do with it?'

'The girl did end up dead just a few weeks later.'

'Look Joseph, I've told you the story as you requested. Beyond that I really don't want to be involved. Pretty feeble and self-interested of me, I dare say. But I've never pretended to be anything else. And now I must go. I have a lunch appointment.'

Celia stood up as if about to leave. I continued to eat grapes at a quite disgusting rate.

'But Celia, you already are involved. You can't keep this thing quiet. Janine must have blabbed about your secret life to Jack before she died, despite her promise to you. And Jack's already spilt the beans to me. Of course, I won't say a word to anyone, I promise. But it's only a matter of time before Jack says something to someone else. It's going to get out.'

Celia turned and arched those finely-pencilled eyebrows and looked at me with what I felt was just a touch of condescension.

'Do you think I haven't realized that. However, it doesn't matter now Joseph, how many cats get out of the bag. You see I've finished. I've handed in my notice. And I'm leaving Charles. So none of it matters.'

'Leaving Charles! What are you going to do?'

'I shall go away somewhere. Sell the house. Give Charles enough to buy a flat. Go somewhere nobody knows me.'

Celia crossed the room, kissed me lightly on the forehead and then departed.

30

Celia was not my only visitor. It seemed solicitude for my well-being was widespread in the Party. I was just returning from the lavatory, the grapes having taken their predictable toll on my insides, when I discovered Jonathan and Julian standing in my room with freshly-shaven heads that had a luminous bluish tinge in the light from the street lamp. Jonathan was waving a black rubber-sheathed torch around as if conducting a son et lumière show with a truncheon, while his ideological twin was lying on my bed with his boots on reading back copies of the *Guardian* cartoon strip. I remember feeling rather amused by this elaborate show of toughness. Somehow I just couldn't really take them seriously as modern-day storm-troopers. A mistake on my part probably. The familiar is often more threatening than we give it credit for being.

'Can I help in some way?' I said.

'Just get your clothes on,' said the one with the torch. 'This isn't a dinner party.'

'I'm glad you pointed that out,' I said. 'I was going to suggest we opened another bottle.'

'Just get those fucking pants on will you,' said the cartoon addict. 'There's an emergency meeting of the Campaign Committee in session. They want to see you.'

'They're a trifle on the besmirched side. I've got a clean pair on the radiator in the kitchen. Do you mind if I just pop down and fetch them?'

'Those will do.'

'But my old granny always said, you never know when

220

you're going to end up on the mortician's slab and think how shaming it would be if . . .?'

'Just get them on.'

'As you wish, I can see it means a lot to you.'

I was not exactly manhandled, but it could fairly be said the two of them took a pretty directive role in my departure from the bedroom and subsequent arrival on the back seat of a car, a 1950's black Volvo that was waiting outside. The torch drove, while the cartoon fetishist got in the back with me.

'Don't try anything funny,' he growled as we snuggled in together. I smiled back and took hold of the leather strap that hung from the roof.

We drove towards the river, VIP style. All the lights seemed to change to green just as we approached them. There were a lot of kids standing around on the streets waiting for something to happen. The sky to the north had a dull reddish tinge. A fire had been started in a derelict warehouse down by the docks. Police cars began screaming and wailing and the kids began to run first in one direction then in another. The revolving lights of the emergency vehicles made them look like they were part of an old movie. As we approached the docks, several streets were closed and we had to make a detour, 'Fascist pigs,' snarled Julian out of the window as we left the fire behind us.

The Community Centre was an octagonal-shaped building reminiscent of a pagoda. At the hub of the building was an open space which could serve as a theatre or a concert hall or a meeting place or simply a thoroughfare. Radiating from it were a number of rooms like the cells of a honeycomb. I was ushered into the domed central section where Ted Clarke was seated behind what looked like upturned packing cases.

'Good evening. This is an unexpected pleasure,' I said, in what I intended to be a loud, confident voice, but which came out just a touch hysterical and overpitched.

'I think we can dispense with the pleasantries,' said Clarke.

'Oh, I never think a little politeness hurts anyone,' I said, 'Do you mind if I sit down? Only I'm supposed to be convalescing.' I helped myself to a plastic moulded chair.

'So you thought you'd be clever with us,' Clarke stood up and took a pace or two up and down a sort of catwalk affair. He was modelling a pair of grotesquely food-stained trousers, along with an off-white nylon shirt that neatly opened to reveal what was his jewel in the crown, a real gem among belly buttons, from which bodily crevice, of doubtful cleanliness, sprouted an unusually virile growth of black hair.

'I don't quite get what you're referring to,' I said.

'You arse'ole. You know very well what I'm referring to. The election addresses have arrived. One hundred thousand of them.'

'Oh good,' I said, 'I saw the proofs a couple of days ago. Looked pretty stylish, I thought.'

'Except you've used the wrong fucking printers.'

'Are you sure about that?' I said.

'A decision was taken by the Campaign Committee on the 2nd June of this year that all election material would be printed by the Cambridge Heath Press as an act of solidarity with the Left and in opposition to witchhunts.'

'Did we agree that? You know it must have completely slipped my mind, I've had so many things to think about lately. I'm afraid I simply went ahead and used the cheapest local printer, just as I always have done in the past?'

'I have the minutes of that meeting right here,' said Clarke.

He slapped a heavy wad of papers down on to the packing case.

'If you say we took such a decision, then I'm sure you're right. In fact, now you come to mention it I do dimly recall something along those lines being said. I just have to confess in the hurly-burly of the campaign, when one has so many little details to attend to, some things get forgotten. Human error.'

'Human error my arse. You're a lying little turd. You made your position quite clear at the original meeting. You lost the democratic vote and so you chose to act in the typical manner of the bourgeois saboteur.' Clarke strutted up and down, hitching his trousers as he went. His snub nose appeared to have receded almost entirely into the fleshiness of his face.

'What I'd like to know is who's orders were you acting under?' He turned on me with this last accusation with a snuffling bristling ferocity.

'Nobody's orders.'

'I don't believe you. I don't believe you've got the initiative to do this on your own say-so. You see, Pink, you've been seen in the company of the enemy. Don't try and deny it. Lorraine Mullins let you put your hand down her knickers did she, in return for one or two juicy little favours? Admit it Pink. You've been taking orders from the other side.'

'That's ridiculous,' I said, 'Mullins would like nothing better than Sayeed's campaign to be associated with Militant. And you know it.'

'Arse'ole,' said Clarke. 'But your little game hasn't worked. Your plot to betray the interests of the working classes has been aborted. The Bluebell leaflets have all been shredded.'

'I think that might have been a mistake,' I said.

'We are not prepared to be associated with an electoral address that has been produced in violation of the democratically reached decisions of our Party. A new order has been placed in the appropriate quarters.'

'But that election address has already cost us over fifty per cent of our total budget allocation. You won't have enough money to produce another. And anyway there isn't enough time to get them printed.'

'Perhaps you should have thought of that before,' said Clarke, squaring his papers. 'There just remains the question of disciplinary proceedings against yourself.'

'What are you proposing? A smacked bottom.'

'An emergency session of the Campaign Committee

has decided unanimously that you should be expelled from all further meetings.'

'Fine by me. But I'm still the agent of this party. I was appointed agent by the NEC and only the NEC can take that away from me. As agent I am still in charge of the day-to-day administration of this election campaign. And one other thing. When this whole business is finished with I shall be calling for a full independent inquiry. I think then it will become pretty obvious who the real wreckers are. And now, if you don't very much mind, I could do with some shut eye. I am still under doctors' orders. I'll be seeing you, comrades.'

I walked out. That was something I'd always wanted to do to Clarke. I was pleased with myself. I was making progress, even if the election was going down the drain fast.

31

The following morning, on my way down to breakfast, I noticed that something was different, had been different since my return from the hospital, but it was only now that the precise nature of the difference clicked. The Baby Burco had gone. So, too, had the stacks of books, the wellington boots and the radiogram. The jumble mafia must have collected during my absence. The hallway now had a desolate, forsaken air, strewn with last year's dead leaves and trails of grey anonymous matter, the detritus of a civilization.

Feeling faintly depressed, I went to the fridge for my diary. I keep it in the fridge, not in order to retard fungal growth, but so that I don't forget to consult it in the mornings. I was busily engaged turning its sticky pages when there came a sound of broken glass and shouting from the road. I presumed it was the milkman playing his usual trick of smashing the odd crate against the front step, so I ignored it. However, further crashings followed in quick succession, suggesting either a large number of crates were being hurled, or some calamity of altogether more serious proportions was taking place. Perhaps the long awaited Revolution had finally broken out and anarchy was loose on the streets. I struggled to my feet, lurched back along the corridor and stood blinking for several seconds in the harsh morning light before fully appreciating the enormity of what was taking place.

A concertina of cars, bumper crunched against bumper, stretched back from the roundabout to the zebra crossing. No-one appeared to be seriously hurt but handkerchiefs were pressed to foreheads, many were tearful, and there was a good deal of general recrimination going on. In particular, there was a lot of angry gesticulating towards the façade of the Labour Party Administrative Headquarters, which was not entirely explicable simply in terms of the British public's mass-media induced socialist phobia.

Charles had unveiled his masterpiece. And it was indeed a rather startling sight. No routine renovation job this. It was a full-blown mural. Enthroned in the centre was a naked woman with a crown of hawthorns on her head and flaccid heavily-veined breasts, one of which hung down a lot further than the other. What I found rather distasteful, however, was not the breasts in themselves, but the fact that the facial features that went with them were quite clearly Celia's. She was seated astride a giant phallus covered in warts and other unpleasant looking cankers and surrounded by a gallery of grotesque creatures crawling out of eggshells, licking anuses, vomiting, defecating, and generally excreting noxious substances. It wasn't difficult to recognize Ronnie Mullins, the late Melrose and several other personalities from the local Party. Alan Sayeed, for instance, had been depicted with considerable prescience in the manner of St Sebastian with an arrow through his heart.

'What do you think?'

'It was only then I noticed Charles lounging by a downpipe, staring at me with a look of immense self-satisfaction.

'It certainly seems to be causing quite a sensation,' I said. 'The traffic has come to a complete standstill.'

'There is no point in tame art. I wanted to provoke a reaction. It was my intention to confront society with an image of its own depravity.'

'Well you've surely done that all right. But I'm not too sure the Maintenance Committee are going to be exactly over the moon. Not to mention the Road Safety Officers and the Obscene Publications Squad and the Campaign for Moral Rearmament.'

'Do you think then that artistic vision should be intimidated by philistines and petty bureaucrats?' Charles towered over me in a somewhat menacing manner.

Not wishing to get involved in this particular line of debate, I asked whether the woman with the long hair on the far right-hand side, grappling with an octopus-like creature that appeared to have a tentacle inserted into her every available orifice, was Lorraine.

Charles relaxed back on to his heels and gave me his condescending poor fool look. 'What I have created here has an emblematic significance that goes far beyond purely temporal associations. I'm not sure how well versed you are in our classical culture, Joseph, but there is a reference to Laocoon in the section you mention which you might have picked up on had you read more widely. What is it that you are finding so amusing?'

'Sorry. Didn't mean to laugh. Only I've just noticed Ted Clarke.' Clarke had been crudely caricatured as a repulsive slug-like creature biting the heads off babies and spewing out the bones. Charles had done a remarkably good job in capturing his truculent bullying expression.

'Laughter is not an altogether inappropriate response to a work of this nature,' said Charles ponderously.

'Dare I ask where I am?' I said, as the police sirens grew nearer.

'You are that tiny figure in the background being stoned by the irate mob,' said Charles with relish. 'If you had permitted me to take your photograph, as I requested, I might have been able to do greater justice to the peculiarities of your physique. As it was I just had to make do with inspired guesswork.' Charles' inspiration was not exactly of the flattering kind. My skin had more wrinkles than Labour's Social Compact with the Unions. But this wasn't the moment for personal vanity. The irate mob in the street looked like they might start stoning the both of us shortly. I decided to get the hell out of it and leave Charles to do the talking.

The jumble sale was held in St Luke's Church Hall, a great barn of a building with a vaulted wood and iron roof beneath which the birds of the air sometimes took shelter in biblical fashion and expressed their appreciation by begatting on each other and shatting on the congregation below. The walls were a bare grey brick and the windows were placed high enough to prevent any little Sunday school child's thoughts from straying to the mortal world.

The sale doors were due to be thrown open at eleven, but from about ten onwards the queue began to snake around the gravestones. Most of the punters were young and middle class and looking for something outrageously ill-fitting for that evening's social extravaganza, but there was also a leavening of the genuine poor.

I had arrived just in time for Meryll's pre-sale briefing. She was wearing her red beret with the combat anorak, the khaki drill trousers and the black fire-escape earrings.

'Rule number one, no-one is to leave their post under any circumstances at any point whatsoever unless they have first spoken to me and I have organized a relief stallholder. Rule number two, remember that it is during the first half-hour of the big crush that theft is most likely to occur. Keep your eyes open. Anyone with a large carrier bag is automatically suspect. Rule number three, there will be no reduction of prices until I give the signal. Let's not forget we're here to make money for the Walthamstow Eleven. Too often in the past we've just given things away to those who can well afford to pay the market price. And rule number four, all takings should be kept in a secure place, well away from the stallholders' own money to avoid the possibility of confusion. Any questions? No. Good. Be ready to take up your positions in exactly seven minutes.'

I had been allocated the second-hand shoe stall. Second-hand shoes were my market niche. They didn't require much in the way of display, so I took the opportunity of wandering over to Pam, who was on women's clothing. She was looking even more red-eyed and snuffly than usual.

'How are you?' I said, in a casual sort of way so as not to seem too prying or overconcerned. I couldn't just ignore her. She was after all carrying my child, even though she didn't know it.

'Oh dear, I'm OK, I suppose,' said Pam in a dejected tone that suggested she was anything but.

'Morning sickness?' I whispered. I didn't want anyone else to hear. Rumours just flew around this Party.

Pam shook her head.

'Back ache, blood pressure, indigestion.'

'No, I'm fine, really. It's just . . .'

'Just what?'

'I'm not so sure I can go through with it.'

'You mean the business of being a single parent. It's certainly a tough proposition. Not something to be gone into lightly.'

'You think I haven't thought about that,' snapped Pam. 'You think I'm being irresponsible.'

'No,' I said. 'I wasn't for a moment suggesting that.'

'Anyway, I've got Meryll.'

'Sorry, I was forgetting about Meryll.'

Pam screwed her face up. She didn't look too happy about the idea of Meryll herself. In fact, she had the look of someone who any minute might start sobbing uncontrollably.

'I'm just so frightened it will turn out a boy.' It was as if she had to squeeze the words out of her, as if they caused her an awful wrench.

'Would that be so bad?' I said. 'Boys need mothering, too.'

Pam leant closer to me. She had a skirt in her hands, a black leather skirt, the hem of which she was fingering nervously, while seemingly quite unaware of what she was holding. She reminded me of a woman I had once watched at the edge of a swimming pool, during an adult learners session. There was the same look of terror.

'Meryll insists I must have an amnio to find out the sex beforehand. If it is a boy she wants me to have an abortion. I'm not sure I can go through with that.'

I felt slightly stunned, slightly sickened. It was a little like the feeling I had when reading about the atrocities committed on Jews during the Second World War. Selecting the sex of one's child. Was it simply a matter of taking control of one's own life. Or was there something rather more sinister behind it. A desire to purify the world by eradicating undesirables.

'Talk about something else, quickly,' muttered Pam. Meryll was descending on us from her position at the rostrum.

'How much is the skirt?' I asked.

Pam looked at me, uncomprehending.

'The skirt in your hand there. The black leather one. How much is it. A niece of mine is looking for one just like it. She's quite slim. I think it would fit. How much?'

'Thirty pounds,' said Meryll, taking charge.

'Thirty pounds? Don't be ridiculous. This is a jumble sale not a fashion house.'

'It's a quality item,' said Meryll. 'You can take it or leave it.'

'But it wouldn't cost that much new,' I said.

'Thirty pounds,' repeated Meryll. 'That's the market price.'

'And since when have we been so keen on market prices in this Party?' I said. 'I thought we were supposed to respond to human need.'

'And what is your human need for a black leather skirt?' said Meryll.

'I just explained it was a gift for my niece. She's an undergraduate at Warwick University. She's finding it difficult to make ends meet.'

'Thirty,' repeated Meryll with a sneer.

This little bit of haggling was beginning to attract the

attention of other stallholders. And I hardly wanted the whole world to know I was buying up Celia's cast-offs. For I was quite sure that was who it came from. I had recognized it instantly. The skirt was, after all, imprinted upon my psyche.

'OK, thirty, but I can only give you ten now. You'll have to wait for the rest.'

Meryll accepted on the condition I also provided her with a written IOU. I put the skirt in my Co-op carrier, in which I also had my other bits and pieces, and slunk back to second-hand shoes. Pam looked at me as if I were mad. Meryll simply looked smug.

Trade was relatively brisk. I sold a handsome pair of size nine brogues made in Street, Somerset, collector's items, to myself, and two pairs of Mothercare sandals, to the general public, in the first five minutes. Wellington boots were a bit slow, but then they tended to come in one offs which meant doing a mix and match job which isn't to everyone's liking. Anyway, the real bargains had all gone by the time Jack White arrived. Which might have explained why he wasn't looking in too good a mood. He could certainly have done with a new overcoat. He elbowed his way straight across to where I was serving.

'What the hell do you think you're playing at, Joseph?'

'Shops,' I said, tersely. We hadn't spoken since the Prince of Wales debacle and I wasn't much in the mood for re-opening lines of communication.

'I can see that for myself. But I was meaning this business of painting rude pictures over the front of the Committee Rooms. Dear God, haven't we got enough credibility problems without trying to impress the general public we're nothing but a bunch of pathological perverts.'

'You'll have to talk to Charles Ronayne about that. It's not my handiwork.'

'I already have. So have the police. The whole thing's being whitewashed.'

'I shouldn't think Charles is too happy about that. He's been at it night and day for weeks on end.'

'Charles has lost his bloody marbles. They've carted him off to the loonie bin. What I want to know, Joseph, is why you just sat on your frigging fanny and let it happen?'

'I had other things on my mind. Look, what do you want from me? My resignation? If so, you've got it.'

'Hold on. Hold on. Not so hasty,' Jack backed off with his hands in the air. 'Always was your trouble, laddie. Too volatile. Too ready to take offence. Look, I've done my best to smooth things over with the authorities. The whole thing is being treated as the work of a psychopath. They don't even know he was a Party member. Not yet. But this campaign is in danger of turning into a fiasco. Even without this latest little act of sabotage. We've got to stop the rot, Joseph. Our livelihoods depend on it, laddie. And time is running out.'

Jack put his arm around my shoulder and gave me a matey squeeze. 'Joseph, you're not sulking are you about the Celia business?'

I said nothing.

'I did it for your own good, laddie. You must know that. It's high time you stopped looking at women through these rose-tinted spectacles of yours.'

I still said nothing.

'Look Joseph, I have concocted a little scheme that could dramatically alter the entire political picture. But I shall need your help to put it into operation. I'm not asking you to do it for me, an old man no longer in the best of health. But for the Party, Joseph. Think of the Party.'

'What scheme?' I said.

'Not here. Too many ears. Let's take a walk.'

32

'Where are we going?' I asked.

Jack was bent low into the wind, clutching his trilby to his head.

'It's three in the frigging afternoon. Where the hell can a man go at this godforsaken time of day? Pubs are all closed. What a piss hole of an area you live in, Joseph. Well, don't just stand there. It's your neck of the woods. Suggest something. Somewhere we can get our heads together.'

'There's a launderette down the road. It's open twenty-four hours a day.'

'A launderette. Is this what we've come to. Squalid meetings in the public wash house. You'll be suggesting park benches next.'

'It's got a vending machine.'

Jack raised his eyes to the heavens. 'Dear God, the launderette be it then. And may my dear mother in heaven not witness what her wretched son has come to.'

The Launderama, as it was called, was empty apart from a rather attractive Oriental woman with a young child and a mountain of washing in a variety of brightly-coloured plastic bags. Jack gave her a look up and down and tipped his hat in her direction. She smiled shyly and hastily addressed her child in some foreign tongue. I got us two cups of coffee and we went and sat in the window where there was a remarkably fine collection of dead flies.

'You know, Joseph,' said Jack reflectively, 'there's something to be said for women of the Third World.

They still appreciate the old male virtues of lust and gallantry. In fact I'm seriously thinking of taking my summer vacation in Bangkok this year. Top-class tarts at rock-bottom prices. Of course, they're born and bred to it. It's a way of life. I'll tell you what's wrong with most of the whores in this country, Joseph. They're all fucked up. Only the very worst sort of girl is attracted into the business. It's no longer taken seriously as a profession.'

The small child had tottered over to us and Jack took the opportunity of patting its head and chucking it under the chin and ogling its mother. The mother came and dragged it away and made apologetic gestures. Jack protested that he loved children.

'Look Jack, I deserted my post at the second-hand shoe stall to be here and Meryll is not going to look kindly on that. She shoots deserters on sight. I take it you want to talk to me about something other than your summer holiday plans.'

'Hold your horses, laddie. Hold your horses. As my old mother used to say. Everything comes to him who waits.'

Jack began rooting in his tatty old leather briefcase. Eventually he produced a large brown envelope which he handed to me with a look of overweening pride.

'This, Joseph, is our salvation.'

I flicked through the contents. It didn't take long for me to ascertain that what Jack had got hold of was a copy of the same Stentor papers that I had originally been given by Lorraine and which had been taken from me by the Chingford police.

'So the dirt has come full circle.' I said.

'What?' said Jack.

'King Lear,' I said.

'Bugger King Lear. This is as nice a little can of worms as you'll pick up anywhere outside the Co-op,' Jack rubbed his hands gleefully together.

'Where did you get it from?'

'What does it matter where I got it from. I've told you before, Joseph, we're not just a bunch of pretty faces in Central Office. We do our homework. But the beauty of

234

this little file of dirt is we can use it to take out Mullins.'

'And what do you expect that to achieve?'

'I seem to be having to spell things out for you today, Joseph, in words of rather less than one syllable. We get rid of Mullins and we leave the field wide open for Sayeed. OK, you might not like it. I'm not saying I like it. But let's face realities. Pakistanis have taken over our restaurants and our corner shops so why not the Houses of Parliament. And whatever our personal prejudices might be. Sayeed is running on the Labour ticket.'

'You seem to be forgetting it's a three-cornered race. You eliminate Mullins and you will be transferring the Mullins' vote to Sayeed's main rival, which is the Tory. The people voting for Mullins would never vote for Sayeed, even if the only alternative was Attila the Hun.'

'And what makes you so sure about that, laddie?'

'The thousand and one doors I've knocked on these past few weeks and the kind of reception I've been getting. The only thing that is keeping Sayeed still in there with a fighting chance is the fact that Mullins is also running, thereby splitting the anti-Sayeed vote. Ironic isn't it? But you start trying to ignore the ironies in politics and you're in trouble.'

Jack looked like a kid whose icecream has just fallen splat on the pavement. He couldn't quite believe this was happening to him.

'Dear God, in that case what was the point in sending all this filth to me?'

'That rather brings us back to my earlier question. Who sent it?'

'I don't know who sent it. It came through the post.' Jack's voice was sulky and embarrassed.

'Has no-one ever told you, Jack, you shouldn't believe that every bit of junk mail that flops through your letter-box has been sent for the good of your health.'

Jack ran his fingers back through his hair and down his face and back through his hair some more. He looked hard across at me. It was the expression of a man who, faced with adjusting his view of the world, opts instead for poking someone else's eye out. 'And why should I believe you, eh? How do I know you're not just giving me this line because of a little emotional attachment you might have for the Mullins camp. There have been rumours flying about concerning you getting your leg over the lovely Lorraine. Nice looking woman of course. I had a crack years ago. In the back of her car. Parked in a side street at two in the bloody morning. Shall never forget it. Almost gave me a hernia. But things were different then. Ronnie was one of us. Not quite the same as sniffing round the knickers of the opposition bang in the middle of the election campaign. To my mind that stinks of treachery, Joseph. Treachery. I didn't want to believe it. Not of you. We've been around together a long time. But there comes a point when all the evidence seems to stack up on the wrong side.'

Jack assumed his sad and world-weary expression. The expression of a man who liked to think well of people but was always finding himself disappointed.

I ignored his Lorraine story. 'Did you notice the writing on the envelope?' I said.

'Joseph, don't tell me you're a graphologist. I don't want to know.'

'It's Clarke's.'

'Fascinating.'

'Clarke sent you this.'

'So Clarke sent me the stuff. So what?'

'You knew it came from him all along, didn't you? I expect it was Clarke who persuaded you it would be such a great idea to use it to eliminate Mullins. For someone who's been in this game as long as you have Jack you can still be remarkably naive.'

'This is becoming boring, Joseph. And you seem to be forgetting I'm your boss. All I want to know is, are you going to put the finger on Mullins for me or are you not? Because if the answer is no then give me that envelope back and you're fired.'

'The answer is no. But if you don't mind I'll hang on to these for a bit. Because you see I know something about all this that you don't. Which is how Clarke got hold of these letters in the first place. And just why it suits Clarke to hand victory to the Tories on a plate. And right now I'd like to go and talk that one over with him.'

'Suit your frigging self,' said Jack, waving his hand dismissively towards me. His attention had already become distracted by the Oriental woman. It seemed one of the washing machines wasn't draining properly.

'Probably a sock in the pump,' said Jack, plunging his hand in. 'Or a giant-sized tampon.'

The woman smiled sweetly at him. She obviously didn't understand a word of English.

33

Clarke lived down a quiet cul-de-sac on the leafy side of the borough. He had a flat in a small private block, the sort of place where you didn't hang your washing out on a Sunday. It had been built in the Thirties with rounded corners, metal-framed windows and long iron balustrades, so it had something of the style of a transatlantic liner. I explained to the hall porter, who wore a serge navy-blue uniform and a peaked cap with gold braid, who it was I wanted.

'And is Mr Clarke expecting you, Sir?' he asked in a voice both obsequious and condescending.

'Not exactly,' I said.

'Mr Clarke does not welcome casual callers. He is a very busy man.'

'We're old friends.'

'With all due respect, Sir, that's what they all say.'

'So call him up if you don't believe me.'

'And what name shall I give?'

'Julian.'

'Julian who?'

'Just Julian.'

The hall porter contacted Clarke on the internal telephone. 'There's a gentleman here wishes to see you. Name of Julian. Shall I . . . Very good, Sir.' He turned back to me. 'If you'll go straight up.'

I took the lift. It was one of the old-fashioned wire and pulley sort with meshing iron gates. It struck me how odd it was that during all the time Clarke and I had been in the same Party together this was only my second visit to his home. The previous occasion was some years back when I had called to collect his contribution to the monthly newsletter that he had failed to deliver on schedule. He had kept me waiting then, in the hallway. Of course, the oddity of his living quarters was not exactly unknown in the Party and was often commented on. He always said that it was necessary for him to live somewhere with good security because he had made a lot of enemies during his union work. It was generally accepted that he was the sort of man who liked to keep his private life very much to himself. Indeed, it was generally presumed he didn't have one.

The lift clanked and ground to a halt. I crossed the small landing and knocked on the door to Number 17, a good long hard knock, the sort of knock that meant business. Clarke opened the door about six inches and when he saw who it was wedged his stomach in the gap. He was unshaven and smelt sweaty as if he had just got out of a rather fetid bed.

'Where's Julian?'

'Julian is unfortunately feeling indisposed so I've come in his place.'

'What do you want?'

'I'd like a word.'

'I don't talk to arse'oles.'

'I was thinking we might try it mouth to mouth, just for a change.'

He went to crash the door in my face, but I had already had the prescience to put my foot over the threshold and one of the most remarkable features of shoes made in Street, Somerset is their resilience. The door rebounded off my forward toecap knocking Clarke off balance. He fell against the far wall, blinking rapidly and raising his forearm like a man who feared he was about to be hit. What most struck me about him though was the slippers he was wearing. A pair of woolly-lined moccasins. Somehow the absurdity of Clarke, the bête noire of the bourgoisie, padding around his flat in a pair of furry moccasins made me realize I need no longer take him seriously.

'You cunt,' he spluttered. 'You fucking cunt.'

'Shall we go through to the living room,' I suggested. 'We

might as well make ourselves comfortable if we're going to have a frank exchange of views.'

I led the way. The living room was furnished with a chunky three-piece suite, covered in cream velvet with gold piping and gold tassles round the base. It made me think of a family of circus elephants such was the disproportion between their huge size and their over-fussy style. The curtains, in dark maroon velvet, were drawn. A gas fire was lit. There was a large roll-top mahogany desk where it appeared Clarke had been working when I knocked on the door. There was an impressive number of dark mahogany bookshelves with serious looking books on. The wallpaper was Regency stripe. But what most amused me were the petite wall lights. The bulbs were shaped like candles and the shades were in fluted silk with the same gold tassles as were on the suite.

'Cosy place you've got yourself here,' I said, sinking back into one of the armchairs and crossing my legs.

'What do you want, you turd? I'm going out. And I have an article to finish first.' Clarke remained standing, fidgeting against the edge of the desk with his fat little sausage-like fingers, breathing heavily.

'People's homes are so revealing of their true natures, don't you agree? They say so much about them that one would never necessarily guess from just listening to their conversation or observing their behaviour in public meetings. Take this place of yours, for instance. Clearly it reveals the serious intellectual who feels safe with books and ideas and working papers and agendas. The surprise is the domesticity, the obvious love of comfort. To me that suggests the intellectual very much set in his ways, rather self-cosseting, spoilt, ill-adapted to change.'

'Shut up, you shitty little arse'ole. Just shut up will you. Say what you came for and get out. Or I shall . . .'

Clarke was shaking with rage. His face was grey and sweaty. He seemed to be having even more trouble than usual keeping his shirt tucked into his trousers.

'You'll what? Throw me out? I hardly think so. But to come to the point of my visit, I'd like to know more about your special relationship with our security forces.'

Clarke backed away clutching at his chest. 'You're off your fucking head, Pink. Security forces. What are you on about?'

'I think you know very well what I'm on about. Actually, I must congratulate you on an excellent job. No-one could help but admire your professionalism. And what a perfect choice Alan was as the candidate. You knew the electorate would hate him almost as much as the delegates loved him. But even so you left nothing to chance. Having nurtured him into the limelight, no opportunity was then lost for destroying his campaign. All in the cause of ideological purity, of course. That was the beauty of it. The rent amnesty business was a bit tricky though, wasn't it? Alan might have aborted on that one before he had been properly exploited for maximum damage potential. But you saw the danger and neatly avoided it. Yes, your bosses must be very pleased with your work. But then they don't know yet about your one major blunder.'

Clarke was busily edging his way along the wall towards the door. He was still pulling at his shoulder and chest like someone trying to remove a hair shirt or possibly locate a revolver in its shoulder holster. At the mention of the word blunder he paused. He diverted towards the sofa.

'What are you talking about?'

'A small mistake. No doubt your bosses are charitable men. They will understand. They will overlook a minor error of this nature. In the context of your long and devoted service.'

Clarke grabbed a cushion and lunged at me. But he was a slow heavy man and I had plenty of time to avoid his blow. He sank on to his knees. I got up and positioned myself with my back to the mantelpiece, legs astride, hands clasped behind my back, the Victorian patriarch. This was, after all, my big speech. It was important to get the delivery right.

'Over-confidence was your fatal flaw. You didn't have to give the Stentor papers to Jack White. You could have approached Mullins directly yourself or through one of your henchmen. But you couldn't resist such a golden opportunity for playing games. The idea of getting Jack to do your dirty work, knowing that he would accept for the wrong reasons and that his actions would backfire on him horribly, now that would appeal to your love of manipulation, your deus ex machina complex. But what, of course, you didn't calculate on was that those papers came from me in the first place. So I knew their provenance.'

Clarke slowly revolved his cumbersome body until he was sitting on the floor. He turned the pale palms of his hands uppermost like a man professing his innocence. His breathing was most odd. It was coming in short panting gasps.

'Don't take it too much to heart,' I said. 'You can always blame the whole muddle on one of your elders and betters. The senior Conservative, for instance, who left confidential papers on the Labour Party subversion plan in the hands of a prostitute. Now that was careless. Particularly as she was later to pass that same information on to Alan himself. I expect you've noticed how he has not been quite so compliant when it comes to following your strategy these last few weeks. Hardly surprising really, is it?'

Clarke said nothing. His head had lolled back and over to one side and his breathing was painful to listen to. It was when I got to this point I realized I hadn't thought out the end of this scenario at all clearly. I had gone to Clarke's with the intention of saying my bit, of relieving my feelings, of establishing my version of the truth. Well, I'd done all that. And the world was still the same place. Clarke might have rolled over but he was not exactly co-operating. And I could hardly involve the police. They were unlikely to admit to having passed the Stentor papers to MI5. And Clarke himself had done nothing illegal by passing them on to Jack White. As for

242

Janine, her death was a closed file. There was no proof for any of her accusations. I was just thinking there was very little left for me to do but slope off home, tail between my legs, when Clarke distracted me by collapsing into the horizontal. It was only then it occurred to me he might be having a heart attack or an epileptic fit or something.

I bent over him and loosened his shirt buttons, those that hadn't popped open already. My knowledge of first aid was limited to a Boy Scout badge I'd obtained at the age of twelve which had to do with tying neckerchiefs around severed arteries and sucking out snake bites. I vaguely considered the kiss of life and rejected it again. Instead I tried gently slapping his cheeks and getting him to say something. But he just groaned.

I reached for the telephone and dialled Docklands General. The switchboard told me I should contact the patient's GP. I told them I didn't know his GP from Adam. I was advised to make a search for his medical card. I telephoned down to the hall porter who gave me the name of a local practice. I dialled this number and was put through to an emergency answering service. Eventually I was told that a doctor would call me back as soon as he was free.

I went back to Clarke. He was muttering something incoherent. At first I thought it was to do with Lenin, but it might equally have been about a need for clean linen, a common doctor-related phobia so it seems. I went and fetched a glass of drinking water instead. He hadn't asked for it but it seemed like an appropriate gesture.

I was just returning with the water when the phone went. It was the doctor who had been contacted by the medical answering service. He was clearly telephoning from a pub, because in the background I could hear a noise of clinking glasses and laughter. I explained the situation.

'Doesn't sound too serious to me,' said the doctor. 'Put him to bed with a couple of aspirin. I expect things will have settled down by morning.'

'But doctor, he's collapsed on the floor, he's a terrible colour and he can't seem to breathe properly.'

'You sometimes get these side effects. Nothing to worry about.'

'Doctor, I don't want to sound melodramatic about this but I really think he's dying.'

'What did you say his name was again.'

'Clarke. Ted Clarke.'

'Not one of mine. Can't help I'm afraid. Against professional etiquette to interfere with the patients of another practice without a written letter of authorization from his usual GP.'

'But what if he hasn't got a usual GP? He's never had a day's illness in his life, so far as I'm aware.'

'He'd better approach his local Family Practitioner Committee for details of practices with vacancies. My list's full I'm afraid. Cheers.' And he put the phone down on me.

I rang the hospital a second time and explained that it was an emergency and couldn't they send an ambulance. I was told that the ambulance service was under great pressure and it would be nearly an hour before one would become available. They suggested that if I was really concerned it might be best to bring him straight in to casualty by car.

So I telephoned down to the hall porter and asked him if he could give me a hand. He didn't sound too keen at first and when he did eventually arrive he'd changed out of his uniform into a boiler suit and a large pair of industrial rubber gloves.

'Can't be too careful these days, can you? What with all this Aids about,' he said, presumably by way of an explanation for his bizarre appearance.

'Aids! This is a heart attack,' I said. 'And I don't think heart attacks are catching.'

'There's a lot more got it than this Government is letting on about,' said the hall porter, knowingly.

This was a subject area I felt we hadn't really got the time to get into.

'If you could just get under that arm, I'll lift him from this side and then between us perhaps we can get him on to the landing and into the lift,' I said.

So we dragged Clarke out of the flat and on to the landing. Getting him into the lift was another matter entirely. It needed the two of us to manoeuvre him and if you didn't hold the mesh doors open they automatically clanged shut. The net result was Clarke's legs got crushed a couple of times. Also the lift was so small there wasn't room to lay him down. We had to prop him up against the wooden panelling as if he were in a vertical coffin. When we got to ground level an elderly woman with two Sealyham dogs was waiting to get in. Clarke almost fell out into her arms. We only just managed to steady him in time. She complained that she'd been waiting for the lift to arrive for a full ten minutes and it really was too bad the way people used it for all kinds of purposes other than the one it was originally intended for. Meanwhile, one of the Sealyhams cocked its leg against Clarke's turn-up. We continued to slide and bump him until we got him into the lobby. I kept thinking he must have died when he'd give this odd little moan and twitch. Not that twitches were exactly a reliable indicator where life was concerned. Weren't chickens notorious for running around farmyards after their heads had been severed from their bodies?

'Have you got a vehicle handy?' I asked the porter. I had parked the van a couple of blocks away, more through force of habit than any real fear that Clarke might report me to the General Purposes Committee.

'He's not going in my car,' said the porter, putting his foot down, and dropping Clarke's foot simultaneously. 'I've only just had the interior upholstery redone in real sheepskin.'

So I ran and fetched the van.

'Back or front?' asked the porter.

'It had better be the back. I don't think he'll be safe in the front. He'll flop around too much.'

I undid the string that tied the rear doors together.

And using the one two three heave ho technique we got him inside.

The porter declined to accompany me to the hospital, so I drove him by myself. All went well until accelerating away from red traffic lights a little too fast, Clarke's body slid into the rear doors and the string gave way. He was halfway out before I knew what was happening. I jammed the brakes on, ran round the back and hauled him in again. The driver behind gave me a curious look and I saw him noting down the van's registration number. But there was no time for explanations.

When I finally got Clarke to the accident service, two stretcher orderlies and a doctor took over. I felt a wave of immense relief and gratitude that at last he was off my hands.

'Is he still alive?' I asked.

'He doesn't look in too good a shape,' said one of the orderlies. I watched them wheel him into a resuscitation unit.

'Are you the next of kin?' asked a kindly-faced nurse.

'No,' I said. 'No . . . I just happened to be there.'

There was nothing left for me to do. I walked back out of the hospital into the cool of the late afternoon. An avenue of plane trees with their scabrous patches and peeling barks stretched from the accident unit to the main gateway. They made me think of a row of lepers begging alms. Not for the first time just lately I reflected on what an unpredictable and arbitary business staying alive was.

34

After humping Clarke halfway across London I was feeling pretty exhausted. However, there was one other little matter I was anxious to clear up before finally calling it a day. It was gone nine by the time I pulled into the Mullins' drive but lights were blazing in every window and anyway Lorraine had never struck me as one of life's early retirers. I tugged on the bell rope. Within seconds the door was flung open and Lorraine was standing there, arms wide, big smile like she was expecting a rampant lover to leap into her embrace.

When she realized it was me her jaw sagged a millimetre or so but she recovered well.

'Joseph. This is a surprise. Come in. You can give me your advice.'

She was wearing a miniscule black bikini, sun hat, enormous dark shades and carrying a tall glass of some frothy green cocktail. I had the distinct sensation of having stepped into a Californian swimming pool scene, except there was no pool in evidence and the temperature outside was decidedly on the chilly side. I made a series of mild protestations about having only come by to drop something off. But Lorraine would hear none of it. It was like we were the oldest of friends between whom there had never been a cross word. She grabbed hold of my arm and began dragging me towards the staircase.

'I really would like a second opinion,' she drawled out of the corner of her mouth, while sucking the evil-looking green substance up a fancy glass straw. 'You don't mind do you? Only you're one of the few men in this world, Joseph, whose opinion I really value.'

She led the way up the stairs. I followed, my head about on a level with her arse. I observed the creases at the tops of her thighs alternate direction like a pair of out of phase windscreen wipers. The effect was hypnotic.

Lorraine's bedroom was an extravaganza of pink satin furnishings, with furry white rugs and a plentiful supply of mirrors. But the dominant impression, overlaying even the obvious nostalgia for Fifties Hollywood, was of entering the hideaway of a clothes kleptomaniac who wasn't too strong on the tidiness front. They were everywhere. Piled high on the bed; in heaps on the floor; hanging out of wardrobes. There was even a sun-dress swinging from a lampshade which created a rather sinister shadow on the opposite wall.

'Well, what do you think?' said Lorraine, peering at herself in the cheval glass, drawing in her stomach muscles and smoothing the flesh over her hip bones with her heavily-jewelled hands, like she was kneading dough.

'Very nice,' I said. I threw the letters on the cluttered dressing table.

'James says I'm too old for a bikini. Says they look best on skinny girls of sixteen. But I saw it in the window of Eloise and just fell in love with it. Ridiculous price. Works out at about twenty pounds per square inch. Jamie says you can buy real estate cheaper than that. But you're paying for the design, aren't you?'

'I've brought your letters back,' I said, pointing to them.

Lorraine swung around towards me, picked up another swimming costume from the end of the bed and held it up in front of her. 'Jamie insisted on me having this backless one-piece thing with slits down the front. He said it was more sophisticated. But I'm not sure it's really me. Shall I slip it on for you. You can tell me what you think. Close your eyes.'

'I said I've brought you your letters back.'

'What letters?' said Lorraine with an affectation of guilelessness that even I was getting a little too long in the tooth to be taken in by.

'The letters between Stentor and your husband.'

Lorraine pouted. 'Oh those. You needn't have bothered.'

'Needn't have bothered.' I couldn't help but give vent to a mild explosion of rage. 'What about the threatening telephone calls. The doing my flat over. The arranging to have me beaten up. Have you forgotten about all that?'

Lorraine put an arm around my neck, nuzzling against me.

'Oh Joseph, I felt really bad about that. They didn't hurt you too much, did they? I was going to visit you in hospital only Jamie thought it wasn't too bright an idea. But you really were silly to hold out on him like that you know. That really wasn't very clever of you. James was convinced you were either planning to destroy Ronnie politically or blackmail him or both. He's not the kind of man you want to play those kinds of games with.'

'I wasn't playing any games. I genuinely didn't have the sodding things.'

'And now they just happen to have fallen back into your lap again.'

'As a matter of fact, yes.'

'Oh Joseph, you don't really expect me to believe that, do you?'

'I don't see why not. But what I don't understand is why two weeks ago it was so desperately important for you to have them and now apparently no-one gives a piss.'

'You mean you haven't heard?' Lorraine withdrew her fingers from my nape and took a step or two backwards. 'No, I suppose you wouldn't have. It was only being announced this afternoon. Ronnie's standing down. He's quitting politics altogether. So those letters couldn't damage him anyway. They're old hat.'

'Ronnie. Quitting. At this stage. Why?' I felt suddenly overcome with weariness.

Lorraine flung herself back on the bed and laughed. When she'd done laughing she sat up with her legs wide apart, took hold of a pair of tweezers off the bedside table and began pulling at the occasional stray pubic hair that showed around her crutch. 'Fucking things grow like weeds. I've tried everything. Wax. Creams. Electrolysis. Nothing works. I reckon it's all the chemicals in the water, don't you? They're making women hairier. You can lend me a hand if you like Joseph.' She gave me a slack-mouthed look and narrowed her eyes.

'Sorry, I'm terribly squeamish about such things,' I said. 'I can't even squeeze my own blackheads without the benefit of a local anaesthetic.'

Lorraine's smile was a little hard around the edges.

'Suit yourself. James wants me to shave the lot off. He likes the plucked chicken look. He's a bit of a weirdo like that. But you wouldn't want me to scalp my pussy, would you Joseph?'

'Why is Ronnie quitting politics?' I said.

Lorraine sighed, swung her legs off the bed, slunk across to the mirror, looked over her left shoulder, the left foot straddled backwards and tightened her buttocks. 'Oh Joseph, you really are the innocent aren't you? Isn't it obvious? Ronnie was only necessary to James so long as he seemed like the best bet for keeping that Leftie trouble-maker Sayeed out. James likes to have a friendly MP representing his point of view in Parliament.

Lorraine looked over her other shoulder, changed legs, made the same clenching movement with her arse.

'And now,' I prompted.

'Now the Tory is doing so well in the canvass returns that the situation has changed. James thinks it's best if Ronnie stands down with a personal recommendation to his supporters to vote Conservative. That way Sayeed is bound to lose.'

'I see. And I suppose the Tory and Stentor have already reached an accommodation as regards the future development of Docklands?'

'Of course.'

'I thought you hated Stentor?'

Lorraine shrugged. 'You can't go on fighting these people for ever. You have to swim with the tide. I was pretty angry about what James did to me, sure I was. But a condition of Ronnie pulling out of this election is that Mr Stentor honours a few past agreements. He's lending us his yacht in the Caribbean for starters. I want to travel a bit. They say it broadens the mind. If I sit around in this dump much longer all I'm going to broaden is my bum.'

She turned away from the mirror and padded flat-footed towards me.

'Oh Joseph, we could have been so good for each other.' She pressed herself close against me. Her breath was hot and spicy on my cheek. I guessed she must have eaten take-away curry for supper. 'So you've got sexual hang-ups. That needn't have been a problem.'

'Sexual hang-ups?' I queried.

'Oh come on, don't be shy about it. It's all around the Party. How you like to dress up in black leather skirts. But that needn't have been a barrier between us, Joseph. I like a man with a bit of imagination. Remember how you promised you'd fuck me in an aeroplane? Think about it. Doing it thirty thousand feet up there.'

'Look, the letters are on the table,' I said. 'Do what you like with them. I'll let myself out.'

35

I'd arranged to meet Alan at the Wellington, a raunchy spit and dirt kind of place right down on the waterfront. By the time I got there it was nearly last orders and crammed full of kids, puking, kissing and punching each other. Most of them looked about twelve, in the last stages of tuberculosis and pissed out of their heads. I pushed my way through the crowds, feeling like a geriatric voyeur at a children's orgy. I eventually came across Alan playing the fruit machines.

'I'd given you up for lost,' he said.

'Sorry. Got a bit sidetracked.'

'Feel pretty whacked myself,' said Alan. The music was of the head-banging, permanent damage to the eardrum variety.

'Why did we choose to come here? I shouted. 'It's like trying to hold a conversation inside a tumble drier.'

'It's also convenient,' shouted Alan.

We manoeuvred ourselves into a quieter little area away from the worst of the maelstrom.

'So, don't keep me in suspense,' said Alan. 'How did the showdown with Clarke go?' He gave me the look of a drowning man clutching at a floating can of lager.

'He's had a heart attack.'

'He's what?'

'Heart attack.'

'You've got to be joking.'

'No joke. I took him to the hospital.'

'Is he . . .?' Alan made a rocky movement with his hand, indicating mortality.

252

'He looked pretty iffy by the time I got him there. But I'm no expert on these things.'

'Jesus H. Christ. Who'd have credited it, eh? Now, if you'd told me Jack had keeled over I'd have said he'd had it coming to him for years. But Clarke. I always thought he was built like a Sherman tank.'

'One of life's little quirks, I guess.'

'I can't say I'm exactly overwhelmed with grief. But did he talk before he . . .?' Alan made the rocky movement again.

'Afraid not.'

'Typical. Typical of my luck. Our last chance down the fucking drain. Mind you, having a heart attack isn't exactly the response of an innocent man, is it? Seems like your visit must have raised his blood pressure somewhat.'

'Possibly. But I'm not sure raised blood pressure would exactly stand up in a court of law as prima faeces proof of guilt.'

'Prima what?' said Alan.

'Faeces. It's Latin for pile of dog shit. Which is the same as saying the evidence stinks.'

Alan laughed in a despairing kind of way. He took a kick at a door post which was just standing there minding its own business. 'Clarke was out to wreck this Party and nothing's going to change my mind about that. The worse thing is I feel such a damn fool for ever having allowed myself to be taken in by him. It seems so obvious now that he was just stitching us up.'

'There's no point in blaming yourself,' I said.

Alan shrugged like someone who wasn't convinced but who hadn't got the energy to argue the point. 'You've heard about Mullins, I suppose?'

'About him pulling out. Yes.'

'With a recommendation to his followers to vote Tory.'

'It's not going to help.'

'It's the final straw that broke the candidate's back. The last nail in the Labour coffin. It's a fucking disaster. And I'll let you in on a secret, Joseph. I haven't told anyone else this, not even Andrea.'

I reeled back a bit. Not more secrets. I wasn't sure I could cope with any more. I'd had it up to the cerebral cortex with secrets. Once people started confessing it tended to be as inexorable a process as a rising tide of vomit.

Alan leant towards me a little unsteadily. He'd obviously been drinking and he didn't usually drink. I steeled myself.

'I want to disappear,' he said.

'I was expecting more to come but no more came. As secrets went this seemed like a pretty harmless one.

'There's an epidemic of it,' I said.

'Epidemic of what?' said Alan.

'Disappearing. Celia's going off to join a convent or something. The Mullins are going abroad. And now you're talking about it as well. If this goes on there'll be no electorate left, let alone any candidates to vote for.'

'Joseph, I'm being serious. I'm not sure I can go through with it. It's going to be a humiliation. I'm going to enter into the political history books as the most goddamn awful candidate of all time. I just want to crawl into a corner and cry.' Alan slid slowly down the wall until he was sitting on his haunches. He looked handsome, passionate, vulnerable and a mess.

'You've got to go through with it,' I said. 'There's no turning back now. You've just got to get out there and do your best.' I spoke in my most practised football-coach manner.

'If it wasn't for your support I'd have quit weeks ago,' said Alan.

'I wasn't too sure whether to take this as a reproach or a compliment.

'I just wish I was more deserving of your good opinion,' I said modestly. I slid down the wall to join him on the floor.

'Only a miracle can save us now.'

'So let's drink to a miracle,' I said.

36

On the morning of the election I was woken by the sound
of Jack's voice over a loud-speaker telling me in no
uncertain terms to get my arse out of bed. I must have
overslept. So I cut the morning ablutions in favour of an
extra squirt of Weleda deodorant, made from only the
very finest natural ingredients and without cruelty to
animals. I had got the idea of using this particular brand
off Celia. I thought if I smelt the same as her she might
be more attracted to me. It didn't seem to have worked.
Unfortunately, I was in such a hurry I forgot to check
that the nozzle was in alignment with the arrow which
meant most of the spray went into my mouth instead of
under my armpits. But this wasn't the moment for
worrying about refinements.

Standing in the street waiting for my arrival was a hot
off the assembly line, white, long wheelbase, open-top
Landrover with a pretty impressive PA system. Alan
was at the wheel. He was looking immaculate in a
sharply-pressed light-grey suit, a red rose in his button
hole, his black hair all slicked back and shiny with coconut oil, and his eyes glistening like a child's. Slumped
next to him and wrapped in his old tweed overcoat was
Jack White.

'Who's daft bloody idea was it we should go around in
an open-top jalopy at this time of the morning in the
middle of the new ice age?' grunted Jack.

'Yours,' I said, getting in the back.

'You're a traducer of the truth, Joseph. And may your
perfidious soul rot in hell.'

'You said it was important the candidate should have maximum exposure.'

'To the people, not the sodding elements. You forget I'm a sick man, laddie. A sick man. By rights I shouldn't be here at all. Which reminds me, have you any news on Clarke?'

'No,'I said.

'Well I think the vehicle's just great,' said Alan. 'And what's more I'm beginning to get a really good feeling about the way this election is going. People have been coming up to me all morning and shaking my hand and wishing me good luck. We're on a roll, comrades. We're on a roll. Our message is at last beginning to get through. I think we're in with a chance.'

'All morning,' croaked Jack. 'It's not even frigging dawn yet.'

'So where do we start,' said Alan, ignoring this last remark and rubbing his hands together.

'We do the Tubes first,' I said. 'Get the early commuters. Then we move on to the factories. Those which haven't been closed down that is. And we aim to hit the main shopping precinct about ten.'

As we pulled away from the kerb Jack leant back towards me. 'Joseph, what the hell have you been drinking? White spirits, witch hazel, TCP? Whatever it is, laddie, your breath smells like a damned apothecary shop. Here. Get some of this down you.' He pulled out a bottle of Gordon's gin from his overcoat pocket. I declined the offer. So did Alan. Jack drank off about an inch and a half before replacing it.

Alan was on great form. He pumped hands, kissed babies, danced a tango with an old age pensioner, flirted, quipped, sympathized, listened to endless tales of woe and made the right connections to the larger political issues. I felt proud of him, proud of his energy, his commitment, his professionalism, and above all this tact.

By late afternoon most of the main concourses of the constituency had been covered. It was decided to make a final round of ward committee rooms to check returns and rally the workers. Also something had to be done with Jack, who was both drunk and claiming to be suffering from acute hypothermia.

All went well until we arrived at the headquarters of Meryll's ward, which also happened to be the ward where Andrea lived. The committee rooms were in Meryll's flat. The walls were covered in posters of Emma Goldman, Rosa Luxemburg, Christina Pankhurst and other heroines of the Revolution. Otherwise the furnishings were pretty much on the utilitarian side. Up one corner was a plastic dustbin of brown lumpy liquid advertising itself as non-sexist, non-rascist, vegetarian cuisine. It didn't look very appetizing but I hadn't eaten since the previous day and was just looking around for a convenient receptacle when Meryll stomped up.

'I'd be ashamed to show my fuckin' face in here if I was you,' she said.

'Are there bowls for this or do we use the common trough approach?' I asked.

'Your wife hasn't turned out. She hasn't even fuckin' voted yet.'

'Ex-wife,' I said. 'You can't hold a man responsible for the actions of his ex-wife. But it's not like Andrea to miss out on the big occasion. She must be ill. I'd better give her a call. Mind if I use your phone?'

'She isn't ill,' snapped Meryll. 'She's already been knocked up three times. She just slams the door and shouts abuse. One worker's got a badly bruised toe. She had to go to Casualty.'

'That's fashion shoes for you. No resilience. You need something robust if you're going to do doorstep work. Look, I'll run along and see what the problem is.'

All the vehicles were in use ferrying the old and lame to the polling booths, so I jumped on a handy bicycle and pedalled off, rosette flapping in the wind.

Andrea must have seen me coming because she was right behind the front door when I peered in through the letter box.

'Go away,' she shouted. 'I don't want to talk to anyone. Just go away and leave me in peace will you.'

She slammed the flap down from the inside nearly trapping my fingers.

'But Andrea,' I said.

'If you don't go away I shall call the police.'

'Andrea, are you being entirely reasonable about this?'

'Reason. What's reason got to do with anything? Was it reasonable for you to destroy my relationship with Alan? And now the two of you are going round hand in glove. As thick as thieves. It's Joseph this and Joseph that. All hunky-dory. Well I hate you Joseph. I hate you. You've ruined my life.'

'Andrea. Whatever your personal feelings might be I do think you have a civic duty to vote. It's going to be a very close result. Your cross could make all the difference.'

Andrea shrieked with laughter. 'Vote. Vote. Vote for what? For a jumped-up newsagent's son who thinks he can save the world by batting his eyelashes and looking charming. You must be even stupider than I thought, Joseph.'

I was kneeling in the porch, my mouth on a level with the letterbox. 'Can't we try talking about this in a civilized manner,' I suggested.

There was no reply. Just an ear-splitting scream brought forth from deep within the bowels. More of a howl than a scream. The kind of noise that you would expect to rend curtains, break windows and tumble chimney pots. Real wall of Jericho stuff.

'Andrea, are you OK?'

Nothing.

'Andrea, is Livingstone with you?'

Still nothing.

'Andrea, please say something.'

More nothing.

'If Livingstone is with you I'd like to talk to him.'

A bottomless pit of nothing.

258

I was beginning to panic when a neighbour came out of her front door and began watering her plants, a somewhat redundant activity as it had rained almost every day for the past fortnight and she only had a scrubby patch of catmint.

'She's not very well,' I said, by way of an explanation, though quite what it explained I wasn't too sure. I stood up, stuck my hands in my pockets, whistled a bar or two of *Oh God Our Help In Ages Past*, and sauntered off down the front path as casually as I could manage. I cycled off to the end of the road and then doubled back along the alley, crept in through the small rear garden and lifted the kitchen window sash on which, fortunately, the latch was still broken. I got my trousers slightly damp negotiating the draining board but apart from this minor mishap it was a soft landing.

I took a couple of steps towards the hallway and paused. I could hear the faint sound of chanting coming from the front room, something along the lines of, 'Kill the Bastard'. As I listened the refrain grew louder and more frenzied. Undeterred, I continued along the corridor and peered in through the doorway. Andrea was kneeling on the sofa furiously pummelling a cushion.

'Where's Livingstone?' I asked.

Andrea looked a little startled to see me but was not discomposed for very long. I think if you'd caught her in the middle of hanging her own grandmother upside down from the ceiling by her toenails she would still have managed to make the intruder feel it was they who were in the wrong, for not knocking first. She grabbed a book off the coffee table and threw it at me. Fortunately, she'd always had dreadful aim.

'Andrea, I insist on knowing what's happened to Livingstone. I am his father. I do have some rights in the matter.'

'He's at my mother's,' said Andrea, with a slow, cold over-articulation of each syllable.

'Fine,' I said. 'Fine.'

I picked the book up off the floor. It was entitled *The*

Primal Scream by Dr Arthur Janov. Of course, I thought. That explains everything. I placed it title down on the coffee table. Andrea had always had a taste for temper tantrums. It was hardly surprising she had finally discovered a therapy that encouraged her to indulge them.

'What do you think I've done with him? Put him into care,' she said.

'Just wanted to make sure everything was OK, that's all.'

'Oh, get out of my way. I'm going out. And those check trousers of yours are bringing on my migraine.'

She pushed past me and slammed out of the front door. Good old Andrea. Dependable as ever.

I left shortly after. The neighbour was still animatedly tending her catmint. She looked a little bemused to see me.

'Pleasant evening,' I said. 'But I think there'll be more rain later.'

By this time I was starving. Emotion made me hungry. And my stomach was beginning to feel like it was cannibalizing itself. I wasn't too drawn to the idea of Meryll's plastic dustbin so I made a short detour to the San Remo. It wasn't seven yet but when I got there the place was in darkness and there was a closed sign on the door, courtesy of Coca-Cola. Now the San Remo was usually open for business three hundred and sixty-five days a year, 6 am till midnight. Something was wrong here. I banged on the door a couple of times. Eventually a window was thrown up a couple of floors above me and a head was stuck out.

'Who eez it making all theez damn row?'

'It's me, Joseph.'

'Jozeef. Is it really you my oldest friend? Why you not say something before. Just a jiffie. I be with you.'

I waited several jiffies. Eventually Dimitrios emerged, undid a vast number of bolts and removed the protective wire mesh.

'Sorry to put you to all this trouble,' I said.

'No trouble too great for my oldest friend,' said

Dimitrios. 'Come in. Come in. We must have a last drink together.'

'A last drink. What is this? What's going on here? Why are you all shut up?'

'Theez are sad times,' sighed Dimitrios. 'Sad times. You partake a little retsina? Cheer the soul.'

'Just a small glass,' I said.

Dimitrios poured two murky tumblerfuls, took a long drink, sighed some more.

'So what's happened?' I said.

'I have to sell. Lock and stock. No choice. Business not so good. Shop front already broken three times this year. Insurance man he don't want to know. Only dossers and pensioners come to the San Remo these days.'

I briefly wondered which category I fell into. But such musings were cut short by Dimitrios' next remark.

'Mr Mullins. He make me offer I cannot refuse.'

'Mullins. I never knew he was interested in the restaurant business?'

' 'Eez my landlord. 'Eez bin trying to get rid of me for many years. He get rid of me and he can sell the whole property to his friend Mr Stentor. Mr Stentor he has plans. Eez going to open big wine bar for smart city people. This whole place eez changing Jozeef, changing for bad.'

'You will be missed,' I said, taking my leave.

'You come on package to Greece, Jozeef. You make me visit. We play chess together beneath the olive trees and drink many carafes.' He took my hand.

'It's a deal,' I said.

The combination of the wine and the lack of food had me feeling pretty groggy by the time I got to the town hall for the count. I noticed there were now three dead goldfish floating on the surface of the left-hand aquarium. It seemed like the local government had got a serious pollution problem on its hands. But right then I hadn't got time for testing the water. Jack lurched up to me and grabbed me by the lapel.

'Our boy's ahead. Only a neck but he's out there in front.'

I went into the central chamber to take a look for myself. And sure enough, Alan's pile of votes was just beginning to inch ahead of the Tory pile. The Democrat was nowhere.

'It's still early,' I said. 'Too early for celebrations.'

The black boxes were still arriving from the outlying districts and being emptied on to the wooden trestle tables arranged in a large oval. On the inside of this oval sat the tellers and on the outside the scrutineers. Such was their look of preoccupation, it was as if they were locked in some obscure form of mortal combat. The counted votes were placed in rows along a table in the centre. I was just settling down to make a long night of it when a message came through from Docklands General Hospital. I was wanted there urgently. Apparently Clarke was still alive and asking to see me.

I rang for a taxi. The driver insisted on talking to me about the wretched state of the nation and how he'd never voted in his life.

'Politicians. They're all the same if you ask me, mate. They're all in it for what they can get out of it. I don't trust any of them.' He seemed to derive some sense of moral superiority from never having participated in the democratic process.

I tried to avoid answering his questions, overtipped him ridiculously and went straight to the hospital enquiries desk. I had forgotten to ask which ward I was to go to. The receptionist, with blonde hair that flipped up at the ends like a Barbie doll's, consulted various lists, looked suspiciously at my rosette, which was somewhat on the droopy side by now, and eventually directed me to D4.

On arrival, I was shown into a small side ward. Clarke lay on his back. He had a drip into his arm, a catheter into his penis, a plastic tube up his nose, and he was all wired up to a series of dials and tracers that were monitoring his every last heart beat and fart. I stood over him. His eyes flickered in recognition.

'How you feeling?' I said.

'Don't give a shit,' he gasped.

'Who doesn't?'

'I don't. Don't give a shit for feelings. Your feelings. My feelings. Anybody's feelings.'

'I see.'

'This place is a dung heap.'

'You asked to see me,' I said, thinking a change of subject might be a good idea.

'A dung heap, Pink. The world is a great big arse'ole. And sooner or later we're all going to get sucked into it.' He struggled up on to one elbow.

'You should be taking it easy,' I said. 'Not working yourself up about these metaphysical problems.'

Clarke snorted a kind of laugh. 'There's something I want you to know.'

'What's that?' I said.

Clarke said nothing for a moment or two. His hand moved feebly across the sheet as if searching for something. I looked away towards the black rectangle of window.

'You were right. I did work with M15. Worked with them for years. But I didn't do it because I believe in the established order. I didn't do it to bolster up the ruling classes. I'm not a fucking collaborator.'

'So why did you do it then?' I still stared at the blank window. But I could see Clarke's reflection as he struggled with the sheets.

'I did it for the Revolution, of course. The Revolution.'

'What Revolution?'

'The Revolution that can only happen when the Labour Party has been smashed.'

Clarke was getting excited. One of his feet was hanging out from under the bedclothes.

'That old chestnut, eh? The Labour Party ameliorates capitalism argument. Well, I hate to tell you this Ted, you being a sick man and everything, but you're living in another time zone. All you're going to achieve by destroying Labour is make life one hell of a lot easier for the hardline Tories. Why else do you think they're so happy to help you?'

Clarke swung both legs out of bed. 'I want to shit,' he shouted.

'Just hang on and I'll ring for a nurse,' I said.

He tottered to his feet and lunged towards me.

'I want to shit on the capitalists.'

He crashed face down on the floor. Tubes pulled out of him everywhere and fluids began to spill.

I shouted for a nurse.

37

It was 2 a.m. by the time I got back to the count. Jack was sitting on the edge of the fountain in the foyer, gin bottle in one hand, gesticulating with the other and singing *Auld Lang Syne*.

'Is it over?' I asked.

'Over. All over laddie. Lost by three hundred votes. A creditable performance. Almost respectable. Come here. Come here.'

'Where's Alan?' I said.

'Forget Alan,' he said. He beckoned me across, put an arm around my neck, bent my head close to his. 'I want to tell you something, laddie. Couldn't tell you before. Wouldn't have been correct procedure. But this is . . .' He took another pull and lapsed into a fit of coughing.

'This is what?' I prompted.

'My swan song,' he croaked.

'You mean . . .'

'That's right. Early pension terms have been agreed. I finish at the end of the month. This is my last count. It's an emotional moment, Joseph. An emotional moment.'

'Yes, it must be,' I said.

'And I'll tell you something else.' He loosened his grip. 'The leadership was expecting a worse result. We have acquitted ourselves with honour. We have been sorely tested and found not wanting. Not wanting, laddie. I shall put in a word for yourself, as my worthy successor.' Saying which, he fell backwards into the water. I pulled him out by the lapels.

'Where's Alan?' I said. The place appeared deserted

apart from a couple of cleaners shovelling rubbish into refuse bags.

'They've all gone off into the night,' said Jack, gesturing vaguely.

'Where?' I said, giving him a shake. But before I could get any sense out of him my attention was distracted by Pam with dyed red hair and bloodshot eyes, hurtling through the swing door of the Ladies. Instead of making the usual detour round the display cabinets, this month celebrating fifty years of civic progress, she plunged straight on into the cordoned-off green area.

'I don't care what you think,' she shouted defiantly over her shoulder, hacking her way through gumtrees and yucca plants and rampant vines. 'I'm going to have it. Whether it's a boy or a girl or a Martian. I'm going to have it.'

The Ladies door swung open again and this time Meryll stepped into the open, adjusting the braces on her camouflage fatigues and spitting venom.

'You've been got at. Some fuckin' bastard's got at you. Just tell me who it is and I'll fuckin' kill him.'

'I haven't been got at by anyone,' shrieked Pam, leaping through pampas grass with Meryll scrambling after her. 'I do have a mind of my own, you know.'

'Bravo! Bravo!' shouted Jack, clapping his hands above his head.

Pam slid down a rocky escarpment constructed out of fibre glass and diverted to the far side of the fountain. Meryll cut through what looked like a glade of watercress and took up position on the nearside.

'It's my baby. Mine, nobody else's. And I'll have it if I want to,' shouted Pam through the delicate plumes of spray.

Jack tottered to his feet and performed a kind of drunken jig, singing, 'It's my baby and I'll cry if I want to.'

'You've been got at,' hissed Meryll.

'Haven't,' said Pam.

'Cry if I want to. Cry if I want to,' crooned Jack.

266

The tiny droplets of the fountain, caught in a through draught, swirled and tumbled.

'Sneaky little cock sucker,' sniped Meryll.

'Filthy minded, frigid bitch,' frothed Pam.

This was too much for Meryll. She took out her anti-rape aerosol from her briefcase and waved it threateningly. Pam countered by removing her sachet of pepper from her coat pocket, which she always kept there in case of emergency. When hostilities broke out it was Jack who got the worst of it, caught as he was in the crossfire. He exited hastily into a handy committee room, with his forearm over his eyes, groping like a blind man, cursing and howling.

It was Jack's departure that snapped me out of my own trance-like condition. I suggested to the combatants, in my most diplomatic manner, that this was getting no-one anywhere, was potentially damaging to the reputation of the Party, and wasn't it time we all went home for cocoa and bed.

Meryll responded to my peace initiative by telling me to go and fuck myself.

I'd never quite understood why masturbation was a celebrationary, positive and altogether desirable activity when undertaken by women, but something worthy only of coarse derision when transferred to the male context. But this didn't seem like the most appropriate moment for debating the issue. The two women were now facing each other across a thin tongue of gravel, grim-mouthed and trembling. Meryll struck Pam hard on the left cheek. For an instant Pam looked so shocked it appeared as if she were going to subside into tears. Then her face suffused with anger and she grabbed hold of Meryll's spiral staircase earrings and yanked on them for all she was worth. Meryll gave vent to a literally ear-splitting scream and ran out into the street with blood dripping from both lobes. Pam was left with a wrenched off earring in each hand looking confused. She sank to the floor, sobbing.

'I've blown it now. I've really blown it now.'

'Don't worry,' I said. 'Serves her right. I expect she'll get over it. And if she doesn't . . .'

'It's not Meryll I was thinking about,' said Pam. 'I couldn't give a piss about Meryll. It's the baby. Do you think it'll be OK? Only you're supposed to be extra careful in the early months.'

'Oh sure,' I said. 'These tadpoles are tough little creatures.' I affected an expertise I didn't possess. 'It'll be fine.'

'It's not a tadpole, it's an egg,' said Pam, with just a touch of belligerence.

'It'll be fine either way,' I said. 'You haven't seen Alan anywhere have you? Only I arranged to meet him here.'

'The last I saw of him he was getting into a lift,' said Pam.

'A lift. What can he want with a lift? There's nothing above here but offices.'

Pam shrugged and threw the earrings into the centre of the pool. It was a rather Arthurian gesture, I thought.

I ran back to the lifts and pressed the call button. There was only one in working order and that trundled slowly down from the top floor, which was a pretty fair indication of where Alan had chosen to get out.

'By the way, I like your new hair colour,' I called, just as the doors were closing.

It was as I had guessed. Alan was out on the flat roof, standing by the railings, staring out over the city.

'Beautiful up here, isn't it,' he said, when he saw me.

'Yes,' I said.

'Helps to see things in perspective.'

'I guess so.'

'From up here we're just ants. And none of it matters. You heard the results, I suppose?'

'Yes.'

'We could have won.'

'Next time.'

'If we hadn't gone out of our way to get up the noses of our supporters we damn well would have won.'

268

'We learn by our mistakes. Occasionally. Even in this Party.'

'Where did you disappear to?'

'The hospital. Clarke wanted to see me.'

'He's still alive then.'

'He died while I was there.'

I wondered whether to tell him what Clarke had said. I decided against it. This wasn't the moment. It just rubbed in the unnecessariness of it all.

Alan said nothing. He tightened his grip on the top railing. A cold wind from down river ruffled his hair. 'It's the kids I feel sorry for,' he said, after a while. 'What sort of world are they going to inherit?'

I thought of Livingstone. I hadn't been putting much in to his present, never mind his future. I determined to make more of an effort. Even if it meant visiting more graveyards.

'So, where do we go from here?' said Alan.

'Don't know about you,' I said. 'But in the short term I could certainly use some food.'

Sucking Sherbet Lemons
Michael Carson

'A splendidly articulate and witty first novel'

Simon Brett, Punch

Benson is fat, fourteen and inspired with Catholic fervour.
He dreams of heaven as a place where Mars Bars grow on
trees . . .

Benson is also a founder member of the Rude Club, at
whose meetings 'irregular motions of the flesh' set off
attacks of guilt that send him scurrying to confession.
After one such attack he finds himself pledging his unclean
soul to the service of God.

But at St. Finbar's seminary the temptations put before the
novices are as great as those of the outside world:
especially from Brother Michael, who entices boys to the
rubbish dump on cross country runs. Expelled from
St. Finbar's, and back at school, Benson befriends the
sixth form's star pupil. Together they attend Benson's first
orgy. It is both the culmination of his sexual insecurity and
the beginning of self-acceptance . . .

'Funny about two notoriously difficult subjects, catholicism
and homosexuality. He is the real thing, a writer to make any
reader, of whatever sexual or religious orientation, laugh'

Joseph O'Neill, Literary Review

**'Graphic but not pornographic, humorous but never
sniggering, this is a marvellous first novel'**
Fanny Blake, Options

'A funny, gay, Roman Catholic bildungsroman'
Philip Howard, The Times

0 552 99348 4

BLACK SWAN

A SELECTION OF FINE NOVELS
AVAILABLE FROM BLACK SWAN

THE PRICES SHOWN BELOW WERE CORRECT AT THE TIME OF GOING TO PRESS.
HOWEVER TRANSWORLD PUBLISHERS RESERVE THE RIGHT TO SHOW NEW
RETAIL PRICES ON COVERS WHICH MAY DIFFER FROM THOSE PREVIOUSLY
ADVERTISED IN THE TEXT OR ELSEWHERE.

☐	99075 2	QUEEN LUCIA	E.F. Benson	£4.99
☐	99076 0	LUCIA IN LONDON	E.F. Benson	£4.99
☐	99083 3	MISS MAPP	E.F. Benson	£3.99
☐	99084 1	MAPP AND LUCIA	E.F. Benson	£4.99
☐	99087 6	LUCIA'S PROGRESS	E.F. Benson	£4.99
☐	99088 4	TROUBLE FOR LUCIA	E.F. Benson	£3.99
☐	99202 X	LUCIA IN WARTIME	Tom Holt	£4.99
☐	99281 X	LUCIA TRIUMPHANT	Tom Holt	£4.99
☐	99348 4	SUCKING SHERBET LEMONS	Michael Carson	£3.99
☐	99306 9	THE UNLUCKY FAMILY	Mrs Henry De La Pasture	£3.95
☐	99340 9	ALL ABOUT ANTHRAX	Ross Fitzgerald	£3.99
☐	99338 7	PUSHED FROM THE WINGS	Ross Fitzgerald	£3.99
☐	99327 1	VINEGAR SOUP	Miles Gibson	£3.95
☐	99368 9	LOVE ON A BRANCH LINE	John Hadfield	£4.99
☐	99362 X	THE RUB OF THE GREEN	William Hallberg	£4.99
☐	99169 4	GOD KNOWS	Joseph Heller	£3.95
☐	99195 3	CATCH-22	Joseph Heller	£5.99
☐	99208 9	THE 158LB MARRIAGE	John Irving	£3.99
☐	99204 6	THE CIDER HOUSE RULES	John Irving	£4.99
☐	99209 7	THE HOTEL NEW HAMPSHIRE	John Irving	£4.99
☐	99206 2	SETTING FREE THE BEARS	John Irving	£4.99
☐	99207 0	THE WATER METHOD MAN	John Irving	£4.99
☐	99205 4	THE WORLD ACCORDING TO GARP	John Irving	£4.95
☐	99141 4	PEEPING TOM	Howard Jacobson	£4.99
☐	99063 9	COMING FROM BEHIND	Howard Jacobson	£3.99
☐	99252 6	REDBACK	Howard Jacobson	£4.99
☐	99351 4	BLUE HEAVEN	Joe Keenan	£4.99

*All Black Swan Books are available at your bookshop or newsagent, or can be ordered from
the following address:*

Corgi/Bantam Books,
Cash Sales Department,
P.O. Box 11, Falmouth, Cornwall TR10 9EN

Please send a cheque or postal order (no currency) and allow 80p for postage and packing for
the first book plus 20p for each additional book ordered up to a maximum charge of £2.00 in UK.

B.F.P.O. customers please allow 80p for the first book and 20p for each additional book.

Overseas customers, including Eire, please allow £1.50 for postage and packing for the first
book, £1.00 for the second book, and 30p for each subsequent title ordered.

NAME (Block Letters) ....

ADDRESS ....

....